GORGEOUS MONSTER

USA TODAY & WALL STREET JOURNAL BESTSELLING AUTHOR
CHARITY FERRELL

Gorgeous Monster

Copyright © 2022 by Charity Ferrell

All rights reserved.

www.charityferrell.com

Cover Designer: Lori Jackson

Editor: Jovana Shirley, Unforeseen Editing, www.unforeseenediting.com

Proofreading: Editing 4 Indies

No part of this book may be reproduced or transmitted in any form or by any means, electronic or mechanical, including photocopying, recording, or by any information storage and retrieval system without the written permission of the author, except for the use of brief quotations in a book review.

This book is a work of fiction. Names, characters, brands, places, and incidents either are products of the author's imagination or are used fictitiously. Any resemblance to actual persons, living or dead, events, or locales is entirely coincidental.

A NOTE FROM THE AUTHOR

Hi reader,

Gorgeous Monster is darker than my usual stories. Cristian Marchetti is a true anti-hero and not for the faint of heart. This story contains graphic violence that could be triggering to some.

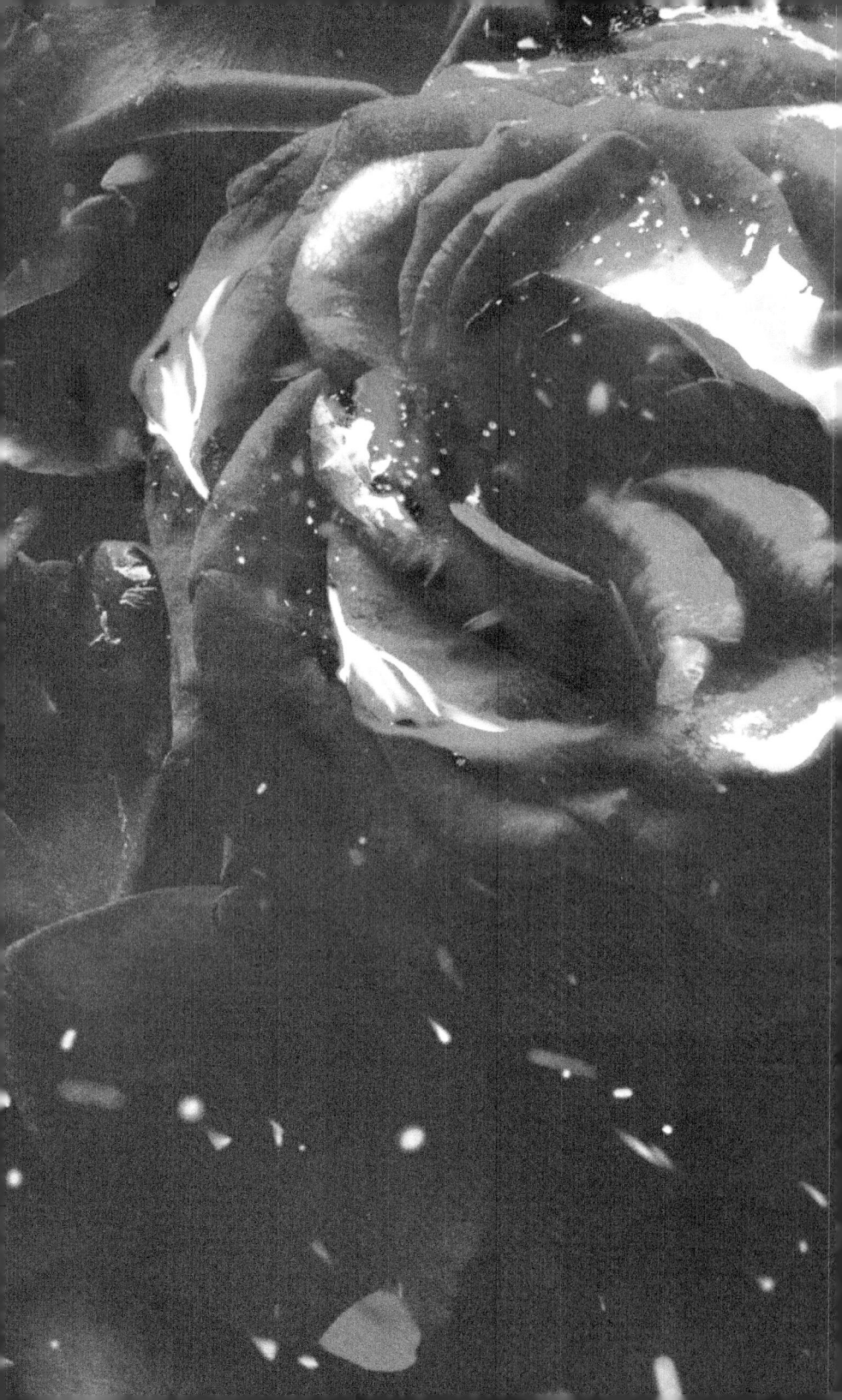

PROLOGUE

NATALIA

I fall in love with the wrong men.

Which is why I'm on my knees with my best friend's father's cock shoved down my throat.

The man who also happens to be the head of a Mafia family.

You might think you know me, but I promise, you have no idea.

I'm Natalia Carprio—the woman who fell in love with two dangerous men and started a war.

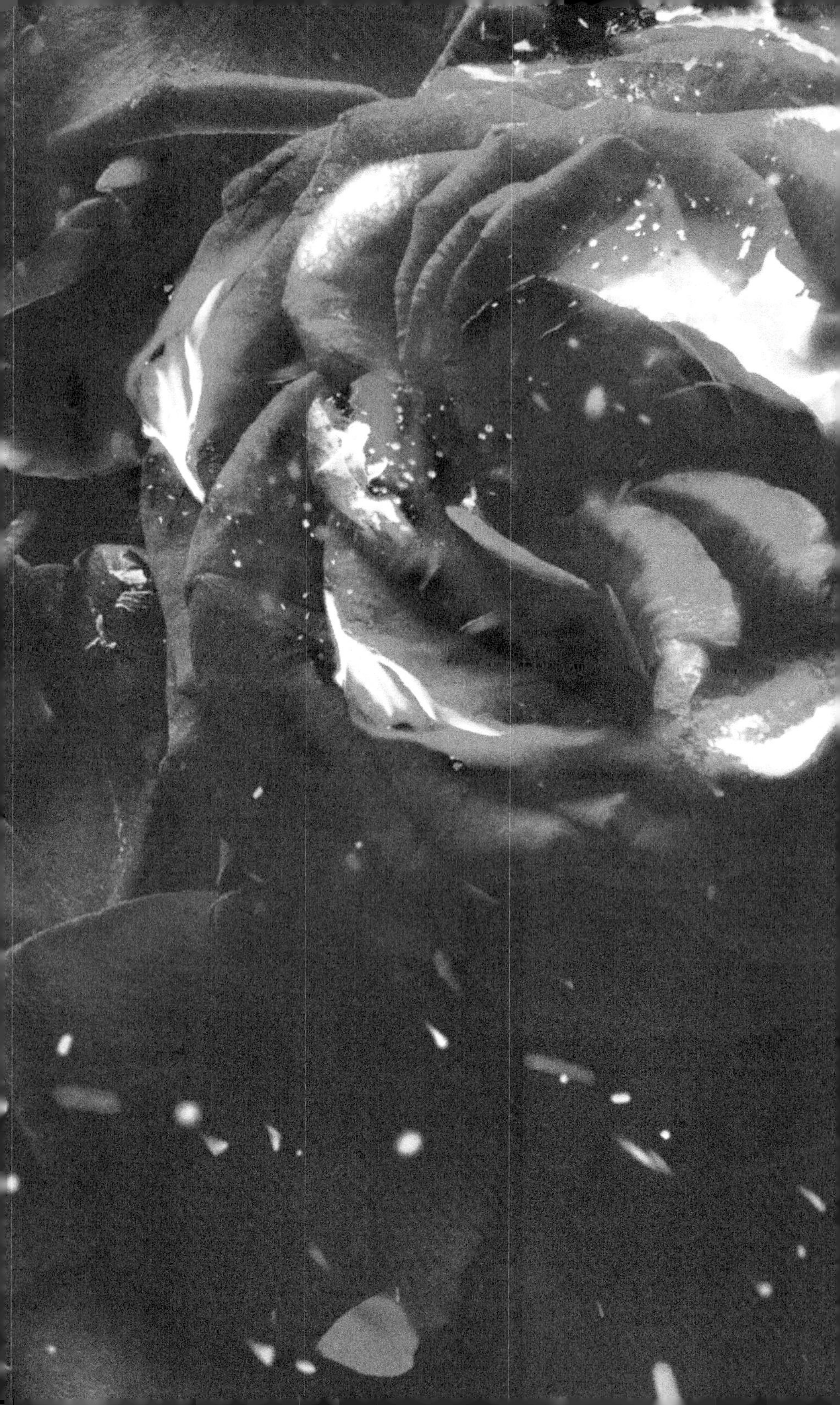

1

NATALIA

I don't want to die.

That's why I'm here, standing in front of Cristian Marchetti's office door.

A door that leads to a room where the devil plays his cards.

The fates of so many lives have been determined within those four walls.

And tonight, mine will be too.

He's expecting me. I requested to speak with him—not his daughter, *him*.

My knock on the door creates the only sound in the Marchetti mansion's foyer. It's a mere hint of a noise, but from the adrenaline pumping through my veins, you'd think I pounded on the thing and demanded entry.

"Come in," he calls from the other side, his tone thick with dominance.

Here goes nothing.

I wipe my sweaty palms down my dress before opening the door and stepping inside the devil's lair.

"Shut the door."

I do as he ordered, and even though *I'm* the one shutting the door, I flinch when it slams shut. I adjust my eyes to the light and scan my surroundings. The room exudes power and wealth from its high ceiling, oak crown molding, and ornate fireplace. The smell of fresh leather, spicy cologne, and cigar smoke hangs in the air.

He silently watches me from behind his desk, as if he's a predator waiting for his prey to fall into his trap and come right to him.

I'm about to beg for my life from the man deemed New York's most dangerous.

A man known for his cruelty and ruthlessness.

Cristian Marchetti.

The boss of the Marchetti Mafia family.

My best friend's father.

My last resort.

His name is only spoken in whispers.

A silent monster, rarely seen but highly feared.

I've been best friends with his daughter, Giana—*Gigi* for short—since I was sixteen, but I have caught glimpses of him in passing only a handful of times. Before his earlier demand, he'd never spoken a word to me, never paid me any mind.

He's the epitome of tall, handsome, and Italian. His thick hair, as black as his heart, is trimmed short. Black stubble covers his smooth cheeks and jawline—a jawline so sharp that he could cut people with it. An olive complexion, one people spend hours in the sun to achieve, complements his sea-green eyes—eyes so scary yet beautiful that they draw you in. Black-inked tattoos spread along his chest and disappear beneath his shirt.

"Natalia."

My stare-a-thon is interrupted when he says my name.

"How can I help you?"

On the drive here, I rehearsed word for word what I'd say. The problem is, I didn't expect him to be so intimidating. Hearing scary stories of monsters is one thing, but encountering one—being in their presence—makes your blood run cold.

"I need your help," I answer with a stressed breath.

"What could you possibly need my help with?" There's a hint of mockery in his tone.

"Protection." That's putting it lightly.

"Protection from?" He scrubs a palm over his jaw. "I need you to be more specific."

"Vinny Lombardi." AKA my lunatic ex-boyfriend who placed a bounty on my head for thousands of dollars.

"Now, why would a sweet girl like you need protection from Vinny Lombardi?" That mockery intensifies.

I chew the corner of my lip. "Women aren't allowed to break up with men in that family, apparently."

I wish Vinny had disclosed that little rule *prior* to me agreeing to be in a relationship with him.

"My favors don't come for free." He steeples his tattooed fingers together and rests them against his lips.

"I'm your daughter's best friend." Surely, that must mean something to him.

His silence confirms it doesn't.

"What's the price then?" I throw my arms up in frustration. "Do you accept payment plans? Give *daughter's best friend* discounts? Or … I don't know … do pro bono work to prevent an innocent woman from being murdered?"

"Payment plans?" Cristian scoffs. "Natalia, sweetheart, you couldn't afford me in your lifetime." He raises a brow. "Which might be fairly short if you have the Lombardi family on your back."

I recoil at his words. "I don't know what else I can give you."

He'd better not say sex.

There will be no sex with my best friend's father—even if he is gorgeous, has a body better than half the men my age, and I've dreamed of having sex with him more times than I can count on my hands … and toes.

He drums his fingers along the edge of the desk, as if running ideas through his head and waiting for the perfect one.

Suddenly, he grabs a pen and points it at me. "Tell me everything you know about the Lombardi family."

"Are you kidding?" I shriek. "They'll kill me."

"It sounds like that's already in your future."

Fair point.

His callous gaze penetrates mine as he waits for a response.

He creates a show of checking his Rolex when I take too long. "The way I see it, you have two options. You tell me what I want to know, which is every fucking detail, and in return, you'll receive protection. Otherwise, handle the Lombardis on your own. I wish you luck because you'll need it."

I raise a finger. "But—"

"There are no *but*s. Agree or get out of my house."

A bitter taste fills my mouth.

I'm no rat, but my life is at stake.

"Natalia, do we have a deal?"

Yes. No. Yes. No.

The two options swing through my head like a pendulum.

I'll be making a deal with one monster to escape the other.

"My offer ends in five seconds."

I stutter, searching for words.

"Five."

I can try to run, but Vinny will hunt me down.

"Four."

To do this or not.

"Three."

And who's to say Cristian will keep his word? I wouldn't exactly call him trustworthy.

"Two."

I have Gigi on my side. He won't kill me because of her.

"One."

"Yes!" My pulse is on fire. "We have a deal."

"Perfect." His smile is sinister as he plays with the pen in his hand. "I'll have a driver take you home to gather some belongings."

"Wait …" I blink at him. "For what?"

"I can't protect you if you're not here."

"I was thinking this would be more along the lines of being protected *at my home*."

"I'm not wasting my resources on someone who's yet to become worthy of them. Want protection? Do as I say."

Without meaning to, I fall back a step when he drops the pen on the desk and rises from his chair. His towering frame dominates the room, making everything else seem so small.

Standing inches from me, he buttons his black blazer, which likely cost more than my college tuition, and nods toward the doorway. I take that as my cue to *get the fuck out*, and when I turn to leave, he follows me. My heart jumps at his closeness. I breathe in the scent of his earthy and manly aftershave while praying I don't trip and fall on my face.

"Dario," he yells when we enter the foyer.

A familiar guy rushes out of the guest bathroom, zipping his jeans, and nearly loses his balance when he brakes to a stop in front of us. "Yeah, boss?"

Dario Leoni is from my neighborhood. He was trouble then, and with the Marchetti influence, I'm sure he's worse.

I tug at the collar of my dress, anticipating Cristian's next move.

Cristian jerks his head in my direction. "Watch Natalia. You can drive her to collect her belongings from her home and *bring her back*. Otherwise, don't let her out of your sight."

"What if I need to use the bathroom?" I ask because it's who I am.

Ignoring me, he keeps his focus on Dario. "You can take your eyes off her if she needs to piss."

"How very nice of you," I grumble.

This time, Cristian acknowledges my remark. His stare is cold, and he bares his teeth while saying, "I think a man saving your life is plenty nice, sweetheart."

I warmly smile at Dario. "No offense to Dario, but are you confident he's the best person to protect me?"

Dario glowers and grunts in disapproval.

My question isn't out of line. Dario is scrawny, has little muscle, and reminds me of Gumby.

Cristian lifts his chin and makes a show of looking down at me, as if I were vermin that just ran over his Italian leather shoes. "My home is Fort fucking Knox, Natalia. And let's not get ahead of ourselves." He clicks his tongue against the roof of his mouth. "You've yet to show yourself valuable enough for better protection. Start a list of every Lombardi secret you know, and then we'll determine the degree of security you're worth. Gigi is in Italy, but you can sleep in her room or the guest room. You know where both are, I presume?"

Good thing this man hardly speaks in public because he's a grade-A asshole.

Not that I'd tell him this. The *need to live* thing outweighs my need for sarcasm. So, I nod.

"Good." He straightens his blazer before adjusting his cuff links. "Make that list, Natalia."

"I'll need time."

"Tonight. If it's lacking, that proves you don't want to live."

2

CRISTIAN

Dario groans when I fist his shirt collar and shove him into a corner, out of earshot from Natalia.

"Touch her, and you'll be pissing blood for the next month," I hiss, tightening my grip.

Dario fails to meet my eyes. "Yes, boss."

Natalia bruised his ego by questioning his competence in keeping her safe.

Not that I blame her. We brought Dario into the family two weeks ago, and he's yet to show his worth, making him the perfect babysitter for the woman who has yet to prove her worth. I consider tonight a trial for them both.

Dario rubs at his neck when I release him. Without granting him or Natalia another glance, I walk out of the mansion and into the night. My chauffeur, Francis, is waiting for me in front of a running Escalade in the horseshoe driveway.

"Good evening, Mr. Marchetti," Francis greets, tipping his hat down before opening the SUV door for me.

I nod in acknowledgment and duck into the leather back seat.

"Why is Lombardi Jr.'s girl here?" Rocky asks from the front seat as soon as Francis shuts the door behind me.

Rocky is my consigliere—ranking underneath my son, Benny. His family has worked for the Marchetti family for three generations. He's been loyal to me since the day I took over after my father's murder. He was at my side when I had to prove that even though I was young, I could run the family better than any of the other incompetent motherfuckers who thought they could do a better job because they were as old as dirt.

I clench my jaw at him referring to Natalia as Vinny's girl. I hardly know Natalia, but she deserves better than Vinny. Hell, the hookers on the corner who blow men and then rob them in hotel rooms deserve better than him. Better than the men they rob, really. I'm shocked the idiot is still breathing with his hotheaded temper.

"She's not his girl." I crack my knuckles and sit back when Francis joins us in the SUV. "He put a bounty on her, so she came to me for protection."

"Since when do we play bodyguard to random bitches?" Rocky huffs, shaking his scarred bald head. "If they aren't family, they aren't shit—"

His shoulders tighten when the barrel of my Glock 19 presses to the side of his skull. I always keep a piece within reach for situations like this.

"That's my daughter's best friend." I grind the barrel into his head. "Call her a bitch again, and you won't have a mouth to do it a second time."

"Sorry, boss." Rocky slowly lifts his hands and rests them on the glove box. "My apologies."

Loyal or not, I won't tolerate disrespect. We will protect whomever I want, whenever I want, and I want no argument out of my men.

I make a point to add extra pressure on his skull before drawing my gun away and sitting back. "*Natalia* will offer every detail the Lombardi moron told her."

Rocky shakes his head. "Vinny isn't dumb. He wouldn't have told her shit."

"Vinny is one of the stupidest motherfuckers in the world. I guarantee you, he told her *too* much."

Rocky only nods—smart enough not to continue arguing with me.

"Information is information." I smirk, ready to deliver further punishment for him mouthing off. "Make sure Natalia doesn't die while feeding me that information. She dies, you die."

Rocky twists in his seat to look at me in irritation. "What?"

"Keep the bitch alive, Rocky." I enunciate each word sternly.

"I thought calling her a bitch was off-limits?" Rocky sounds like a teenage girl bitching rather than a man in his fifties.

"Off-limits to *you*. Nothing is off-limits to me."

He forces a composed expression on his face. "You're using her to get to Vinny, aren't you?"

"Yes," I reply with no shame.

I will squeeze everything out of Natalia.

Then, she will become bait.

"Mickey, Mickey, Mickey," I taunt. Like a vulture, I circle the stupid motherfucker who owes me a hundred grand. "I've given you enough time to bring me my money."

"I'm trying, Cristian!" Mickey screeches, spitting out blood. "I'm trying!"

"Trying, huh?" Without allowing him a chance to reply, I slam my fist into his face and smirk in satisfaction at the sound of his nose cracking. "Word is, you're shooting my money up your veins."

Junkies are the worst people to owe you money. They think of their next high over their lives.

"Fuck!" Mickey cries, flinging his head back as blood gushes from his nose.

We took Mickey from his deli an hour ago after he admitted

he *still* didn't have my money. We dragged him into the warehouse, kicking and screaming, and shoved him into the chair. After pulling the burlap bag off his head, I provided him the same opportunity I do to other men who have disrespected me.

A chance to save himself.

I told him the rules of my Seven Seconds game with a shit-eating grin. A game I created a decade ago because, over time, murder had grown boring. I've yet to lose a round of Seven Seconds.

I gave Mickey seven life-saving seconds to run and dodge the single bullet I'd shoot at him. Most men at least attempt to save themselves. But I didn't even have to waste a bullet on Mickey. The imbecile tripped and fell on his face before making two steps. He then crawled back onto the chair and begged me not to kill him.

Men begging and crying for their lives becomes a goddamn headache.

My wife. My kids. My fucking Pomeranian.

It's laughable that these men assume I care about their lives.

That I have a heart worthy of compassion.

I've murdered men.

Thrown dead bodies into the Hudson.

Watched men's skin dissolve off their bodies after I poured acid over them.

Then, as if I were an average family man, I'd attend my daughter's dance recital with no regrets.

You wrong me, my family, or my business, you die.

"Please," Mickey pleads, raising his dirty hands. "Don't make my kids grow up without a father, Cristian. You have kids!"

I place a palm on my chest over my heart in fake sincerity. "You weren't thinking about your children when you chose not to pay me."

"Give me three days!" Drool slides down his chin. "I'll go to every bank for a loan on the deli tomorrow." He groans in pain, struggling to keep his eyes open. "I'll even give you half the deli."

"No one wants your piece-of-shit deli," Rocky shouts before taking a bite of the roast beef sandwich he took from said deli.

"It generates good money! I'll give you every cent it makes until you're paid back."

Out of patience, I shoot Mickey in the face. His head jerks back on impact before his body slumps in the chair. Blood leaks from the cracks in his skull and begins puddling on the concrete floor.

"Burn down the deli with his body inside," I instruct Rocky. "Leave a suicide note in his car, apologizing for being a worthless father." I gesture toward the blood. "Make sure this is scrubbed clean."

I spit on Mickey's dead body before tipping the chair over. His body collapses onto the floor with a *thud*. Motherfucker took too much time out of my night when I had more important shit to do.

Rocky nods, an evil smile on his lips. "I'll call our boys Lorenzo and Luca."

Just another day in the office.

3

NATALIA

Things are working out in my favor for the first time in days.

With Dario as my protection, I'd opted out of going home yesterday. Instead, I'd borrowed clothes from Gigi's closet. Cristian didn't come knocking on the locked guest room door last night, demanding a list, so I got a few hours of sleep.

And this morning, I padded down the marble staircase, and Cristian was nowhere to be seen. When I realized the coast was clear, I grabbed a blueberry muffin from the dining room before making myself comfortable on the couch in the living room.

So far, the day is looking up.

Not sure how long that'll last, though.

"This shit is disgusting," Dario says, staring at the TV in repulsion while sitting on the other end of the couch.

I sweep my arm toward *Dr. Pimple Popper* on the screen. "This is coming from a guy who literally kills people for a living."

Dario hasn't admitted to killing anyone, but it's what you do in this life. You can't be in the crime world without committing at least one murder. Vinny explained that's how all families work. If they do differently, they're not a family worth being feared.

Our attention leaves the TV when the front door slams shut. Panic charges through me.

This is it.

Time to hand over my failure of a list.

Time to find out if I'm worthy enough to keep alive.

But who's to say he won't kill me after I give him the list?

Crime families aren't exactly known for being honorable.

"Yoo-hoo!" a woman shouts. "Where is everyone?"

My muscles loosen at the familiar voice of Helena, Cristian's older sister and Gigi's aunt. I turn to see over the back of the couch while Helena continues yelling for Dario. She walks into the living room, a Gucci bag swung over her shoulder, and the shopping bags in her hands bump into her with each move she makes.

"Dario, my brother—" Helena flinches, pausing for a moment when her gaze settles on me. "Cristian demanded I bring outfits for his dinner date tonight." She scans the burgundy-walled room, searching for someone else.

Dario points at me with his phone. "I'm assuming it's her."

Helena dramatically gasps as if she were a soap opera star. "Natalia?"

I violently shake my head. "It's definitely not me."

Helena drops the shopping bags and pulls her phone from her purse. "Cristian!" she shouts into it. "Who is this woman I'm dressing?" She nods, listening to him, and worriedly stares at me. "Natalia?"

I wave my arms and make a slicing motion across my neck. "No, it's not Natalia."

"She said it's not her," Helena tells him before quieting again. "All right, all right." She nudges the phone in my direction. "He wants to speak with you."

I take the phone from her as if it were a bomb. "Hello?"

"Pick one of the fucking dresses, Natalia," Cristian orders. "Be ready at eight."

The call ends.

I slowly hand her back the phone. "I guess it is me."

Helena's eyes widen. "That damn brother of mine."

Helena brought five dresses in different sizes in hopes that one would fit me, along with four pairs of heels.

Each dress is sexy, designer, and black. As if the monster wants me to match the color of his soul. After trying each one on, I choose a knee-length cocktail dress with a deep slit up my thigh and pair it with strappy black Louboutin heels.

Helena became the mother figure in Gigi's life after her mother was murdered. She also became one for me when I was with them—taking me to spas and helping me pick out prom dresses and apply for colleges. She's kind and a bit on the dramatic side, and like Gigi, she doesn't seem to fit in this world.

"Natalia." Helena sighs as I stare at myself in the floor-length mirror. "I don't know how you got yourself mixed up with my brother, but be careful, honey. Sweet girls like you should stay away from men like him unless you're looking for heartbreak … or death."

I look away and run my hand down the dress.

"I'm surprised he's taken an interest in you. You're young for the women he typically dates."

"Whoa." I raise my hand. "I am *not* one of Cristian's *women*. He's doing me a favor and letting me stay here."

She blinks at me. "A favor?"

I nod.

"My brother doesn't do favors without a price, Natalia." Her voice softens as she squeezes my shoulder. "What's the price for you?"

I chew on the inside of my cheek while racking my brain for

a response.
How much does Cristian share with Helena?
I decide to go with honesty. "Information."
She sighs again, worry creasing her forehead. "That's not his price with you, Natalia. I know my brother. He wants more than information from you."
"I have nothing else to give him."
Helena wrinkles her nose.
"Oh my God," I gasp, smacking her arm. "I'm not sleeping with my best friend's father."
She eyes me skeptically. "I will pray for your soul, Natalia, because my brother will crush it with his bare hands."

Helena's words haunt me after she leaves.
What's Cristian's play here?
He's up to something.
Just as he said, his favors aren't free.
Everything with Cristian comes at a price.
What's my price?
My next visitor for my dinner makeover is Carmela. Her dress is shorter than mine, her heels higher. Unlike Helena, there's no kindness. I have no idea whether she's part of this family, but she seems to fit into this world.
She's in charge of hair and makeup, but her job doesn't last long. When she yanks a brush through my hair, assaulting my poor scalp, I stop her.
"I can do this," I say, pressing my hand over the brush.
She jerks away from me, mutters, "Thank God," under her breath, and throws her supplies back into her bag. She doesn't say another word to me before leaving the bedroom.
Carmela is not a Natalia fan.
I roll my eyes and steal a straightener from Gigi's bathroom to finish my hair. My winged eyeliner takes me three attempts to

perfect, thanks to my shaky hands. I finish my makeup with cherry-red lipstick and pucker my lips into the mirror.

This isn't the first time I've gone to dinner with a man in the Mafia.

But it's the first time the man isn't my boyfriend.

I shiver, wishing I knew how terrible Cristian's intentions are.

At eight o'clock sharp, there's a knock on the door. Dario is waiting for me when I open it. His gaze travels down and back up my body, his smile building shrewder by the second.

I snap my fingers in his face.

Dario shuffles backward. "Mr. Marchetti requests you meet him in the car."

Of course.

The monster doesn't come to you.

You go to him.

I follow Dario downstairs, and he stops to wave me out the door. The humidity is sticky when I walk out. My hair will be a hot mess by the end of the night.

An aged man is standing in front of a black SUV, waiting for me.

No sign of Cristian.

"Miss Natalia," the man says, waving me over.

He opens the door when I reach him and assists me into the back seat, where Cristian already is. His attention is on his phone, and he doesn't pay me a glance as I make myself comfortable.

I've had shared rides with Uber riders who acknowledged me better. He's the one who asked—no, *demanded*—my presence for dinner, yet he's acting like my company is a nuisance.

The only sound during the drive to who knows where is the classical music flowing through the SUV's speakers. Cristian types on his phone and periodically speaks to the driver in Italian—a language I wish I'd picked up on, so I could eavesdrop on their little conversation.

I clutch the door handle, ready to barrel-roll out of the SUV, when the driver pulls into the busy parking lot of L'ultima Cena.

If you want authentic Italian food, you go to L'ultima Cena. That is, if you have deep pockets, an influential last name, or you're a man the public is terrified of. Otherwise, it takes months to book a reservation. It's also Vinny's favorite and most frequented restaurant.

L'ultima Cena translates to *the last supper*. It's an appropriate name for a restaurant that caters to men in the crime world. They'll easily book a private room and then clean it up if there's a murder—for an extra fee, of course. This restaurant is known for serving many men their last supper.

"I can't go in there," I frantically tell Cristian while smacking my hand against the seat in front of me.

He ignores my panic and calmly adjusts the collar of his shirt. "You have no choice."

"This is the Lombardis' favorite restaurant."

"It's also my favorite." His smirk chills me to the bone.

Without another word, Cristian opens the door and steps out of the SUV. I'm shocked when he holds out his hand to me. I cross my arms and refuse to take it. My heart clutches in my chest, warning me to stay in the vehicle if I know what's best for me.

Cristian can dine alone for all I care.

This city is too small.

I've dined here with Vinny countless times.

If people see me with Cristian, there will be talk.

Vinny will receive a text within five minutes and know where I am.

Then, I will join the list of victims who had their last supper at L'ultima Cena.

"We can do this one of two ways, Natalia," Cristian says, his voice and face tight. "Either you get out of this car willingly or I drag you out of it."

"Drag me out, then." I have more confidence than I should, arguing with a mob boss.

But I might win this one.

Cristian is a man who maintains a low profile.

Dragging a woman from his car isn't low profile.

Neither is bringing Vinny Lombardi's ex-girlfriend to his favorite restaurant.

Shit, maybe I won't win this one.

Cristian slams the door so hard that the car shakes, and he storms around the SUV. I yelp when he swings my door open.

His face burns as he climbs into the back seat and invades my space. "Natalia, do not fucking test me."

We're so close that I breathe in the cinnamon on his breath—can practically taste it. I shiver when his chilly hand clamps around my bare thigh. His palm is rough but soft—a man who gets his hands dirty but makes sure to moisturize after.

"And dragging you out in this dress will give me a delightful view of your pussy." He gives my thigh a firm squeeze that will definitely leave a bruise. "Your choice, sweet Natalia. You have five seconds."

My head buzzes at everything going on around me—Cristian so close, his touch, the car beeping from Cristian having the door open. All of it is too much.

I hate being at his mercy.

There's nowhere for me to run or hide.

"Five." His face hardens.

He stretches farther into the seat, closer to me, and moves his hand from my thigh to my face. I can't stop myself from shivering with desire.

"Four." His strong fingers close around my chin. The grip is so tight that I'm unable to break from his hold.

"Three." He clenches his jaw.

"Two." He drops his hand to grip my elbow.

His actions are so rapid that it's hard for me to keep up.

"One."

He jerks back, taking me with him, and I nearly topple out as he literally *drags* me from the car, just as he threatened.

A wicked smile spreads along that evil face as he helps me regain my balance. "Are you ready to follow orders now?"

My cheeks redden in embarrassment.

People are staring, so I stubbornly nod.

Cristian pats my head as if I were a fucking dog. "Good girl."

He waves to his driver before resting his palm on the base of my back, guiding me toward the entrance. On our journey, we pass vine-covered walls, a waterfall, and grand statues. A doorman sprints over to open the door and escorts us inside.

My hair rises along the back of my neck as goose bumps cover my arms.

Is my reaction from the wind or from what just transpired with Cristian?

This man, forcing me into a restaurant I'm terrified to enter, screams every red flag in the book. My problem is that red flags are my favorite attribute in a man. I can't blame it on daddy issues because my father is kind. I'm just attracted to power-hungry, crazy-ass men.

We walk together naturally, moving as one, neither of us straying off pace. I hate how my body turns on me and warms at his touch—*craves* more of his touch.

Confusion fills me when Cristian guides me to the hostess stand instead of a private room. The hostess squeals when she sets her eyes on Cristian. She shoves another hostess away to help us and brushes her hand along Cristian's arm while guiding us through a brick pathway.

Since Vinny always took us to a private room, I've never had time to appreciate the beauty of the interior. I admire every inch of the restaurant—the breathtaking stonework, extravagant Italian artwork, and the low lighting, which creates the perfect ambiance.

People watch us and whisper as we pass.

"The table you requested, Mr. Marchetti," the hostess says with a cheeky grin. "I ensured I kept it open all night for you."

His *requested* table is smack dab in the middle of the dining room.

What the fuck?

Cristian waves off the hostess, disregarding her. I gawk when he turns into a chivalrous bastard, pulling out my chair and waiting for me to sit before taking the one across from me.

This is too date-like for my liking.

What is this man up to?

He's so hot and cold.

Evil, then decent.

"Good evening, Mr. Marchetti and his exquisite date. I am Oliver, and I will be taking care of you tonight," our server greets us with a thick Italian accent. He settles a wine bottle flat in his palm, as if he were presenting it at an auction. "Your usual Domaine Leroy."

Oliver is an attractive man, no older than his thirties. His black hair is slicked back, and he's wearing a white button-down shirt with *L'ultima Cena* stitched into the left corner of his chest.

"Thank you, Oliver," Cristian says, his tone just as dismissive as it was with the hostess.

"A glass for both?" Oliver asks.

"Yes," Cristian answers for us.

Oliver pours us each a glass and places the bottle in the ice bucket. Cristian smiles in self-satisfaction as he orders our dinner before allowing me a word.

"Excuse me," I say, leaning toward him when Oliver walks away. "I have a voice."

Cristian grabs his glass of wine. "You can use that voice when you decide not to play childish games in the car."

"Why are we here?" I attempt to ignore the curious stares and moan at my first sip of the wine, savoring the hints of black cherry and smoke.

"To eat," he replies in a bored tone.

"Why are we eating *in public?*"

"So people can see us."

"Why?"

"To know you're with me."

My heart thuds as I take in his mocking smirk. "*Why* do they need to know I'm with you?"

Jesus. Can this man ever give a straightforward answer?

"You ask too many questions, Natalia."

"You don't answer enough questions, so stop with the bullshit, Cristian."

He skims a finger along the rim of his wineglass. "Vinny needs to know that you're dining with me."

"Why?" If I have to ask him why one more time, my head will explode.

"They'll want to kill you more."

I replay his answer through my brain, as if I'd misheard him, and gulp my wine in one swig. "Why would you want that?" I snatch the bottle of wine and refill my glass until it's close to overflowing.

"I'll be your last resort."

"What the hell does that mean?" I down another glass.

"I'm all you have now, Natalia." He leans forward, so impassive for a man revealing how twisted his brain is. "Cross me, and you're dead." He tsks. "No more Mafia men for you to run to for protection."

I recoil at his words, and a tremor shakes through my body.

I've made a deal with the devil.

And when he's done, he'll dispose of me.

He rakes his gaze over my face with no shame and smirks. "On another note, you look beautiful."

I glare at him. "I appreciate you providing a nice dress for me to die in. Might as well look pretty at my death."

"Doubt a pretty dress will make up for your brains being blown out, but, hey, your body will look good."

I pour another glass. "Does Gigi know her father is such a cruel bastard?" I drink the wine in one swallow.

"My daughter knows who I am."

I blow out a breath, in need of more answers. "You want people to think we're dating?"

He scoffs. "Sweet Natalia, I don't date. I fuck women and then send them on their way."

With the glass in my hand, I wave it toward him. "You know what I mean."

"The Lombardis need to think I'm fucking you and that you're giving me pillow talk at night. They fear men like me knowing their secrets."

I place my hand over my frantically beating heart. "I'm the sacrifice?"

"You came to me." He shrugs as if my life means nothing to him.

"You promised to protect me."

"I didn't agree to do it forever."

"When you're done with me, then what? I'm thrown out to the wolves?"

"We'll speak of that problem when it arises." He levels his gaze on me. "So, steer clear of becoming a problem for me. Your life will last longer."

"I could tell Gigi—"

He speaks over me. "Gigi is the only reason I haven't traded you in exchange for something more valuable from the Lombardis."

"There's something more valuable than my life?"

"Absolutely."

I shut my eyes as the alcohol hits me. "You kill me, and she'll hate you."

"She won't know it was me."

I scrub a hand over my face. "What did I get myself into?"

"A world you should've stayed out of."

4

CRISTIAN

Sweet Natalia.

She seemed so innocent at sixteen when she and Gigi became friends. But the few times I watched her on camera, wandering my home, curiosity flashed on her face. That interest was what most likely drew her to dating the Lombardi boy. And then what led her straight to me.

Natalia hardly speaks during dinner.

To me at least.

She has no fucking issue sharing a conversation with Oliver. Oliver is the owner, Stefano's, grandson. Stefano pays me a generous fee to remain in business. His price will triple if Oliver entertains Natalia for one more goddamn minute.

Natalia orders another ten-thousand-dollar bottle of wine before I demand Oliver to go away.

And now, I'm dealing with a tipsy Natalia.

She asked what she got herself into, but *what the fuck* did I get *myself* into?

I'm at dinner with a woman half my age, and I can't take my eyes off her.

As a man rarely impressed with women, my allure in her confuses me. I hate how my body reacts to her—how my cock jerked in my pants when I climbed in the back seat after she refused to leave the SUV. I didn't scare her. In fact, it seemed my anger turned her on. My thoughts scramble, straying from exploiting her as my new pawn to fucking her.

Desire bled from her, and it took more restraint than I'd had in years not to spread her legs and enjoy her as my appetizer.

I need to fuck someone before I fuck my daughter's best friend.

Before tonight, I hadn't walked through the grandiose entrance of L'ultima Cena in over a decade. I don't dine here regularly. When I do enjoy a meal here, it's when I'm doing business or I want to put a bullet through someone's head. But I made an exception to that rule with Natalia. Vinny needs to be angry and terrified that she's with me.

People gaped as if they'd never seen me before. In hindsight, many of them haven't. I don't do what I do for attention. I do it for the money, the power, and to preserve my family's legacy.

Natalia received just as much attention. Women envied her, and men drooled, the fuckers staring at her ass and tits. They wanted what I had, and that only turned me on more.

We hardly touch our food. I didn't come for the food or the hospitality, so I don't give a shit. An hour passes, enough time for Vinny to be told of our whereabouts, so I stand and tell her it's time to leave.

She half shrugs, and I'm surprised with how stealthily she rises to her feet, given how much alcohol my little nuisance has consumed. I don't take her hand—because fuck that—but I clasp mine around her elbow, tighter than I should. She doesn't pull away.

We remain the center of attention as I lead her out. The hostess pest attempts to speak to me, something about her number, and I act like she doesn't exist.

Francis is already out of the Escalade, and he opens the door. I release her to him, as if she were someone's crying child I needed to hand back, and get into the car. Unlike the ride here, Natalia doesn't grant me silence.

"Oh my God," she gasps. "I remember you now." Her attention is on Francis. "You walked in on me making out with a guy after picking Gigi and me up from a party."

I jerk in my seat, seeing red. "Party? What fucking party did Gigi go to?"

Leave it to the Mafia roots, but our children don't indulge in fun lifestyles. We're strict. Most of our children are homeschooled, and they don't have outside friends. Gigi is the exception. I carried the guilt of her growing up without a mother. In this world, most of us lose our fathers first, not our mothers. Mothers are the glue to Mafia families.

Natalia waves away my questioning glare. She's pushing me to the edge of my restraint. I ball up my hands to stop myself from grabbing her by her hair, pulling her back, and telling her what happens to women who disrespect me. I'd then give her a choice—get the fuck out of the car or suck my cock.

It's a short fifteen-minute drive to my home. I live close enough to the city that it's easily accessible but far enough to be given privacy. I wasn't lying when I told Natalia it was like Fort Knox. The heavy gates swing open, and we arrive at my estate.

The perimeter wall, gate, and security station prevent trouble from breaching my home. While I ensured our compound was secure, Benita, my late wife, worked on the interior.

Francis drops us off at the double doors, and I step out of the Escalade. Natalia follows me, and I bite back all my anger as we walk through the expansive entryway. Francis turns to park in the six-car garage.

"Your list," I say harshly, removing my suit jacket and draping it over a chair. "I want it now."

I want it now so that I can get rid of you.

Rocky walks out of the dining room, making himself known, holding a glass filled with dark liquor.

The two of them trail behind me into my office.

"Boss," Rocky says, raising a brow. "You want me to sit in?"

"No," I reply, circling my desk.

"But she could—"

"I think I can fight her off," I reply with a scoff, rolling up the sleeves of my white button-down.

Rocky likes to sit in and listen to my meetings. Sometimes I allow it. Sometimes I don't. He's loyal, but I trust no one to hear every word that is said in here. Rocky strives to please me, hoping to become my second-in-command, but everyone knows that goes to Benny.

He can hate all he wants, but this reign stays in the bloodline. It started with my grandfather, then my father, and now me. Benny will take over when I die.

Rocky reluctantly nods, exits the room, and shuts the door behind him.

No business is done with an open door.

Natalia snorts out a laugh and drops into an Italian leather chair that costs more than her life. Many men have lost their lives there. Always choose dark leather furniture if you plan to kill people in your office.

I target all my attention on her and scowl. "Something you find funny, sweetheart?"

"The way these men bow down to you"—she rolls her eyes—"it's ridiculous."

She's definitely drunk.

I grind my teeth before laughing. It's filled with edge and impatience. "How about I also make you bow down to me?"

Her face flushes. "What?"

"I'd love for you to drop to your knees and bow down to me."

Still in my chair, I wheel it out from under the desk. Her whiskey-brown eyes refuse to meet mine as she averts her attention to her heels when I stand. She draws in a deep breath as I stalk toward her. I inhale the sweet smell of her—the perfume I had Helena pick up during her shopping trip—and the expensive wine we drank still lingers on her lips. Smacking my hands down on the arms of the chair, I crouch into her space, closing her in.

She shudders. I'm unsure if it's desire or fear that caused it. She winces when I reach forward and harshly rub at her jawline.

I brush my lips against her cheek before whispering, "Keep running that smart mouth, and that's exactly what you'll be doing."

She gasps when I delve my hand into her thick hair and sharply jerk her head forward.

"You're pushing the wrong man, Natalia," I sneer. "You think Vinny is scary? You do not know the carnage I'm capable of." I tighten my hold when she attempts to tug out of my grip, and I unleash a callous laugh before releasing her.

My cold eyes cast down on her. She flinches when I tap my hand against her cheek.

"Have I made myself clear?"

"Yes," she whispers.

I stand, shuffling backward a few steps, and rest against the front of my desk, crossing my ankles and arms. "The list?" I make a *hand it over* gesture.

"It's in my room."

"Rocky," I yell.

Rocky comes barreling into my office.

"Go into Natalia's room." I peer at Natalia. "Where is the list?"

"I can get it," Natalia replies, her voice low, as if she doesn't want Rocky to hear. "I don't want him in my stuff."

"You're forgetting the part where I give a shit about what you want," I hiss, looking down at her. "Now, tell me where it is, or I'll have him search the room for it. I promise, Rocky isn't careful with people's shit."

"Sure am not," Rocky says, his voice tinged with humor.

Natalia acts as if Rocky weren't even in the room. "It's on the vanity … in an envelope."

"Grab it," I order Rocky. "And don't fucking open it."

"Yes, boss."

Rocky walks out of the room in long strides.

Natalia pretends to inspect her nails as I inspect her.

She's a beautiful woman—an Italian man's dream. Hell, she's a dream for any man with a beating heart and working dick. Thick hair runs past her elbows in a sheet of black—my favorite color. Full breasts, curvy hips, and plenty of ass. If it wasn't for her smart-ass attitude or being my daughter's best friend, I'd say she's perfect.

When she and Gigi became friends, they'd sit by the pool in bathing suits. I lost count of how many men I'd punched when I caught them looking.

"I'm not looking at Gigi," they'd insist. "I'm looking at her friend."

Rocky reenters the office, holding the envelope as if it were a winning lottery ticket. In actuality, it's a golden ticket to kill Vinny. I inch my finger forward, telling Rocky to hand it over, and when he does, I tell him to get his ass out.

Rocky stares at me grimly, not enjoying being excluded from this conversation, but he's smart enough not to question me.

Natalia sits silently in her chair, her arms hugging her stomach as she chews on her plump lower lip.

I hold up the envelope. "Time to learn if you're worth that ten-K bottle of wine … let alone my protection."

She stays quiet, but the nervousness is clear on her face as I open the envelope.

Her handwriting is sophisticated, all straight lines and legible.

1. He likes to gamble.
2. He goes to his parents' Hamptons home when he wants to clear his head.
3. He's doing business with the Corobras behind his father's back.

   4. Detective Hedgekins and Officer Bean are on their payroll.
   5. There you go, jerk.

I notice how she didn't name a single name other than the Corobras. If anyone ever found this letter, no one would know who *he* was.

I crumple the pathetic list in my fist and drop it onto the floor.

"Natalia, Natalia, Natalia," I say, walking around her as if I were a shark who smelled blood. "I told you, you needed to prove your worth."

"I wrote you a list," she yells, gesturing to the balled-up paper. "I did exactly what you'd told me to do."

"Your list is pathetic," I snarl. "I already know all that shit."

Her every muscle is tense. "What else do you want from me? To make stuff up to have a good enough list for you?"

"Cut the bullshit. Give me every address of the Lombardi's. Their home addresses, vacation homes, businesses—any place you've been with Vinny, I want the address."

She returns to chewing on her lip.

"Natalia." I smack my hand onto the desk, causing her to jump. "If you don't start spouting out addresses, I will shove that paper down your fucking throat."

She stares at me, looking almost sober, as if she hadn't drunk one sip of alcohol. This is the moment it truly dawns on her.

That her life is not safe in my hands if she's invaluable.

I don't care about her, friend of my daughter or not.

"Thirteenth Avenue. Brooklyn. That's his main address."

"And what else?"

"I … I don't know."

I slowly withdraw my Glock 19 and place it on the desk. "You'd better think real fucking hard."

"Burly's Cleaners … through the back," she replies, her eyes glancing back and forth between the gun and me. "You walk through the freezer, and there's a door in the back. That's where Vinny meets with the Corobras."

"What do they run through there?"

She lowers her eyes.

"Natalia. What. Do. They. Run?"

"They stash drugs and cash in there. That's all I know." She blows out a ragged breath. "I wasn't involved in Vinny's work. He took me there once, maybe twice, when he made a quick stop. I was never there long, and he hid a lot from me."

"And where's the Hamptons home he *clears his head* at?"

"It's either 306 …" She pauses and thinks before shaking her head. "No, I think it's 308 Cod Maple Drive."

I observe her, watching her every move—how she speaks, how her fingers twitch, and how she chews on her lip when put on the spot—and run her words through my head, memorizing them.

"Please don't kill me," she pleads, her words barely audible.

My hungry gaze meets her doe eyes. "Sweet Natalia, I never make promises."

I spent two hours grilling Natalia on every question I had about the Lombardis and their inner workings. She told me their addresses, what safe codes she knew, who Vinny associated with, and what he said behind closed doors to people on the phone when she was with him.

Learning people's secrets—especially when you can use them toward an adversary—is such a high. Stronger than any glass of liquor. Vinny telling her that information further proves he's an idiot.

Natalia looked ready to fall out of her chair from exhaustion when I finally stopped my questioning and told her to go to bed.

The wicked never sleep, so I'm still in my office when Benny knocks before stepping inside.

Benny has never shied away from how we run our family and business. He was twelve the first time he saw me kill a man and then seventeen when he shot a bullet through the head of his first. Call it father-son bonding. I know Benny will be a good leader when he steps up. But he still needs time. There is still decency lingering in his heart, which I blame his mother for. He needs to release all of that before taking over the reins.

There's no place for good-hearted men here.

We're raised to be loyal and learn respect for those who deserve it. And then we teach what happens to those who become disloyal or disrespectful.

"Natalia?" he asks, a scowl on his face that closely resembles mine.

I arch a brow.

"You and Natalia?"

I can't avoid a conversation about this woman for one second.

If one more person brings her up tonight, I'm throwing her out the window to spare me the goddamn headache.

I drop my pen and recline into my chair. "She came to me for help."

"You told me to stay the fuck away from her years ago." He shuts the door and collapses onto the chair Natalia sat in.

"I did, yes."

"That rule doesn't apply to you?"

"No rules apply to me."

He massages his temples and blows out a long breath. "Is it trouble with Vinny?"

I nod.

"What's he doing to her?"

"The Lombardis want her dead. I didn't ask for too many details." I don't give a shit about them.

"She asked for protection, and you didn't bother asking her *what* exactly she needs it for?"

I shrug.

His brow furrows. "I warned her about him. If only you'd let me ask her out—"

"You have a wife locked in. Asking her out would've ruined that."

I contracted Benny to marry Neomi Cavallaro. He is free to fuck anyone he likes but not date them. I'm unsure whether that will change when he ties the knot with Neomi. Nor do I care. All I care about is him fulfilling the contract.

"Fuck those plans," he hisses. "I'll marry Natalia instead."

My nostrils flare, and I raise my voice. "Natalia is not part of our world. She will not be your wife."

He slumps in his chair, looking like a weak man—something I loathe—and curses under his breath. "Why didn't she come to me?"

"You know exactly why she came to me and not you."

"Unless she's *your wife*, you can't protect her either." He huffs. "The family only protects wives and children."

"We'll cross that bridge when we reach it."

Then, I change the subject from marrying and protecting Natalia and tell him all the information I dragged out of her.

"Let's keep this between us for now," I tell him when I'm finished.

"Vinny will lose his shit." Benny shakes his head. "He loves Natalia. He's *obsessed* with her."

"Let him come to me." A rush of satisfaction hits me at the thought.

5

NATALIA

The guest room in the Marchetti mansion, like the rest of the home, screams wealth. It's on par with a suite at the Palms in Vegas. A suite I had the luck of staying in once with Gigi, compliments of Daddy Marchetti.

Benny accompanied us, of course.

So did Bruno, Gigi's bodyguard.

Gigi's safety has always been a top priority for Cristian.

And with that being said, when he found out about the Vegas trip, he flipped his shit.

I stretch out on the California king bed in the softest sheets I've ever slept on. My splitting headache reminds me of what happened last night.

Dinner, people staring, Cristian's office, my list of Lombardi *secrets*.

Too bad that alcohol wasn't strong enough to make everything a blur. No, I remember every detail. Cristian ruined my ability to get blackout drunk when I needed it the most. *Asshole.*

Initially, I kept my list short, as any smart girl would when a Mafia family wanted her dead. The odds were already against me, and I didn't want to add more trouble. I wouldn't be in this mess had Vinny kept his big mouth shut. He loved bragging about his family's notoriety, and my dumbass listened. I was his girl—surely, no one would kill the Lombardi prince's girl.

Well, except for the Lombardis.

But Vinny would want me dead, even if I were blind to his world. He believes no one is allowed to leave him. In his eyes, breaking up with him is just as much of a betrayal as telling secrets.

When I sluggishly returned to the guest room last night, I found another shopping bag from the city's most upscale lingerie shop. If you want a pair of panties that cost as much as a month's salary, Amor Lingerie is the place to go. A Post-it with, *Your pajamas*, was taped on the outside. When I dragged the contents out, there was a variety of lingerie—every piece black.

Why a man would do all this for someone he planned to murder is beyond me.

I changed into the lingerie and locked the door—for obvious reasons.

"Good morning, Miss Natalia!"

My attention shifts to the door at the gentle knocking on the other side.

"Mr. Marchetti is ready for you to join him for breakfast," Miriam, the Marchetti housekeeper, calls out.

Of course.

Cristian is summoning me via his employees again.

Does that man even wipe his own ass?

I change into a maxi dress I found in the closet with the tags still on. I have no idea whether it's for me, but I'm assuming Cristian provided it, given it's black.

After brushing my teeth and hair and checking my reflection in the mirror, I plod down the staircase, barefoot, as if I were on my way to a root canal. Or an execution. Yeah, that's a better comparison.

Cristian is sitting at the head of the expansive dining table when I walk into the dining room. His posture is perfect, a cup of coffee in one hand and the newspaper in the other. An entire buffet of breakfast options is spread along the table.

"Have a seat, Natalia," he instructs, jerking his chin toward the empty chair next to him, his eyes not leaving the newspaper.

Unlike me, he doesn't look like he woke up feeling like he'd spent all night on a nonstop roller coaster. This morning, he's wearing a black suit, sans tie, and the white shirt underneath his suit jacket is half-unbuttoned, drawing attention to his tatted chest.

Cristian isn't your typical older man or what you'd expect your best friend's dad to look like. The man has aged well, especially for one who lives a stressful life. There's a two-decade difference between him and Vinny, but Cristian could almost pass as Vinny's age. Vinny's father, the head of their family—with his protruding belly from too much Italian food and not enough exercise and the wrinkles that form every time he scowls—looks nothing like Cristian.

No, Cristian is a man who consumes everyone's attention. He's a gorgeous man—a gorgeous *monster*.

"Good morning to you too," I grumble, shuffling into the room and taking a seat two chairs down from him—the more distance between us, the better.

"Next to me," he demands, his eyes remaining on the paper.

I grab the rolled-up cloth napkin and place it over my lap. "I'm good here."

"Next to me, Natalia."

I ignore him.

He drops the newspaper, and it lands on the table with a *smack*. I refuse to grant him the reaction he thirsts for—the panic he normally receives from others. But you don't have to look at Cristian to endure the intimidation that burns through him. You can feel it. Smell it. Almost taste it.

His coldness. His scorn. His *fury*.

I swallow, staring at the burgundy drapes covering half the windows in front of me.

I maintain my refusal to glance at him, but that doesn't stop me from wincing when his hands grip the back of my chair. I shudder when he drops his head and presses his lips against my ear.

"You can either stand and do as I asked or you'll regret it," he snarls, his voice thundering through the room.

"You didn't ask. You ordered," I correct, lowering my hands and clenching the napkin.

"Stand, or I will force you up."

I yelp when he yanks the chair out, and I jerk forward.

"It's up to you." His voice grows harsher with each word. "You have five seconds to decide."

Him and his five-second bullshit.

"Natalia, it's easier to move seats, trust me," Benny says, strolling into the dining room and sliding his phone into his pocket.

Heat creeps up my face at Benny witnessing our little breakfast game. As if this wasn't awkward enough. *No way am I moving now.*

"Then, I suggest you do it yourself," I bite out.

Benny groans and throws his head back.

It happens so fast. Cristian moves my chair next to his. He doesn't bother sliding the two that had separated us, so that brings me even closer to him.

"There," Cristian says, rubbing his hands together as if he just finished a job. "That's better."

Benny shakes his head and takes the seat opposite Cristian. Benny is his father's son through and through, but while Cristian's soul is nothing but evil, Benny has a sliver of integrity. I'm sure that'll change the more he's sucked into this life. Vinny was the same.

Italian ancestry runs deep in Benny's blood, and it shows. He's a growing carbon copy of his father: similar height, black hair as dark as mine, and sporting a small amount of facial hair.

Cristian picks up his newspaper, as if what just happened was no big deal.

Gretchen, one of their housekeepers who's around my age, walks into the room—as if she'd been waiting for the scene to end before interrupting.

"Miss Natalia and Benny, we have fresh-squeezed orange juice on the table," she says, her voice chipper. "If you'd like a coffee, I can bring that for you."

"I'll stick with the orange juice," I answer with a smile.

"I'll have a coffee. How I normally take it." Benny winks at her.

"Of course," she says, flashing Benny a smile. "Coffee coming right up."

"Keep your hands to yourself with Gretchen," Cristian grumbles to his son when the woman leaves the room.

"What are you talking about?" Benny asks.

"You know exactly what I'm talking about. If I have one more employee quit or attempt to kill themselves because you couldn't keep your dick in your pants, your ass will serve me coffee."

Benny snags a slice of bacon and turns his attention to me. "Natalia, my dad said Vinny is giving you trouble."

I nod. "Trouble is an understatement."

"What kind of trouble?"

I sigh, wondering how much I want to say. "Showing up at my house, the gallery, threatening texts galore. I changed my number so he'd stop, but somehow, he figured out the new one. As soon as I discovered the bounty on my head, I came here."

I rented a hotel room a few times but found someone following me. I asked Bonnie—my boss at the art gallery I work at—for a few days off so I could hide from Vinny until I figured out a plan. That plan ended up with me begging for Cristian's protection.

"Let me see the texts," Benny says, holding out his hand.

I pull out my phone from my dress pocket and hand it over to him.

He reads Vinny's string of text messages out loud.

Vinny: Natalia, make this right, or I will END YOU.

Vinny: I'm sorry, baby. I'm just going crazy over losing you.

That one causes Cristian to scoff.

Vinny: SWEAR TO GOD, IF I SEE YOU WITH ANOTHER MAN, I WILL SLIT BOTH OF YOUR THROATS. HIM FIRST, SO YOU CAN WATCH HIM BLEED OUT.

Vinny: I'm sorry, baby. Please call me back.

Vinny: My father knows you know too much. You know what he does with people like that. If you keep ignoring me, then say good-bye to your life.

Vinny: CRISTIAN MARCHETTI? YOU FUCKING CUNT. You'd better count your days.

Cristian releases a cruel laugh at that one.

He and Vinny are definitely in the running for the Craziest Psychopath award.

Cristian plucks my phone out of Benny's hand, throws it on the ground, stands, and slams his foot onto it. The screen cracks and pieces fall off. Then he picks up the phone and drops it into the orange juice decanter.

"What the hell?" I shriek. "Why would you break my phone?"

Cristian straightens his sleeves and sits back down. "Buy a new one."

"Like I have the money to waste on a new phone when I had a perfectly good one."

Cristian relaxes in his chair. "I'll buy you a new one."

I roll my eyes. "The last thing I need is to be more in debt to you."

Cristian runs his thumb over the handle of his coffee cup. "Consider it a favor for the less fortunate."

I reach for the decanter, stick my hand inside, and extract my phone from the orange juice. "Every favor has a price … isn't that your motto?"

"Eat." Cristian snatches the entire bowl of eggs and dumps it onto my plate. "That will keep your mouth busy, so you'll shut the fuck up for a minute."

I narrow my eyes at him. "Is it poisoned now that you got the info out of me?"

"Poisoning eggs is too boring of a way to kill someone."

"My dad probably won't kill you, Natalia," Benny says. "It'll make my sister mad, and my sister is the only person's feelings my father cares about hurting."

Probably doesn't sound too promising.

"Gigi doesn't need to know everything," Cristian comments with a shrug.

"I'm surprised Gigi doesn't know about your little romantic candlelit dinner last night," Benny adds.

"Romantic dinner? Whoa," I say, holding up my hand and shaking my head. "There was no romantic dinner."

"That's not what I heard." Benny gestures to my broken phone. "It seems that isn't what Vinny heard either. My father not killing you doesn't mean you're protected."

"That's not what your father said," I say, shooting a quick glance to Crisitan.

Benny shakes his head repeatedly. "We protect no one unless they're family."

I grab my fork, needing something to do with my hands, and play with my eggs. "Can't you … adopt me or something?"

Benny snorts.

"I'd never have a daughter stupid enough to date a Lombardi," Cristian says. "Try again."

"You can marry into the family, though," Benny says with a smirk.

My eyes widen. "W-what?"

Benny's eyes are on Cristian now. "She can marry into our family."

"Benny," Cristian warns, "I'm going to poison your fucking food if you don't shut your mouth."

"Marry me," Benny says to me.

Cristian slams his hand down onto the table. "Benny, I swear to God. Your name might be on the goddamn family tree, but that doesn't mean *you're* protected right now. I'll smash your face into that plate of food."

Benny acts as if his father threatening him with violence isn't out of the ordinary. "It's true. Vinny doesn't just want her dead now. He wants her alive, meaning he plans to torture her, and technically, he has the free will to do so."

I hold in a breath, covering my mouth at the realization of Benny's words. He's right. Vinny won't let me go with a simple gunshot. No, he'll make me suffer before killing me. He will make me regret leaving him and going to Cristian.

"Do you think I give a fuck about technicalities?" Cristian snarls.

"I do," Benny says. "And so will Gigi."

"She'll get over it," Cristian snaps. "I can buy her a new friend."

Benny shakes his head. "Gigi will never speak to you again."

Cristian grabs the newspaper and opens it, as if he's over the conversation. "Gigi will never know."

"Uh, yes, I will."

Cristian lowers the newspaper, and our attention darts to Benny. He holds up his phone, so it's facing us.

Gigi is on FaceTime, and she speaks in the sweetest voice I've ever heard from her. "You know Natalia is my best friend. I'd be heartbroken if I lost her. Let Benny marry her, and I promise, I'll marry anyone you choose for me."

"Are you fucking out of your mind?" Cristian's nostrils flare. "If Benny marries her, we'll lose the deal with the Cavallaros." He smacks his palm against his forehead. "And here I thought I raised intelligent children. Neither one of you will succeed me. I'll hand it over to the first goddamn man I find in the subway before either of you receives it."

"Then, you marry her," Gigi says with no humor in her voice. "You don't have a deal to marry anyone."

"What?" I shriek.

"Hang up the fucking phone," Cristian tells Benny.

"What—"

He snatches the phone from him and hangs up on Gigi. "Benny, I'll deal with your ass later. Natalia, eat your fucking food."

6

CRISTIAN

When I woke up this morning, I didn't expect the first person I'd want to use my gun on today would be my goddamn son.

Benny knew everything would change if he involved Gigi, so that's precisely what he did. Now, I either have to terminate his engagement with Cavallaro—an arrangement years in the making—or marry Natalia off to someone.

Marrying her off to someone else it is.

No one said who she needed to marry, just someone within the family. I could give her to Gigi's pet hamster for all I care.

"Natalia marrying someone in the family is the only way she'll be fully protected," my idiot son says when we're alone in my office. "Rival families know wives and children are off-limits unless they want a fucking war."

"Fine." I stand from my chair, done with this time-wasting discussion, and wave for him to leave my office. "Go collect Natalia."

I'll solve this issue and proceed to more pressing matters than who Natalia can say *I do* to.

Benny is silent for a moment, stunned at my caving in, and rises to his feet. "All right." He leaves my office.

I snap my fingers and yell, "Dario, get your ass in here."

Dario was recently promoted to a high-ranking soldier after successfully blowing up Foreplay Gentlemen's Club last night. We had been kind enough to ensure all the dancers were out of the building, giving them five hundred dollars each before they left. Dario and Benny tied the owners—the Peterson twins—to chairs inside their office and then ignited the low-budget club. I had grown tired of them promising money and not delivering.

Their deaths were a terrific investment on my part. I got rid of the brothers, profited twenty-five thousand from their biggest competitor, and increased said competitor's monthly rate for their new strip club monopoly in the area.

Dario doesn't bat an eye at murder and jumps when I bark, but I wouldn't consider him competent enough to rank anything higher than a soldier. Sure, it's easy to kill a man. But planning the perfect murder that's clean and doesn't trail back to us takes brains.

Dario hustles into my office. "Yeah, boss?"

I hold up a finger, leaning against my desk, and wait until Benny returns with Natalia before breaking the news.

"Congrats," I say.

Dario straightens his stance, as if preparing for another promotion.

I jerk my chin toward a confused Natalia. "You're marrying her."

"What?" Natalia's face floods with horror.

Dario's gaze moves from me to Natalia, and a smile builds along his lips as he feasts his eyes on her. "Really?"

Eagerness swims in Dario's eyes—to be expected. What's not expected is that my trigger finger suddenly itches to blow his brains out at the way he's staring at her.

"Whoa," Benny hisses. "Dario is a soldier. He can't protect her."

I sneer at my son. "You wanted her married in the family so

bad." I throw an arm out in Dario's direction. "Dario is a soldier in this family. Problem solved."

"I'm not marrying him," Natalia says like a stubborn fucking teenager. "He used to fuck my cousin."

I look at my watch, bored with this nonsense. "I don't care if he's fucked your entire family."

Natalia shakes her head violently. "No, I won't do it."

"Don't be ungrateful," I tell her. "Marry him, or as Benny said, you won't be protected."

Natalia is still shaking her head. "I won't do it."

I cock my head to the side. "There's nothing else I can do for you then."

"Dad—" Benny starts, but I interrupt him.

"Natalia, pack your shit. Dario will take you home." I motion toward the doorway. "Now, all of you, get the fuck out of my office." I cast my eyes to Natalia. "Beg Vinny for a quick death when he gets his hands on you."

I did what they'd asked and found someone for her to marry.

Not my problem she declined my very generous offer.

I could've tried to hand her over to Malfoy—my man who eats a piece of skin from every one of his victims.

I thought I could use sweet Natalia to my advantage, but she's become a problem.

And what do I do with problems?

I squash and bury them.

7

NATALIA

I will die at the hands of a man.
Which man those hands belong to has yet to be determined, but my money is on one of these goddamn New York terrorists who find murder their favorite pastime.

Marrying Dario isn't happening. The maniac once stabbed a guy in the school cafeteria for taking the last basket of fries, and my cousin said he enjoys role-playing murder scenarios during sex. Hard pass on that.

When Cristian makes it clear that he can't help me unless I become Dario's wifey, I leave his office, return to the guest room to gather my few belongings, and walk downstairs.

I hear a loud conversation from Cristian's office, and Dario is waiting for me at the front door. Without a word, he leads me outside to a black sedan, and I slide into the passenger seat.

"You know," Dario says as he drives through the estate gates, "I'd be a decent husband if we got married." His eyes stray to my chest for a moment, and he licks his lips before returning his gaze to the road.

Since I don't want another Mafia man to have me on his hit list, I say, "I'm sorry, Dario, but I can't marry someone I don't love."

"We could learn to love each other."

I shake my head. "I'm sorry, Dario."

"Vinny is known to always get what he wants," Dario says, using a different angle. "He killed a man over a parking spot once."

"I know," I whisper.

I was there.

Men in the criminal world know how to pamper their women, but nothing outweighs their ruthlessness.

For our first anniversary, Vinny said he wanted to make it memorable. He bought me a diamond necklace from Tiffany's, wined and dined me at L'ultima Cena, and booked us a penthouse suite at The Mark Hotel. Even though we'd had dessert at L'ultima Cena, I was craving my favorite ice cream from the shop by my apartment. He took me there and then shot someone over a parking spot.

It was the first time I'd seen Vinny kill someone. I knew what his job entailed but never witnessed him—or anyone—kill another man until that night. He told me not to tell anyone what happened, and I agreed. After that, Vinny decided I was trustworthy, which opened the floodgates of him telling me more.

That was when I should have run, but Vinny said that I could never leave him, or he'd go to hell and back to make sure I was brought back to him.

The mob life had always interested me, but I was smacked by the reality of it. All I'd seen before was Gigi's life—the life Cristian had given her. She had the luxuries, the name, people feared her, and she was protected. I quickly learned that I wasn't Gigi. I wasn't a Mafia princess who'd be protected from these dangerous men.

Dario cuts the engine and sighs when we reach my apartment. "I'll walk you up."

I unbuckle my seat belt. "You don't have to do that."

"I'll check your apartment. Make sure everything is okay."

Unlike his marriage proposal, this offer I don't refuse. I nod, and we step out of the sedan.

My apartment is a duplex in Astoria. Monique, the seventy-year-old widowed neighbor, owns the building, and I've rented from her for the past two years. I stayed with Vinny most of the time when we were together, but when I moved back into my place after our breakup, he kept showing up at night. That was when I realized Vinny would make my life hell before allowing me to walk away from him entirely.

We walk along the side of the building and up the stairs that lead into my apartment. Dario is close at my back, his chest brushing along mine as I ease my keys from my purse. When I unlock the door and walk into my apartment, I don't feel safe.

At least I have Dario behind me.

I stroll into the apartment and start hitting the lights.

"Natalia, baby."

I stop dead, fear thrumming through my veins, and slowly turn to face Vinny in what seems like slow motion. My good-looking but callous ex will kill someone without blinking an eye —and that's what the expression on his face screams he's prepared to do.

Vinny blocks the door, a sadistic smile plastered on his lips, and from the inside pocket of his suit jacket, he slowly drags out a gun, a silencer connected to the end. His cold eyes creep up and down my body. "Cristian sent *this joke* to protect you?" His gaze flicks to Dario as he releases a mocking laugh. "How pathetic."

Vinny's words are said through clenched teeth. My heart races so hard that I'm waiting for it to fall to Vinny's feet as we make eye contact. His eyes are a storm as he prepares to unleash his anger, and I'm terrified of how much damage he'll cause. His breaths are so loud that I can hear them from across the room.

Vinny might be several steps down from Cristian, but Dario has nowhere near his smarts, stature, or degree of malice. Vinny and Cristian were born into their wicked bloodlines—the evil runs through their veins.

Dario steps forward to block Vinny from me. "I'm marrying Natalia, Vinny. You touch her, and you'll start a war with everyone in the Marchetti family."

Dario's words ping straight off Vinny, as if he hadn't even said them.

Vinny strokes his smooth-shaven chin. "If I touch *her*, huh?"

"Yes." Dario straightens his stance, stupidly believing he can win this fight with someone who was forced to kill his first man at twelve to prove himself to his father.

"Leave," Dario continues, "or Cristian will have your ass."

My palms are sweaty as my gaze darts to every angle in my apartment for the best escape plan. It's out the front door—go figure—so I'm pretty much fucked unless Vinny moves.

Vinny bitterly chuckles and looks at Dario. "Will Cristian care if I touch you?"

Without waiting for a response, Vinny shoots Dario in the head. I whimper, realizing I'll meet an identical fate as Dario. Dario groans and collapses on the carpet, blood pouring from his skull. I nudge my foot against Dario's body, muttering his name, but nothing.

"You disloyal fucking whore," Vinny yells, stalking toward me.

I stagger backward, screaming at the top of my lungs in hopes of someone hearing, until my back meets the wall.

Vinny steps over Dario's body as if it were nothing but a pile of dirty laundry.

"Vinny!" I cry out, holding up my hands. "Let me explain."

I'm scrambling for words, fighting to keep my brain straight so he doesn't shoot a bullet through it. Vinny's large frame blocks any line of direction toward the front door, so it'd be impossible for me to run past him.

Think, Natalia. Think.

Outsmart the man.

"Explain what?" Vinny asks through gritted teeth before reaching out and wrapping his hand around my throat. "That you are a traitorous slut who needs to die?" His grip isn't tight, so there's no struggle for me to breathe or talk.

"I'm sorry," I whisper. "I was scared."

Spit flies from his mouth, hitting my chin, as he screams, "You thought you were scared then."

"Please," I plead, sticking my hand into my bag. "I wanted to talk to you, so I came back, knowing you'd be here, waiting for me."

Vinny's face twists with conflict.

The man is a psychopath, *but* he feeds on the pleasure of people begging him.

"Please," I repeat, softening my voice.

"Natalia, you have no idea what you've done," he bites out, running his thumb along a vein in my throat. The gun hangs from the fingers of his free hand. "What the consequences of your actions will be."

Panic claws at me, and my next move will either save or kill me. "Please … release me, and I'll go wherever you want. I'm done running."

When he pulls back, I draw out the pepper spray from my purse, kick him in the balls, and spray the shit out of him. He stumbles back a step, and I dart away from him and start running.

"You bitch!" he shouts, covering his eyes with one hand.

He raises his other arm and starts shooting, blindly attempting to hit me. I flee from the apartment, sprinting to the sedan, and jump inside.

"Fuck!" I scream when I find the key isn't in the ignition.

It's with Dario.

I kick off my sandals, slide out of the sedan, and run for my life. My feet hurt as they hit the hot pavement, slamming against gravel and litter until I hit a busy road. Vinny once told me that the best criminals always conduct business behind closed doors, so I need to go somewhere crowded. Vinny won't pull out a gun and kill me with a large audience. Otherwise, he knows his father will hang him by his balls.

I pause, bending at the waist to catch my breath, and that's when I realize I don't have a phone.

Fucking Cristian and the orange juice.

I run to a gas station and hope that Vinny isn't anywhere behind me. The door to the gas station *dings*, and all eyes shoot to me—a frantic, barefoot woman, wearing a shirt sprayed with blood.

"Honey," an elderly woman whispers, taking a step toward me, "are you okay?"

"Ma'am, do you want me to call 911?" the young guy behind the counter asks, holding up his phone.

"I need to call a cab," I say, still out of breath.

"Did you kill someone?" a snot-nosed kid holding a juice box asks. "You'll go to jail for that, you know?"

As much as I'd love to ask for a ride, Vinny is connected to a lot of people. There might even be someone in here affiliated with him.

"Your phone—can I see it?" I ask, stumbling toward the clerk.

"Uh … sure," he mutters, holding it out to me.

I don't call a cab.

Instead, I take the phone and dart out of the gas station. I spot a man talking on the phone and unscrewing his gas cap. Before he enters the pump into his truck, I jump inside.

"What the fuck?" he screams as I slam on the gas and take off.

"Sorry," I yell out the window.

I speed back to the iron gates.

From one monster to another.

What a shit show I've made of my life.

Javier, Cristian's guard at the gate, is shocked to find me returning not only alone but also in a rusted pickup truck that I prayed wouldn't break down on my drive to the mansion.

Cristian makes me wait fifteen minutes before allowing me inside, and I pray harder that those fifteen minutes weren't spent preparing for my death.

He's standing in the foyer when I walk inside. He, Benny, and Rocky are all staring at me in question. I can hear my heartbeat blasting through my ears.

"Where the fuck is Dario?" Cristian roars.

He doesn't ask why I returned in a random truck, or why I'm wearing a bloodstained shirt and no shoes, or why I look like I just spent a week on *Survivor*.

He doesn't care about any of that.

The high-ranking Mafia men are shooting daggers in my direction, and now, I have to tell them one of their men is dead because of me.

"He's dead," I say in a throaty voice, my eyes on Cristian's soulless ones.

"What do you mean, *he's dead*?" Cristian steps toward me.

I scramble back, just as I did with Vinny, and back myself against the wall.

Cristian looms over me, the toes of his shoes meeting my bare feet. "Did *you* kill him?"

"No!" I shriek, attempting to tip my head back for a better look at Cristian so that he can see the truth on my face. "Vinny shot him!"

"That doesn't mean he's dead, Natalia." He raises his voice. "Did you even *try* to help him?"

"Dad—" Benny says, and even though I can't see anything past Cristian's massive body, I picture him walking in our direction when Cristian holds up his hand, stopping him.

"He was shot in the head and wasn't moving," I argue. "Vinny might be dumb, but he knows how to kill someone. He killed Dario and then tried to kill me."

"Unfortunately, it wasn't the other way around," Rocky comments.

"Fuck!"

I jump when Cristian's hands slam the wall on each side of my head.

"Motherfucker!" His icy stare stays on me as he drops his hands and backtracks a step. "Rocky, go to Natalia's house and clean up the mess."

Rocky salutes him and walks out of the mansion.

Cristian grips my elbow and jerks me forward. "Take off your shirt, Natalia."

"What?" I stutter.

"You aren't wearing a bloodstained shirt into my office."

I motion toward his office. "You literally kill people in there, and *they bleed*."

"Natalia." Cristian grits out my name as if he wants to rip me into pieces. "Take your fucking shirt off and walk into my office before I'm wearing your goddamn blood."

I shift from one foot to the other. "I'll go upstairs and change."

He doesn't release my elbow when I attempt to slip around him. "I said, my office." His eyes are cold as he smirks. "You don't have anything we haven't seen before, trust me. I don't want you to take off your shirt so I can jack off to the image of it later. I don't want blood in my office, *and* I need to make sure you're not wearing a wire."

I attempt to yank out of his hold, resulting in a squeeze from him. "I can't exactly do that with you holding me."

He tightens his grip so hard that I know it'll leave a mark, and then he releases me, pushing me back as if I were a rag doll.

I quickly pull my shirt over my head, standing in front of them in only a black lace bra—one Helena brought over. The scrap of fabric doesn't leave much to the imagination. The men go quiet as they stare at me. My nipples pucker at how they cast their eyes down my chest. I drop the shirt to the floor as Cristian reaches forward, and his callous palm presses against my chest, between my breasts. With one swift motion, he runs it between, under, and over my breasts—as a man in an airport would do to search someone.

It's not gentle or intimate.

It's rough and so Cristian Marchetti.

Embarrassingly, I wonder if that's how he is with his lovers.

As if he's happy with what he sees, he turns around and stalks to the office. Benny does the same, his strides long. As do I, my sore feet taking slower steps.

"Natalia, sit your ass down," Cristian orders when I enter the room.

I won't argue with that demand. My feet need a good rest. I plop down onto the chair and cross my arms, hiding myself from them.

Cristian glares at me. "I should've kicked you out when you asked for help. Now, I have a dead soldier, and my son is over here with a hard dick, wanting to marry you."

Benny wanders to the bar cart, pours himself a glass, and doesn't bother correcting his father.

Cristian rubs the space between his dark brows. "Tell me what happened."

My shoulders relax for the first time in hours, and I tell them everything.

Cristian's eyes don't leave mine as he consumes my every word, and Benny downs two glasses of liquor.

"Benny," Cristian says when I finish, and his son sets his glass down. "Drop the truck off somewhere and collect the security footage from the gas station. Hopefully, they haven't turned our little car thief in yet. Pay the clerk for a new phone and make sure there's no police paperwork on this."

When Benny leaves the room, Cristian steps toward me. His

feet hit mine—as he did in the foyer—and he bows his head to whisper in my ear. "You're becoming more trouble than you're worth, Natalia. And do you know what I do with trouble?"

"What?" I whisper.

"Dispose of it."

8

CRISTIAN

If Natalia Carprio doesn't stop giving me headaches, I'm putting a bullet through her pretty little face.

Dario is dead—further proving his smarts were limited.

And now, it's time to use his death to my advantage.

I pick up my phone, and pleasure hits me as I listen to the ringing. I wait for a man as heartless as me to answer.

"Vincent Lombardi," I say as soon as he does. "Your son is becoming quite the problem for me."

"So I've heard," Vincent replies with a huff.

I trace the rim of my whiskey glass. "I have something he wants."

"I know."

"He killed one of my men."

"I know that too." A brief silence passes. "What do you want, Marchetti?"

"One of your men in exchange for the death of mine. Fifty K for the woman." I consider that a reasonable offer.

It's a win-win for me.

A lose-lose for Natalia.

The woman is turning into a liability.

Dario was killed.

My men, including my son, want to fuck her.

And, hell, I've thought about fucking her more times than I'd like to admit.

She's trouble, and she needs to be disposed of.

Might as well profit from it.

Plus, giving her up will provide me with something I want.

"I can't just hand over one of my men for you to murder."

"An eye for an eye, Lombardi." I relax in my chair. "Tell your son to quit being so trigger-happy, and we won't have these troubles."

"That's bullshit, Marchetti. That woman is my son's ex, and he simply wanted to speak to her. Your man stopped him from doing so."

"Vinny was unprovoked. He could've taken her without killing my man."

"Fine," he grunts. "I'll meet you behind the Seminole warehouse."

"Be there at eight."

When I hang up, I smirk with satisfaction.

Tonight, I will lead my daughter's best friend to her death.

Tonight, the monster inside me will come out.

With the ease of a man who excels at manipulation, I wait until after dark to tell Natalia that I'm personally escorting her home to collect her belongings. I'm chaperoning because Vinny knows not to fuck with me.

Her face gives off nothing when she nods and says, "Okay."

Four crime families run New York—the Marchettis, Lombardis, Cavallaros, and the O'Connors. In a perfect world, we respect each other and how we handle business. But that doesn't mean there haven't been problems. Most of those issues are with the Lombardis. Vincent Lombardi is the boss, but his eldest son, Vinny, will take that title when he steps down.

Word is, Vinny has been bragging behind the scenes of wanting to create chaos, break contracts, and attempt to be *king of the city* when he steps into his father's position. Dealing with an idiot like that sounds like a headache. It's better to kill him now than worry about it later.

The Cavallaros have real estate I want, so that's why Benny pulling out of marrying Neomi isn't a fucking option—especially if tension between the Lombardis and me grows. They'll be forced to take sides, and I need them to take mine.

But if Vincent has a brain, he'll listen to what I have to say and logically decide to keep his family and operations safe.

Natalia is in the Escalade's back seat with me, and Rocky is driving. Benny usually accompanies us on business like this, but he'd try to save Natalia from the inevitable. The less bullshit I have to deal with tonight, the better.

"Wait." Natalia smacks her hand on the back of Rocky's seat. "This isn't the way to my apartment."

"We have a brief stop to make," I explain in a relaxed tone. "I prefer to run all my errands in one swoop."

She doesn't reply, but her shaky breaths echo through the SUV.

Rocky nor I mutter another word. Eventually, Natalia will realize the chances of her returning to her apartment are slim to none. I hope Vincent spares her a quick death, but knowing him, he'll hand Natalia over to his idiot son like a birthday present. And everyone knows, Vinny's dick gets hard when he beats and tortures those who have crossed him.

"You son of a bitch!" Natalia screams when Rocky turns into the back alley of the old warehouse. "You're handing me over to him, you fucking bastard!"

Rocky chuckles in the front.

Like Vinny, he enjoys others' pain.

Mutilation is his favorite pastime. The man gets off on chopping up bodies and delivering the parts to unsuspecting family members. Good for me. Even though I've done it, it's a tedious job. Rocky calls it therapy, but we all know the man needs to be in a fucking padded cell, not therapy.

I grunt when Natalia lunges toward me, her nails going in every direction as she claws at me. I allow her a few blows—give her a little something before meeting her demise. When I've had enough, I snatch her wrists and stop her.

"Sweet, Natalia." I rub at the nip her nails gave my lip, noticing a small trickle of blood. "Have you forgotten who's in charge?"

"How could you do this?" Her voice cracks as every inch of her body shakes. "I'm your daughter's best friend—"

I place a finger over her trembling lips. "You are nothing to me."

I'm tired of her thinking I care about her being Gigi's friend.

Rocky steps out of the Escalade and opens Natalia's door, and she screams insults as he drags her out of the seat. His arms are tucked underneath her armpits, holding her up, and her feet drag along the concrete. I rub my thumb over my lip again, collecting the small amount of blood, and bark out a laugh as I join them outside.

A sedan is parked feet away from us, and all four doors open simultaneously. A bright spotlight above us puts everyone's actions on full display. I tune out Natalia's shit talking as Vincent—a dark red cane in his hand—and Antonio, his middle son, ease from the car. Vinny and a younger man then join them. I snort as my eyes lock with Vinny's bloodshot eyes, courtesy of Natalia's pepper spray.

His murderous glare slides from mine to a combative Natalia.

Not that she's making any leeway. Rocky has her arms pinned behind her back with one hand, and his free arm is looped around her waist.

Vinny's eyes tighten as he stares at her.

I'm unsure who he wants to kill more—Natalia or me.

By instinct, I already know the guy standing next to Antonio is their sacrifice. Baby face, no older than twenty, and most likely made some petty mistake that pissed Vincent off.

Natalia screams, and Rocky's hand leaves her waist to cover her mouth.

I ignore her, wishing I'd brought a muzzle for her loud-ass mouth, and motion toward the young man. "This the one?"

Vincent—a stalky man, no taller than Natalia—says, "It is," in a stern and sure-of-himself tone.

"What does he mean?" the poor guy frantically asks, his gaze panning from me to Antonio and then to Vincent. "The one what?"

I pull my gun from inside my suit jacket, a silencer on the end, and shoot the man in the head. Unlike the bastards surrounding me, if the person means nothing to me, I don't mind making their death quick.

Natalia screams behind Rocky's palm, and she kicks at him to free herself. In her head, she's most likely seeing the young man's fate as her own.

"Your son sure loves to run his mouth to the women he fucks," I tell Vincent. "Business with the Corobras—drug smugglers all of us agreed not to associate with since they lace their drugs with shit that are killing people in our city." I tsk underneath my breath. "The other families won't be happy about that."

There's a twinge of recoil from Vincent at my words. From his reaction—a reaction he does his best to mask—my guess is, Natalia was correct about his son doing business with them behind his father's back. But as a boss, it's of great importance to display how emotionless we are.

And Vincent, a man who's been in charge for four decades, usually excels at being unreadable. But not tonight. I catch every flash of anger pass over his red face and the way his hand tightens around the top of his cane. If this were any other man than his son, Vincent would've killed him as soon as the words left my mouth.

"What the fuck?" I hear Antonio hiss to his brother, glaring at Vinny.

I haven't paid another glance at Vinny.

The stupid motherfucker doesn't deserve my attention yet.

Snapping my fingers, I gesture for Rocky to bring Natalia to me. She paused her struggling to watch the scene but starts back up when Rocky yanks her toward me.

"The code to Vinny's safe is Natalia's birthday." I chuckle, rattling off information Natalia had given me, and this is the moment I finally slip my gaze to a fuming Vinny. "At your home in Brooklyn … Thirteenth Avenue, am I right?"

My eyes flash in victory. Vinny, a few inches taller than his father, is fighting for restraint harder than Natalia is fighting for her life. The man has a temper on him, and I'm hoping he falls right into my trap.

Come to me, motherfucker.

Let me shoot you between the eyes.

But Vinny doesn't. For the first time in his pathetic life, he uses his fucking brain.

What a shame.

Time to up the ante.

"All this information has come from this one here." I step to Natalia's side, causing her to freeze in place, and tap the gun against her temple. "Burly's Cleaners … through the back."

I can practically hear Vinny's breathing from here.

Can feel it whip through the air and sing to me.

"You said fifty thousand dollars, Marchetti." Antonio interrupts my theatrics with calmness. "Hand over the girl, and this business is over."

Now, that is a real leader.

I shake my head and press the gun against Natalia's head simultaneously while ignoring her cries. "I've changed my price."

"To what?" Vincent fumes.

I move my gun from Natalia's head and point it at Vinny. "Him."

"The fuck?" The tight cord of restraint Vinny held snaps, and he starts to charge toward me.

I lightly brush my finger along the trigger of my gun, but before I can pull it, Antonio steps in to protect his hotheaded brother from his death.

Antonio aims his gun at me. "Cut the shit before I blow your head off, Marchetti."

"Do it." Thrill storms through my body. "There are things I need to argue with my father about in the afterlife." My tone turns bored. "Plus, my son would become a monster, avenging my death." I shut an eye. "My guess is, you'd lose at least half your men."

A sharp laugh escapes me when from the back of the warehouse, four of my men make their appearance. The Lombardi men are the target of their AKs. If the Lombardis want to try to kill me, all three of them will die immediately after.

I never said I wasn't one to play dirty.

I do what needs to be done.

"Marchetti, this is out of line," Vincent says, shaking his head. "This isn't the way we conduct business."

"It is when your son kills one of my men." I waggle my finger at him. "That changes the rules." I smirk and train my gun on Vinny, my eyes directed to Vincent. "I know it's extreme to tell another boss to sacrifice their son—"

"I'd die before I gave up my son," Vincent says, stabbing his cane into the concrete as he advances a step in my direction. "If you came here thinking that would happen, you're crazy."

"Oh, what I just said is a sliver of what he told Natalia. He gave her so many secrets." I ignore Antonio's gun on me and peer at my pawn. "I know where the guns … the cash is."

"Sweet Natalia." I say her name as mockingly as possible. "She told me so much, and I'll fuck more information out of her." I return my gun to her and slip it underneath her dress and between her legs.

Her body shakes, her teeth chattering, as tears fall down her cheeks. She opens her mouth, but it's as if she can't form words. Or she doesn't want to say the wrong ones. I keep the gun beneath her dress, and she jumps forward when I drag it over her panties. It's as if that move jerks her back to life, and she returns to struggling with Rocky for release.

"Vinny, Natalia will be in my bed night after night. And each time I spill my cum inside her, she'll tell me more about your small dick and moan out all your secrets."

"You motherfucker!" Vinny snaps. Meeting the end of his patience, he darts toward me.

This time, it takes Antonio *and* Vincent to restrain Vinny.

Vinny bares his teeth at me as Natalia screams at Rocky while squirming in his hold. I grin, loving how Vincent is registering what a hothead his son is. Out of all of us, Vinny and Natalia are the only ones showing their emotions.

Vinny's gaze isn't on me.

It's anchored on Natalia.

His hands are balled into fists, and he looks ready to explode.

A sheen of sweat is visible on his forehead as he stares at her like she's a toy who's been on his Christmas list for years. I dramatically yawn before dipping my head down and kissing Natalia's neck. She thrashes in Rocky's hold, but she doesn't have even half the power of him.

This is the moment I realize how much Natalia means to Vinny.

He loves her. He will kill for her. And he will die for her by my hands.

"Cristian, you called me, and we made an agreement," Vincent says.

Vinny's temper lessens to listen to his father.

Vincent signals to his dead man and shouts, "I delivered my end of the agreement. Don't you dare disrespect me with this juvenile game." He gestures toward my men, waiting for someone to make the wrong move. "You're wasting everyone's time. I'll see the girl on the streets eventually."

A whimper bursts from Natalia at Vincent's comment.

"Yeah, bitch," Vinny spits, his eyes never leaving Natalia. "You wait until I get my hands on you. We'll have some real fun."

Natalia goes back to being frozen, still, as she watches her ex stare her down, as if he wants to set her on fire.

Antonio releases his brother to run his hands through his hair. "Jesus."

"You can't protect her forever," Vincent says. "It'd be in your best interest to hand her over. She means nothing to you."

I remove the gun from under Natalia's dress. "Oh, she means everything to me." I run the gun over her cheek, and she trembles as I cruelly stare at Vincent. "I will marry her."

"The fuck you will!" Vinny roars, and that cord finally springs free as he charges toward me.

My guys step closer to the enemy, but I hold up my arms, stopping them.

I want to see what his next move is.

Antonio snatches the back of Vinny's shirt and tugs him back to his side.

"You have something else to say, Vinny?" I yell. "Feel free to attempt to murder me. Until then, Natalia will become my wife. The longer I have her, the more info I'll drag out, detail by detail."

The night is getting later, and it seems no one will take any action tonight.

I jam the tip of the gun into her cheek before drawing it back and playing with it in my hand. "Until next time, gentlemen."

"You're nuts if you think I'm marrying you," Natalia shouts as soon as Rocky throws her in the back seat with me.

I point out the window. "Should I hand you over now then? He offered fifty thousand dollars for you, but you're worth more than that to me. But if you're going to have this attitude, then we can make the exchange with them, and I'll at least be richer." I relax into the seat, proud of myself for my good behavior and not putting a bullet in Vinny's head. "I look forward to fucking you on our wedding day."

"You won't touch me," she spits.

"Then, I look forward to fucking another woman on our wedding day."

She winces at my response. "Why do you want me to marry you? I thought you wanted me dead."

"You see, Vinny put Vincent in a dangerous predicament. Vincent knows the longer you're with me, the more I'll know. He wants you dead, and I want Vinny dead. That can happen in two ways. Vinny kills you, which is a way for me to start a war with the Lombardis, *or* Vincent grows sick of his shit and asks me to hand you over in exchange for his son. But you will not be loose until I have Vinny."

"Why do you want him so bad?"

"That's none of your concern."

"You're using my life to get it."

"Should have stayed away from men who can kill you." I tap on the seat for Rocky to drive. "Let's go."

9

NATALIA

The bastard planned to hand me over to the Lombardis as if I were nothing but a rat.

Technically, I *am* one since I gave Cristian information on Vinny, but I didn't *rat* Cristian out.

I thought the monster sitting next to me was deceitful before, but now, it's clear that his word is that of Judas Iscariot. Under no circumstances can he be trusted.

I rotate, resting my back against the car door, and fix my glare on Cristian. "You're a disgrace to the male population."

It's dark, so all I can make out is his profile.

But I don't need to see him to detect the frustration rippling through him.

He wanted Vinny.

He wanted Vincent to take me home and do whatever he deemed fit for my rat self—rape, trafficking, homicide. Cristian didn't get what he wanted, and I'm sure that doesn't happen often.

"Watch your mouth when speaking to me," he says in a menacing tone.

I don't want to watch my mouth.

Cristian needs me for something.

So, now, I'm going to take this opportunity to talk to him any way I'd like.

"Why?" I ask, almost taunting. "You won't kill me yet. I'm a pawn for your *who has the biggest balls* contest." I tap the edge of my mouth. "Or guns since it seems you psychopaths prefer not to get your hands dirty like *real* men. You shoot guns because you're pathetic—"

I gasp as my head smacks into the window when Cristian's hand wraps around my throat, blocking any further insults directed at him.

His large hand nearly spans my entire throat, and he crowds me. "I have murdered men with these bare hands, sweetheart." His hand clenches tighter around my neck. "I don't need a gun to kill someone." He lowers his head until his mouth is nearly against mine. "Keep pushing me. You thought dying at the hands of Vinny was scary? Mine would be much worse."

When he releases me, pushing me back, I hold my throat and pant out breaths.

He straightens out his suit. "Now, shut up like a good little wife."

When we return to the mansion, I'm running my hands along my throat.

I'd bet my last life left that there will be red marks tomorrow.

"Natalia, come with me," Cristian orders as if I were one of his men.

"Fuck off," I reply, rushing toward the stairs, the guest room my destination. "I've had enough of your psycho ass tonight."

It's been a day … a night … an *everything*.

I yelp when he snatches my elbow, pulling me back, and I fall into his chest.

"I haven't had enough of *you* yet."

What is it with men in power?

Why do they assume all of us will fall at their feet and worship them?

I attempt to pull out of his grasp, but he tightens his hold.

Fear.

It's what fuels Cristian.

He grips you tighter and tighter, pulls you in closer and closer, until he has you exactly where he wants you—at his mercy.

"I said, come with me," he says through gritted teeth.

I throw my free arm up. "Sure, fine, whatever. My night can't get any worse than almost being sold to a mob family."

I shouldn't have said that. Knowing Cristian, he'd find that a challenge and make it worse.

His hard body brushes against mine as he leads me up the stairs, down a hallway, through a narrow walkway, and into a second wing of the house. It's as if we were in Hampton Court Palace, like the home was built for someone to get lost inside.

He releases me with no warning, so I nearly bust my ass when we stop at a door in the back of another hallway. A keypad is drilled into the handle, and Cristian blocks me from watching him punch in the passcode. The door beeps once, then twice, and he opens it.

I follow him inside since not only does he seem to expect that of me, but I also want to know what lies behind that door —as if I were on a game show, waiting to see whether I'd won a prize.

It's either good or bad.

No in-between with this man.

The room is rich with the scent of Cristian.

The monster's bedroom.

"I told Leona to have your belongings moved from the guest room to here," he says, unbuttoning his jacket, slipping it off his arms, and draping it over a leather ottoman in the corner of the room.

I linger in the doorway, as if stepping in would sign my deal with the devil. "Who's Leona?" All my time here, and I haven't heard that name mentioned once.

"The woman in charge of caring for my wing of the house," he answers like it's common knowledge I should know.

"I didn't think we'd do the *husband and wife* thing behind closed doors."

He stands tall, in front of the largest bed I've ever laid eyes on, and folds up the sleeves of his white button-up. I eye the man who just declared himself my future husband, my thighs tingling, and desire spirals through me harder than with any other man I've been in the same room with.

More than Vinny.

More than every crush I had in high school.

I want this man—the man who didn't give a shit about my life thirty minutes ago. There is seriously something wrong with my brain. Vinny's stupidity must've rubbed off on me.

He smirks, scrubbing a hand over his tan skin. "Sweet Natalia, I don't fake marry women."

"Yet that's exactly what you're doing with me."

"You will treat me like your husband, Natalia." His voice and eyes harden.

I motion back and forth between the two of us. "How long will we keep up this charade?"

"Until I say so."

"And when we're done?" The words fall out of my mouth between hard breaths.

"We'll talk about that then," he replies with such ease, and I wish I had the peace of mind he did, but his life isn't on the line like mine.

I gulp. "You can't kill your wife."

He advances a step in my direction, and my entire body tenses as he stalls in front of me in the doorway.

He tucks a strand of my hair behind my ear, and shivers run up my spine. "Wrong, sweet Natalia. No one else can kill my wife. No one said anything about me."

I stare at him, speechless, as he slips past me, leaving me alone in the monster's den.

10

CRISTIAN

I walk downstairs to a quiet house.

I only have a few live-in employees. Leona, who's worked for me for decades and doesn't come out much. Miriam, my cook and housekeeper, and Gretchen, Miriam's daughter. Gretchen started only a few months ago after the last girl slit her wrists when Benny told her she was only a good fuck.

My fucking kids.

I'd once thought they were my biggest headaches.

Then, the dark-haired beauty upstairs tiptoed her way into my life.

Benny lives in the other wing of the house, and when Gigi isn't roaming around the world with my aunt, she has her own area.

Some dons have their men live with them, but I greatly appreciate my privacy. I have around-the-clock employees who guard the gate and two who live in the guesthouse and switch shifts, watching the mansion's perimeter.

I find Rocky in the living room, surrounded by silence while staring straight ahead into a black-screened TV. I whistle for his attention, and he grunts while pushing himself off the couch and onto his feet.

Without my asking but knowing me well enough to understand, he follows me into the office and shuts the door behind him. I pour two glasses of much-deserved bourbon, the glasses clinking together as I hand one over to him. Rocky rests his back against a wall as I swallow down the contents in one swig.

"What's the plan now, boss?" he asks as I pour myself another.

I shrug. "Looks like I'm getting married."

Another glass down.

Another drink poured.

I can tell there's something Rocky wants to say, but he's hesitant to release the words.

He stares into his drink, searching for words that won't piss me off.

His voice is thick when he finds them. "I'm concerned about war with the Lombardi family."

I chuckle. "I'm not."

I love a good war.

It keeps me young.

Keeps me thriving.

Keeps me king.

"I thought maybe you were considering Carmela …" His voice trails off as if he doesn't know how to finish his sentence.

Carmela is Rocky's daughter, the woman I sent to do Natalia's hair before dinner.

Most men in our business would balk at their daughters fucking a man they're not married to, but I'm the boss. Rocky was happy when I brought his daughter to my bed and allowed her to suck me off until I came down her throat.

No way would I let a motherfucker even *think* about Gigi in that way.

That's why I've yet to marry her off like so many men in our family have done to daughters even younger than her. I'm waiting for her to come to me with a selection. My daughter won't be traded as a business deal.

My son? Yes.

Married or not, Benny will do whatever the fuck he wants.

But there are certain restrictions on Mafia wives, and Gigi would break nearly every single one of them.

But just like Rocky thirsts for becoming my right-hand man, he also aims for me to take Carmela as my wife. I've considered it. She does everything I ask with no argument. She sucks dick like a champ and obeys my every word. But as much as I appreciate submission and begging, that power dies when the person surrenders without argument.

I enjoy women with tight pussies who let me take them any way I want. But I also want those women to have a smart mouth and a backbone. Which is why I haven't remarried after Benita's death.

That will change.

And I don't know where Natalia will fit into that mold.

Deep down, I don't want her to fit into that mold since I don't plan to keep her for long.

It's past three in the morning when I return to my bedroom.

I'm not a man who sleeps much.

I acquire what is necessary to keep my body functioning, but there's too much to be done, too much on my mind, for me to shut my eyes and relax.

The only light comes from a lamp in the corner on the table next to the ottoman. The ottoman that Natalia is curled up on with a book in her hand and a blanket covering her lower half. She drops the book as I shut the door and lock it.

I didn't give her direction on what to do before I left the bedroom earlier, but I at least expected her to be in my bed … *our* bed.

Do I feel bad about the Vincent situation? No.

It's what happens in this world, and she means nothing to me.

And right now, with the way she refuses to pay me a glance, she's telling me the same thing.

"Why are you over there?" I walk deeper into the room and remove my watch and cuff links, setting them on my nightstand.

"This is where I'm sleeping."

"All right."

Where is the Carmela submissiveness when I need it?

I don't look at her again as I stroll to the bathroom, undress, tuck my Glock into a drawer, and shower. I think of the woman in my bedroom as the steaming water pours down my body. She's poked at my every nerve the past few days. She became an annoyance, then a headache, and now, she's a pawn.

It's a shame, really. Vinny should've made her his wife as soon as he could.

I'm sure Vincent wouldn't allow it, though. Most marriages are chosen via contract—always for the benefit of the family. From the fire in his eyes when he saw me with Natalia, I know Vinny wanted Natalia to be more than his girlfriend, but Vincent wouldn't allow it.

Vinny probably liked Natalia for the same reason I even considered this marriage charade. She's gorgeous, and I'm sure, being the spitfire she is, she's a good fuck.

I want Natalia to bow down to me.

To see her on her knees, looking up at me with those brown eyes.

My cock twitches at the thought of it.

I walk back into the bedroom with a white towel tied around my waist. Natalia sucks in a ragged breath, those beautiful eyes of hers widening as she discreetly sweeps her gaze up and down my body.

"How many men have you fucked, Natalia?"

Those defiant eyes of hers harden as they flash back to mine. "None of your business."

"How many?"

She pinches her plump lips together and stays quiet.

I raise my voice. "Excuse me?"

"Three," she finally answers.

"Good. That's a short list of men I need to kill."

She winces. "What?"

"If you've fucked my wife, then you need to die."

"That was *prior* to you."

I shrug. "Again, if you've ever stuck your dick into my wife, then you die."

Her tone turns harsh. "And what about you … and *your* women?"

"If you want to hunt down every bitch I've fucked and kill them, go ahead." I smirk. "I'll have Rocky clean up the mess for you."

"You are ruthless."

"Tell me something I don't already know, sweet Natalia." I drop my towel when she opens her mouth to talk more shit, but her words are swallowed down as she inhales a deep breath.

It's as if the towel hitting the floor knocks some sense into her, and she slaps her hand over her eyes. "Jesus, do you mind?"

"No."

She slowly drags her hand away from her eyes.

I watch her watch me.

My cock twitches, and her nails dig into her blanket as she fights the urge to lower her eyes.

"Considering you've fucked three men, I'm sure seeing a cock is nothing new to you," I add.

And even though it's the last thing I should do, I lower my hand, taking her eyes with it, and wrap it around my growing erection.

How am I this hard over this woman?

Over my daughter's friend?

I stroke myself once while staring at her.

Her eyes are entranced on my cock, her tongue sweeping over her bottom lip.

I give myself another slow stroke, my cock hardening every second, and I wish I could replace the hand with the woman's across from me.

The room swells with desire so deep that I can smell it, and we haven't even touched yet.

She doesn't take her eyes off me.

"Do you want something, Natalia?"

"Gigi will hate me," she whispers.

"Gigi suggested we marry."

"As a ruse." A harsh pant accompanies each word.

"Suit yourself then." I give myself another stroke and control the groans forcing their way up my throat.

"Can you stop doing that?"

"What?"

Her eyes leave my cock, and she looks at me while gesturing to my hand.

I'm not normally a man who jacks off in front of women, but I do when she's practically salivating for a taste, debating on her next move.

"I fuck women, Natalia." My voice and cock harden. "If you don't want to fuck me, that's fine. But warning: I will get it elsewhere if not from you. I'll even be kind enough to give you a heads-up."

Fuck. Just get your ass over here and wrap those pretty lips around my dick.

She stares at me with a fire burning in her eyes and smirks. "That's so sweet. I will extend the same courtesy." She says her words with a sense of self-satisfaction, as if she's proud of herself.

I stop my stroking. "If you want him *and yourself* to die, then go ahead. The five minutes he lasts won't be worth your lives. I can promise you that."

She turns silent as her eyes wander back to my erection and settle there for what seems like an eternity.

As the desire intensifies, I return to stroking my cock. "If you want it, Natalia, it's yours."

I'm sure she's sucked cock before.

She was with Vinny.

I want her mouth, her pussy, her everything at this moment.

I'm not a man with many weaknesses, but the woman in the corner, her wide eyes and mouth staring at me, has become one.

I freeze when she slowly slides the blanket off herself, stands, and walks toward me.

11

NATALIA

I, Natalia Carprio, am an idiot.
 I'll admit it.
An idiot who's taking short steps toward this dangerous man and practically salivating as I do it. At this point, I should tell Cristian to pistol-whip some sense into me.

All the boundaries I promised myself I'd keep from this monster are shoved into that dark corner.

This is a man who's threatened my life countless times.

A man who was prepared to sell me to a mob boss with no apologies.

And my best friend's father.

All reasons for me to run for my life—*literally.*

Instead, I'm walking toward him, each step fearless and consumed with desire.

It's impulsive, and in the back of my head, I'm positive regret will swoop through me in the morning.

His cock is thick and long—the largest I've ever seen.

"If you want it, Natalia, it's yours."

Mine. For tonight at least.

But will I do the same for him—give myself over for tonight?

If so, will he return the favor?

I remember the nights Vinny just wanted a quick blow job, and our intimacy was over. With Cristian's cruelty, I wouldn't be surprised if he blew my brains out after I blew him.

Stupid, stupid, Natalia.

But Cristian, he has this pull to him.

A pull that will make anyone bow to his feet.

Cristian's breathing is controlled. His arms are flexed, his hand still circled, but not moving around his thick cock, and my fingers ache to touch him, to feel what I know will give me an experience I've never had. We make direct eye contact, his half-lidded eyes trained on me before skating his gaze over my barely covered body. The black bralette and cheeky boy shorts that Helena brought over are completely see-through, hence why I assured I was covered when he returned to his bedroom for the night.

As soon as I reach him, Cristian closes those masculine hands over my shoulders, putting heavy pressure on them. "Get on your knees, Natalia."

I gulp but stand firm. "I don't take orders."

"You do now."

And only because my insides are burning for him, urging me to surrender all rationality, do I slowly drop to my knees. The monster's face relaxes in satisfaction. The carpet is soft and warm against my legs.

When I'm settled, Cristian's hands drop from my shoulders, and he rubs the head of his cock over the seam of my wet lips. "Suck this cock like you're a woman convincing a man to marry her."

My bottom lip tingles. "I'm not convincing you to do anything. I'll suck your dick because I'm horny, not because you're demanding it."

He plunges his large hand into my hair. I wince when he roughly tugs the long strands, wounding them around his wrist, and he yanks my mouth so close to his erection that my nose presses against his stomach.

"I don't give a fuck what your reason is."

Desire overtakes my sanity.

All my attitude.

All my disdain toward him.

His hold still tight on me, he grants me an inch of space, so I can breathe without him nearly suffocating me. I run my tongue along the length and grin against his cock when he shudders.

I'm attracted to men who show what they want in the bedroom since I'm a woman who does the same. I savor the intimacy of pleasuring someone until they fall apart, moaning my name and orgasming so hard that they can't stop thinking about it the next day.

I lick, kiss, suck on the tip and groan when he tugs on my hair.

"Put my cock in your mouth and suck it like a good girl before I shove it down your goddamn throat."

His cock twitches when I take his entire length into my mouth and taste the saltiness of his pre-cum. His head falls back, his long fingers clenching into my hair, and I control my gag reflex when his tip hits the back of my throat. I've never sucked off a man of his size, a cock filling my mouth so deep, and just as I'm relaxing my jaw and hollowing out my cheeks, he pulls my hair back.

This man and my hair.

"Look at me when my cock is in your mouth."

I do, and he stares down at me with hunger in his eyes.

I suck him, not caring about the consequences.

Not caring what people will think.

It's Cristian and me.

The king and his sacrifice.

"Mmm …" he groans, slapping my cheek in approval. "At least I know my future wife can suck this cock well."

He thrusts his cock deeper into my mouth, and his hand

releases my hair, moving to the back of my head and cupping it. He controls my pace, rough and aggressive. "Just like that, Natalia." His voice turns somewhat praising. "You're going to make such a good wife."

He drops his head again, his desire for eye contact crumbling as I push him to the brink.

"Fuck," he moans. "Don't move that sweet mouth of yours."

At first, I don't understand what he means. But then he grips my head so hard that I couldn't move it even if I tried. And this beautiful but dangerous man fucks my face the way you'd imagine a man like him would.

Out of control, possessive, dominating.

Like he's marking his territory.

I choke a few times, but he doesn't stop his relentless pounding into my face.

I'm so turned on. Wetness pools between my legs. My heart skitters with desire. His cock swells in my mouth, and I wait for his cum, wait to taste every bit of him, but he suddenly stops.

"What?" I mutter against his cock.

He slides his cock from my mouth and grips my elbow. I yelp when he hauls me to my feet, but I stay that way for only a few minutes before he carries me to the bed and tosses me onto it.

Everything happens so fast. I'm in the middle of the bed, and then he closes his hands around my ankles as secure as shackles and drags me to the edge of the mattress to reach him. He jerks my legs apart before settling between them. His hand quickly glides up and down his cock.

Fast. Frantic. Just like his breathing.

Just like he fucked my face.

He groans loudly, the entire room practically vibrating with his release of pleasure, as he pumps his cum onto my stomach. Then, he's the one falling to his knees—a view I never imagined seeing—and uses his elbows to spread me wider.

He plants his hands on my thighs, tight in his hold, and his head lowers to my core. I shudder, my body ready to fall apart as he traces a finger through my slit.

"So wet, Natalia."

There's no warning before his fingers—I'm not sure how many—surge inside me.

It hurts, but it feels so good.

It throbs, but I need more.

This was worth it.

So fucking worth it.

Now, instead of his groans filling the room, it's mine and the sound of how wet I am as he thrusts inside me.

He slows his pace and softly kisses each of my thighs, shocking me that a man as malice as him can be so gentle. But then that monster returns when he bites into the skin, and I release a string of curses.

"Since you walked into my office that night, I've wondered how soft this pussy is."

He sucks my clit before drawing a path down my slit, so close to my crack, and then his tongue meets his fingers, still inside me. He continues his stroking, his tongue accompanying each thrust now.

I learn Cristian is just as evil with his tongue as he is with everything else. Just as skilled and calculated.

I can hardly breathe, every pant becoming harder and harder as he eats, fingers, and bites at me. It's rough but oh-so damn good.

Sweat slides off my body, and the wetness from between my legs dampens the sheets.

I cup his head similar to how he did me, only not as rough. No one can hold that amount of power but him. I ride his mouth as his tongue ignites every feeling in my body. He eats my pussy as if he were a man on death row and it was his last meal before his execution.

Cristian might hate me, might want me dead, but right now, all he wants is for me to come undone beneath him.

I moan when he stops licking.

"Who is eating your pussy, sweet Natalia?"

My body is nearly overheating as I arch my back. "You."

"Who?"

"Cristian." I push my thighs closer to his mouth.

"Who?" His voice hardens.

I slap my hands against the sheets. "I don't know what the hell else you want me to say."

My brain is hardly functioning, and he wants to play goddamn trivia.

"Your future husband." His teeth dig into my skin as if he wants to rip it apart, and the pain only adds to my pleasure. "Your future husband is eating this sweet pussy." He nips at the same spot. "Now, tell me, whose tongue is inside your pussy?"

"My future husband's."

Right now, I'd tell him every damn detail of the Lombardis along with my Social Security and bank account number if he asked. I am dying for his tongue.

"That's fucking right."

Another slow lick.

"And who is the only one who will eat this pussy?"

My nails dig into his hair. "My future husband."

His hand cups me between my legs with a similar roughness he gave while fucking my mouth. "Who owns this?"

"My future husband."

Jesus, I didn't talk this much when he was fucking my face.

His fingers move inside me again, and he massages my pussy with his tongue.

Bursts of nonstop pleasure hit me *again and again and again.*

It's good.

So, so good.

Gone are thoughts of death, of Vinny, of the mess I got myself into. The ways his tongue and hand are pleasuring me consume my brain.

"Don't stop," I moan. "I'm close, so close."

He swings my legs over his shoulders, and his licking turns more relentless.

Warmth and waves of pleasure plow through me. My legs shake as he finishes me off, not letting loose until my entire body is trembling, and I'm moaning his name as if it were the winning lottery numbers I needed to remember.

As he slows his pace, he reaches up and levels his hand on my stomach, feeling my frantic breathing. He rubs his finger through his half-dried cum as he rises, coating the tip.

"Mmm," he groans before sliding it inside me.

My head is spinning, and I don't realize how dangerous his action is. I rotate my hips into his touch again, exhausted. I could gain the energy if he wants to keep pleasuring me, but he slips his finger out.

"Open."

I do as he said.

He slides the finger he used to rub his cum into my mouth.

"Suck. Taste how good we are together."

I wrap my lips around it as hard as I did his cock.

We don't kiss.

We don't fuck.

What just happened was personal yet impersonal at the same time.

"You're sleeping here. Get your ass under the covers."

"But—"

"Try to argue, and I'll fuck your face until you can't breathe this time."

As I settle myself on my side, facing away from him, my mind drifts to what will become of this.

How long will the man sleeping next to me keep me alive?

I wake up to an empty bed.

An empty bed that smells like Cristian and sex.

My jaw is sore.

My throat is sore.

My thighs are sore.

I still feel the sting of his bite mark.

Still taste him in my mouth.

How long will this be my new life?

How long will I wake up in this bed before Cristian disposes of me?

I need to decide and come up with a plan.

Will I stay with Cristian and see what my life will become?

Or will I run from him?

I slip out of bed and shower before walking downstairs, barefoot, following the harsh voices coming from the dining room. The room goes quiet when I join Cristian and Benny.

Cristian is drinking a cup of coffee, an empty plate in front of him, and glaring at his son.

"Morning, Natalia," Benny says before stabbing his fork into a waffle and shoving it down his throat.

The composure in his voice makes me question if he knows of his dad's little arrangement that went wrong last night.

Which reminds me … I need to call Gigi. Even with her being out of the country, we talk a few times a week on the phone and text every day. I'm sure Benny told her about their father stomping on my phone, but I need to speak to her.

Cristian says nothing, gives nothing, nor does he look at me. As if the man's tongue wasn't between my legs less than six hours ago.

My future husband looks every bit the king he is—another tailored black suit fit as if he had been born into it like a second skin. Two buttons are undone, exposing some of his chest tattoos. I want to trace my finger over them, read each one, and ask about their meaning.

He's my type—dangerous, destructive, the guy your parents want you to run far away from. I had an aunt who once told me the men I choose to love will be the men who forge my demise. She said I was just like my mother before she gained some sense and chose a good man like my father.

My mother chose the safe man and was still murdered.

Albeit not by him, but we meet our fate when it's our time.

And that's been locked into my head from the day my father told me how my mother died.

But my aunt was right.

Vinny or Cristian will be the death of me.

But will I be the downfall of them as well?

Cristian? No.

Vinny? Possibly.

How dare Cristian not acknowledge me when I slip past him and pull the chair out. I might've been submissive last night—because orgasm and all that—but his behavior has me feeling argumentative.

I collapse into the chair as Cristian says, "Natalia, get up and sit your ass down next to me."

Ignoring him as he did me, I pour myself a glass of orange juice.

Cristian slams his fist onto the table, causing it to shake, and half of my orange juice spills out of the glass. "Place your ass in this chair before I spread you out on this table and let everyone watch me fuck you into obedience."

My eyes widen in horror.

His finally meet mine, as if daring me to call his bluff.

I want to shrink in the chair and allow it to swallow me whole.

Benny chokes on his bite.

"Natalia." Cristian's voice booms through the room. "Now."

I pull myself out of the chair, not wanting another argument or more talk of him *fucking me into obedience.*

When I pass Cristian, he reaches out and brushes his hand

underneath my dress. It's a simple touch but speaks volumes. Shame eats at me like a sickness, my stomach tightening as I grow wet between my legs.

"Good girl," Cristian praises, as if he were about to place dog food in front of me and take me on a walk around the block.

When I sit, he returns to acting like I don't exist.

I'm not sure what women Cristian controlled before, but there's certain behavior I'll accept. Him making a scene like this isn't one of them.

"Benny, you look handsome in your suit." I grab a strawberry, stick it into my mouth, and suck on it. "I've only seen you out of it once—the hot tub in Vegas, where we were practically naked. Remember?"

Benny scrubs a hand over his face, as if he doesn't want to deal with his father's wrath, but tough shit. He's deranged, so they shall take all the shit talking they deserve.

I moan as I bite into the strawberry. "I remember telling Gigi I'd sleep with you someday."

It's a lie.

But, hey, if a lie is what it takes to turn the tables on Cristian, a lie is what I will say.

"Natalia," Benny says in warning, and even though I don't peek at Cristian, I can feel his eyes burning into me, seething, wanting to make me pay for each word said.

"Natalia." Cristian repeats my name as his son did, but there's more edge crackling through it, a deeper threat, a *run for your life* tone. "Keep talking and you'll be responsible for me cutting off my son's hand." He inches into my space and lowers his voice, so I'm the only one who hears him. "Vinny might've been okay with your smart-ass mouth and childish behavior, but I am not that man."

"Vinny." I smile at him with forced playfulness and wrap my hair around a finger. "God, Vinny. I remember all the times he said he owned me during sex as well."

I'm being reckless.

Cristian presses his fingers into the wood of the table. He could very well pull out his gun and shoot me as easily as he did the guy last night. But at least I'd die with some goddamn dignity.

"Benny," Cristian barks, "get the fuck out of here and go outside."

Benny stands, rolls his eyes, and says, "Stop the games, Natalia."

Cristian massages his temple before grabbing my orange juice glass and crashing it against the wall.

The man sure has some beef with dinnerware.

The air in the room feels heavy against my lungs when he slowly stands from his chair. My back straightens, a flush of fear driving through me, and I'm proud of how steady I keep my breaths.

He takes the few steps toward me and stops behind me. The weight of his back against the chair pushes into me like a thousand bricks.

He winds my damp hair around his wrist as he had last night. When he bows his head into my neck, his lips brush my earlobe, and his tone is bone-chilling. "I'm still not against killing you."

Stupid me, following my pattern of making irrational decisions, I grab the knife in front of me and hold it out for him. "Do it, then. Your threats are growing old."

This might be the most senseless move I've ever made.

Dumber than trusting Vinny.

I'm calling his bluff, and it'll either result in my murder or him realizing I'm not a goddamn doormat.

With the silence and agility of a lion on the attack, he grips his hand over mine on the knife handle and clenches it so tight that I wait for my hand to break. I gasp, fighting to hold back his move's effect on me.

I attempt to pull away, but his grip is too firm. His hand is steady as he forces us to drag the edge of the knife along my jawline.

"There are so many ways I can use this on you," he hisses into my ear with a callous laugh.

I whimper when he lowers the knife and presses the tip into my neck. The pressure is light, but it's still there.

This man is a literal psychopath.

And my handing him the knife might make me one as well.

12

CRISTIAN

I will end up killing this pain-in-the-ass woman before we even make it to the altar.

Natalia irritates every single one of my goddamn nerves.

Hell, even nerves I never knew existed.

And that's saying a lot, coming from a man like me.

I run the knife over Natalia's throat.

A rupture of pleasure seeps through me when she shudders.

I won't slit it.

At least, not *right here*.

Under us is a one-of-a-kind rug imported from Italy. Even the best dry cleaner in the world can't clean blood from wool.

And because I'm the monster everyone says I am, I nudge the tip of the knife into her skin—it's gentler than what I'd use with a man who crossed me, but still enough pressure to pierce her skin. She jumps, and a single drop of blood surfaces from the puncture. Her breath is so loud that I wouldn't be shocked if Gretchen could hear it from the kitchen.

Hell, if Benny could hear it from outside.

With the confidence of the twisted man that I am, I run my thumb along the wound of her neck and play with the blood between my fingers. She exhales when I press the finger into my mouth and groan.

She stares at me, wide-eyed and in disbelief.

I lower the finger from my mouth, bring it to her lips, and then push it into her mouth. There's no stopping my grin when she bites into my finger, no doubt creating her own puncture in my skin.

I fucking love it.

I draw back and release my hold of the knife, and she tips forward. She grunts when I yank the knife from her and toss it onto the table. It clatters against Benny's plate.

I misjudged the little pest in front of me.

When she came to me, scared for her life, I saw her as weak.

But sweet Natalia is starting to prove herself.

Her newfound bravery might be a result of her knowing she'll die soon, so she might as well go down shit talking. But she's playing with fire and will be the only one burned between us.

I will marry her.

Our little matrimony will bring me closer to getting what I want.

When she keeps that pretty little mouth shut for longer than five seconds, I return to my seat, ignoring the broken dishes. I sit, and Natalia squirms in her chair. She stares at me, unblinking, as if she needs to keep her eyes on me, waiting for my next move.

I clear my throat and level my tone. "Are you done pushing my buttons so we can talk about the wedding?"

She throws her head back and mockingly laughs. "Yes, let's go from the man who wants to marry me, holding a knife to my throat, to nuptial plans. Sounds very compos mentis."

"A little knife play never hurt anyone ..." I wipe a hand across my mouth and smirk. "At least, not me."

"You were born in the pits of hell, weren't you?"

Yes.

I was born into this family, and we've been ruthless for decades. Mercilessness runs through our cold veins, and cruelty is ingrained in my twisted genes. From the moment I took my first breath, I was the future of the Marchetti family. My aunt once said that my mother added venom to my formula.

I reach across the table, snatch a handful of muffins from a basket, and throw them onto her plate. "Eat something other than goddamn strawberries. I need a healthy wife."

"Is a wedding necessary?" She takes a muffin. "Can't we go to the county building or a drive-through?"

It's comical that my little nuisance here assumes I *want* to spend an entire day getting married when I have more important shit to do. But it's customary to have a large wedding where we spare no expense.

"Not if you want our marriage to be believable. Everyone will already be suspicious with me marrying again, your being Gigi's friend, and your affiliation with the Lombardis."

I hold her gaze, showing her my distaste, giving her a moment to realize how repulsive I find her association with them. My mother referred to them as the cockroaches of organized crime. They were untrustworthy fucking idiots and failed to pay debts. It's improved some since Vincent took over, but they're still scum. Scums who need to die slow deaths.

"They'll be suspicious and think it's weird regardless," she mutters before popping a bite of muffin into her mouth. "Trust me, marrying you doesn't sound too alluring."

"Marrying me prevents your throat from *actually* being slit by someone else." I rub my knuckle over my neck at the same spot where I had the knife against hers. "Although, if last night was any indication of my future with you, I'm certainly not complaining."

She glares at me, her thick black lashes nearly hiding her eyes. "That was a moment of weakness and will not happen again."

"Fine by me. I don't beg for pussy." I cross my arms. "What are your plans today?"

She perks up in her chair at the subject change. "I need to get clothes from my apartment, so I don't have to wear these ridiculous cocktail dresses—"

"Those dresses cost more than your life." I pause to correct myself. "Not technically since the Lombardis were willingly to pay a high price for you."

This time, she flinches at my response but quickly composes herself. "Those are nice for going out but not for everyday wear."

"Someone will take you to your home."

"Then, I need to go to work."

"Do you still plan to work?" I ask dryly with a frown.

Natalia's job makes her vulnerable. She can easily be taken, blown up, or shot there. If something like that were to happen, it'd take time *and* be harder for us to point the finger at the Lombardis. If Vinny kills my wife, my family will expect me to avenge her.

"Yeah," Natalia answers as if I should've already known the fucking answer. "My life doesn't stop just because I have a madman after me."

"It kind of fucking does."

"To clarify, *bills* don't stop."

The thought of having someone sit at the gallery and babysit her is a waste of a man, a terrible use of resources. Any of my guys would also be upset if I had them sitting in an art gallery all day instead of handling business. It'd be a goddamn headache to deal with.

"I'll pay them." There we go. Problem solved. Headache gone.

She scrunches up her nose. "Hard pass on the *sugar daddy* offer. I need you to keep me alive, not support me financially."

"How about I do both."

"How about not."

"Natalia, you going there is a waste of my man's time."

"Then I'll hang out with you."

"Nice try."

"It's the gallery or playing go-to-work with Cristian day."

"Fine. Go to the gallery. It'll keep you out of my hair."

Normally, I wouldn't give in so easily, but the woman is grating my goddamn nerves. The less I'm dealing with her right now, the better.

"What are *your* plans today?" She grabs the water glass in front of her and takes a sip.

"Tracking down the other two men you've fucked and killing them." I shrug.

She rolls her eyes. "Funny."

"I find it amusing you think I'm joking."

Her back straightens. "You can't kill them! They were innocent, stupid boys I went to high school with."

"Not so innocent if they were fucking you." I run my thumb over my lower lip.

I knew as soon as I married Natalia that I'd kill those men, but after last night, that vengeance rope has tightened. Now that I've had my hands on her and tasted her sweet pussy, the thought of killing them gives me an even stronger high.

"And what about Vinny?" Natalia's voice turns frenzied. "Are you leaving him out of your *everyone who fucked Natalia* murder spree?"

I pop my knuckles. "I'm waiting for Vinny to come to me."

Her cheeks redden. "Vinny can be brutal … cruel." She shuts her eyes, as if replaying a moment with him.

She thinks Vinny is cruel.

I can't stop myself from laughing bitterly. "There is no one crueler than me in this city. Vinny might play it off like he is, but let me put a barrel in his mouth and see how tough he is then."

Vinny is a mean motherfucker, yeah.

Teeters along the sadistic side from what I've heard.

But he's no match for me.

I saw him with Natalia, witnessed how weak he was when I touched her in front of him. He cares about her, making him reckless and an easier target for me.

"Why don't you just handle Vinny and leave the others alone?"

"That's not my style, sweetheart." I pull myself from my chair again and stop next to her.

She tilts her head to the side. "Do you not want a say in the wedding?"

I can't help but scoff at her question. "I couldn't give two fucks about our wedding. All I care about is that it happens." I slide my hand into my pocket, grab a phone, and drop it next to her on the table. "Here's your new phone, which you don't deserve. It has a new number. I programmed Gigi and me as your emergency contacts."

Before she can reply, her attention swings to the guy walking into the room.

"This is my nephew Luca," I explain. "He'll watch over you today. Try not to get him murdered."

I kiss the top of her head, walk out of the room, and lick my lips.

Every part of Natalia really does taste delicious.

13

NATALIA

I'm riding shotgun in Luca's Suburban.
When we walked out of the house and to the SUV, Luca instructed me to sit in the back seat. That felt too *mob boss Cristian* for me, so I took the front. Luca, a tall guy who appears to be around Vinny and Benny's age, didn't physically remove me, like his hotheaded boss would've done. He must be *somewhat* more levelheaded than crazy Cristian.

Luca, who I've learned is Helena's son, drives us to my apartment and goes inside with me. To my relief, there isn't a raging Vinny waiting. Vinny must assume Cristian isn't letting me out of his sight now that I've become a hot commodity to the psychopathic men in this city. I change my clothes and pack two suitcases, and Luca helps me put them in the back seat.

Now, it's time to call Gigi.

Something I've been dreading all morning.

My new Cristian-provided phone is the latest iPhone model.

I tightly grip the phone as it rings in my ear. I don't know how much Cristian or Benny has told her about my situation … or me possibly marrying her father.

"Hello?" Gigi answers, her voice bubbly and excited. She

might be a Mafia princess, but she has the voice of a Disney princess.

"Hi," I say, her voice putting me at ease.

"It's about damn time you called."

I laugh. "Your father stomped on my phone and threw it into orange juice."

"Ugh, that sounds like him."

I chew on my lip. "Did he tell you that …?" My voice trails off, and I wait to find out *what* she knows.

"That you're marrying him?" Gigi finishes for me.

"Yeah … that."

"He didn't. Benny did."

"Are you okay with that?" I gulp. "Do you think it's weird?"

Luca snorts, providing his answer to that question, and I glare at him.

"You're marrying him so you don't die. I'm plenty okay with that. It's not like you two will actually date and be intimate." She squeals. "I'm trying to clear my schedule here to come home for the wedding."

I'd love to see Gigi, but the only plan I want to make now is to stay alive. Unfortunately, Cristian seems to be my only savior. I'm not sure how Cristian could be referred to as a *savior*. The man is far from a saintly Samaritan.

He's my monster in shiny armor.

My guardian devil.

"Let me know when," I tell Gigi. "We'll pick you up from the airport."

"Who's *we*?" Luca snaps.

"You and me." I motion back and forth between him and me. "Or whichever babysitter I'm scheduled with for the day."

Gigi tells me about Italy, rants about wanting her father to torture Vinny, and lists her plans for us when she returns home.

When I end the call, I look at Luca and say, "We need to make a quick pit stop."

Luca shakes his head repeatedly. "Nah, I was told no pit stops." He pushes his black Ray-Bans up the bridge of his nose.

"But—"

"No."

"The pit stop is *my father's* home. Cristian won't mind."

"Cristian minds anytime we don't follow orders."

"We'll be ten minutes, *max*."

"No."

Groaning, I text Cristian.

Me: Tell Luca to let me stop by my dad's house.

My phone beeps with a response minutes later.

Cristian: Is that necessary?

My father needs to know I'm getting married, for fuck's sake.

Me: Yes! Either have Luca take me or I'll steal another truck and go there on my own.

Luca's phone rings, and he side-eyes me after looking at the caller's name on the screen.

"Hey," he answers before pausing. "Yeah, okay. Got it." He ends the call and glances at me in annoyance. "He said you can have five minutes."

I tighten the seat belt across my body. "I'll take as long as I damn well please."

"You'll take *five minutes*," Luca corrects, staring at me with a look that confirms he'd rather be out committing crimes than playing chauffeur to little ole me. "Or I'll throw you over my shoulder and escort you out, per your fiancé's demand."

I roll my eyes and direct him to my father's house.

It's a Saturday morning, so I know he'll be home.

Every Saturday, he sits in his office and works on the book he's been writing for years. Who knows if he'll ever finish it, especially since I've walked in a few times and seen him staring vacantly at the screen, as if the story would hurt to write.

When I was fifteen, I started sticking Post-its of motivational quotes on his computer screen.

You can do it, Dad!
Write away!
You got this!

Anytime I asked what his book was about, he'd say it was a secret and then wink.

My stomach is a ball of nerves as we pull onto the street. I spot my father's Buick and point Luca toward it. He nods and veers into the driveway of the two-story brick home, needing lawn TLC. My father is a man who'd rather spend his time with his nose shoved in a book than perform any type of manual labor.

I grip the door handle but then stop.

I don't know when Cristian and I are getting married.

Hell, I don't know if we'll even make it that far.

I step out of the Suburban and look back when Luca does the same.

"You can stay out here."

Luca shakes his head.

"Let me guess. Another *boss's order?*"

"Yes, and also another *make sure there's no one in there who'd murder you*," he replies with a smug expression. "Trust me, you'd rather I be in there than not. I don't pussy out like Dario."

"Don't speak ill of the dead."

"I'm speaking ill of the stupid."

"Wow, I'm convinced all of you were born without hearts." I walk toward the front door and collect the key I grabbed from my apartment earlier.

Luca is behind me. "It's the best way to stay alive, Natalia. Feel nothing, care about only a few."

I unlock the door. Soft jazz music hums through the house from my father's office as we walk toward it. His office door is open, but I gently knock before entering the cramped room. Bookshelves line the back wall, and he's sitting behind his desk with stacks of paper everywhere but on the keyboard.

He lifts his gaze from the computer to me. "Oh, hi, honey."

His voice is nervous as he gives a worried glance to Luca behind me. "I've tried calling you, but it keeps going straight to voicemail."

I inch into the room. "I got a new number."

His shoulders tense when I circle the desk until I'm behind him, and I hug his shoulders. He peeks up at me, raises his hand, and gently squeezes my arm.

Fredrick Carprio raised me as a single father after my mother was murdered when I was six. He struggled as a teacher, then a principal, and we lived paycheck to paycheck. Then, he landed the principal position at Fenimore Preparatory School and got a raise. I got free tuition at one of the top prestigious schools in the country, and things finally started to look up for us.

"I'm getting married," I say as soon as I pull away. The words leave my mouth so quickly that you'd think they came out as one.

My father slides back from his chair, the wheels clicking against the wood floor, and looks at me with sorrow. "I know."

I expected more of a shocked reaction. I haven't brought many men around my father. He refused to meet Vinny and made every attempt to change my mind about being in a relationship with a *dangerous man like him.*

I should've listened. They say your parents always know best, but I was blinded by what I thought was love.

When I first fell for Vinny, I fell for him hard. I fell in love with someone who wasn't the real Vinny.

At least with Cristian, I know what I'm getting from the beginning.

He's not a man who puts on a façade.

No, Cristian shows he's a monster through and through with no apologies.

"Cristian left twenty minutes ago and broke the news." My father runs a hand through his thinning black hair.

"He ... asked for your permission?"

My father slowly rises to his feet. "Cristian Marchetti isn't a man who asks for permission from anyone." He shakes his head, squeezing his eyes shut. "How did you get yourself into this mess, Natalia?" He then rambles. "I knew it was a bad idea, allowing you to have a friendship with his daughter. But he said if I didn't—" His eyes widen, and he snaps his mouth shut.

My heart lurches in my chest. "If you didn't, what?"

Jesus.

Did the man threaten to kill my father over some playdates?

"Nothing," my father mutters, flicking his chubby hand through the air. "It's not important."

The hell it isn't.

I scowl at my father as Luca leans against the wall, crossing his arms, now entertained. "What, Dad?"

"He just said …" My dad stops and shrugs, and his gaze pings to Luca. "He said forbidding you from being friends with Gigi wasn't an option." His shoulders slump. "Cristian Marchetti gets what he wants, and he wanted you to be friends with his daughter."

"You didn't want us to be friends?"

My father's forehead wrinkles. "No."

"Then, why'd you allow it?"

"That's the past, Natalia." He continues to shake his head, as if on autopilot. "I told you from the beginning to stay away from these men when you first started seeing Vinny."

"I'm learning that now," I grumble.

"Vinny is harmless compared to Cristian. Cristian is …" He pays a glance to Luca, as if wondering if it's safe to badmouth his boss in front of him. "He's manipulative … calculated." My father's tone grows frantic. "Vinny is a Boy Scout compared to him."

Luca's attention leaves his phone. "Watch your mouth about my boss. That's my only warning, old man."

I reach out and clasp my hand around my father's. "I will be safe, I promise. He's my only resort to stay alive."

"I love you, Natalia," he says with desperation before clutching me into a tight hug. "Please stay safe for me."

After getting my undergrad in art history at NYU, I started working at Aurora Galleria.

It's a small art gallery in Brooklyn. I became interested in art after finding pieces of my mother's work in my father's closet. I'd been snooping in there to get a sneak peek at my Christmas presents. She was a lover of all things art, and it helped me feel closer to her. Eventually, I talked him into hanging her art canvases back up throughout the house. He'd taken them all down after her death because the reminders were too hard on him. That action helped us both on our healing journeys.

After that, I started taking all the art classes my father could afford—painting, ceramics, sketching. I love art, but I'm not the *best* artist. I'm better at recognizing art and appreciating the artistry and skill that goes into it. So, I decided to become a gallerist instead of the artist.

I'm in the gallery, taking inventory with Bonnie, and Luca is sitting in the corner. Bonnie hasn't questioned why Luca is in the gallery with me. Nor did she when Vinny would come in with me either.

People know who the Mafia men in this city are. They know to respect them. They also like them in their businesses. It's almost like a sense of protection.

Bonnie is a sixty-year-old woman whose husband passed away last year after a heart attack. She spends almost every waking minute either at the gallery or with her grandkids. The more people—customer or not—in the gallery, the fuller her heart is. She's a people person, and her number one person is gone. That's why I try to pick up as many hours as I can. She enjoys the company.

Everyone's attention slips to the door when it chimes, and

I frown when Cristian walks in. All conversation ceases. It's what the man does—stops people in their tracks. He walks in with such arrogance that you'd think he owns the place. His broad shoulders are pulled back, his neatly trimmed, stubbled chin held high, and his eyes roam the room as if taking it all in.

The gallery is an open floor plan, so unless you go into the back room or office, you see almost every inch of space. The walls are white so as not to distract away from the artwork hung along them, and the floors a light walnut.

I stare at him in awe, in appreciation, as if he were the most expensive work here. His suit, the same one from this morning that I didn't have the opportunity to appreciate since so much was happening, is precisely tailored to his body. Black sunglasses conceal those cold eyes of his. I frown deeper when I see Rocky following him, the permanent scowl he always wears plastered on his face.

Luca jumps to his feet as if he'll be fired for not doing his job and quickly slides his phone into his pants while walking in Cristian's direction. I trail him, my pace faster, so I reach Cristian before him.

The smell of his cologne envelops me as I grab the cuff of his white sleeve, lift on my heels, and whisper-hiss, "What are you doing here?"

My head is spinning.

He shouldn't be here for so many reasons.

Cristian peers down at me, his face blank, and removes my fingers off him, one by one, as if I were a pest. "Can't a man visit his future wife at work?"

His question isn't a whisper like mine.

Cristian practically shouts his words, as if making an announcement for the entire building to hear that we will have impending nuptials.

Bonnie gasps behind me, and I can imagine the shock on her face. "Wife?"

I tug on Cristian's sleeve again. "This was supposed to be more of a transactional situation."

That makes me sound a little too *Pretty Woman*, but whatever.

"Was sucking my cock part of this *transactional situation*?" Cristian smirks, self-satisfaction laced with every word of his response.

And that makes it more *Pretty Woman*.

Luca chuckles. Bonnie drops her clipboard.

He can't say I sucked his cock in my workplace.

We'll have a little chat about that, or next time he's in a business meeting with his murderous colleagues, I'll tell them he ate my ass.

An eye for an eye, Monster.

I don't reply, deciding against provoking him further in fear of what he'll say next.

Cristian smirks at my lack of argument, knowing he's won this round, but he doesn't detach my hand from him this time. "We're going to lunch."

My stomach growls at the thought of food, but a twinge of nausea weaves through any desire to eat. The last time I stepped into a car with this man, he planned to hand me over to the Lombardis, like keys to a used car.

Hard pass on enduring that trauma again.

Cristian won't receive any brownie points for changing his mind last night. It wasn't done from the kindness of his heart.

I drop his sleeve and perform a dramatic turn, motioning toward the gallery. "I'm working."

Cristian plays with his fingers, as if bored. "And I don't give a fuck. You have to eat."

I gulp, searching for an excuse to escape another death scare. "We have customers—"

Cristian's eyes scan the room. "I don't see any customers."

Bonnie frowns.

I cross my arms. "The gallery is busiest at lunch."

Cristian strides deeper into the gallery, passing me, and all eyes are on him.

"How much is this?" he asks, pointing at a canvas on the wall without even bothering to look at what *this* is.

"Five hundred—" Bonnie starts to answer, but I interrupt.

"One thousand dollars."

Bonnie grins.

"I'll take it." Cristian points at another piece. "And this one?"

"That's our most expensive piece—" I answer, but Cristian interrupts me how I had Bonnie.

"I'll take that one too."

"It's three thousand dollars," Bonnie stutters.

"I don't care how much it is." Cristian rubs his hands, ignoring Bonnie, and levels his gaze on me. "There. Now, you have enough sales for the day. Let's go."

I stare at him, speechless, and bite into my cheek.

That's the largest sale I've ever had in the gallery. The three-thousand-dollar piece has been taking up room for six months now, and we weren't sure if it'd ever sell. Sadly, it won't go to someone who truly appreciates it, though. Cristian doesn't give one fuck about what the art is. He's buying *me* to leave with him.

How will I get out of this one?

Cristian snaps his fingers at Bonnie. "I'm assuming you work here?"

Bonnie's blue eyes widen as she nods while her hands straighten her short blond hair. "I own the gallery."

"Can she take a lunch now?" he asks. "I think with those sales, she deserves a nice, long lunch."

"Of course," Bonnie says. "Take all the time you want."

Cristian won, of course.
He paid for the paintings in cash, so I'm sitting in the Escalade's back seat next to him. Like last time, Rocky is driving instead of Francis.

Not a good sign, my people. Not a good sign.

Rocky would happily cart me to another back alley.

I peek a glance at Cristian. It's a shame such a beautiful man has such a bitter heart. No humanity resides in those ice-cold veins of his. His blood is diluted with venom and deprivation. He's proven countless times that he's not a man to turn your back on.

Yet knowing all these things about him, my dumbass is marrying him. My pulse races when he's near—out of fear *and* desire. As he stroked himself last night, I watched him with need and desperation. Then, I experienced the best orgasm of my life when his face was buried between my legs.

Hell, am I just as depraved?

"My father said you visited him this morning," I say.

Cristian stops typing on his phone. "I did."

I gesture back and forth between the two of us. "He isn't happy about this."

"I don't give a fuck." He returns to typing.

"He also said you basically forced him to allow me to have a friendship with Gigi."

I'm not angry with him for forcing the friendship. I love my relationship with Gigi, and no harm was done to my father. It's the frustration of Cristian bullying and threatening those to do what he wants.

Cristian drops his phone into his lap and strokes his stubbled jaw. "Is that what he told you, huh?"

I nod.

"It seems he failed to mention that I paid him twenty-five thousand dollars to do so."

"What?" I jerk back and hold my palm toward him. "You *paid* him for my friendship with Gigi?"

"My daughter liked you," he says in a bored tone. "Gigi's feelings were hurt when your father forbade a friendship with her, so I rectified the situation. I saw you as a positive influence." His jaw clenches, and his voice is firm. "That is, until you became involved with the Lombardis."

"*Rectified the situation?*" I shift in my seat to face him. "Do you think you own everyone?"

Cristian keeps a straight face. "If I want to own them, then yes."

The nerve of this man.

I jut my chin out. "You don't own me."

He offers an amused laugh. "Not yet."

"You'll *never* own me."

Cristian reaches out, his muscular hand cupping my bare knee, inches under the hem of my skirt, and I shiver.

His lips form a cunning smile. "I will own every inch of you soon enough, Natalia."

"What are we doing here?" I ask when Rocky pulls into the rear parking lot of L'ultima Cena.

The bright side of our destination? It's not a murderous alley.

The dark side? The restaurant is known for its Mafia affiliation, sketchy meetings, and missing persons *last seen here* reports. A place where you can get lasagna with a side of homicide. It's not a safe space.

Cristian stretches out his arms and straightens a cuff link. "Lunch."

Alexa, please teach this man how to elaborate.

My face burns with frustration as I jerk my thumb toward the restaurant. "This isn't the lunch I expected."

"Then, quit having expectations."

"I was thinking more along the lines of a Big Mac."

My breathing hitches, and I stupidly don't pull away when he reaches out and rubs the pad of this thumb over my bottom lip.

"Rocky, get out," Cristian demands before roughly digging the tip of his finger into my lip.

Rocky jumps at the order and is out of the SUV in seconds.

"Just like we're improving your taste in the cock you suck, I'm upgrading your taste in lunch as well." He roughly digs the tip of his finger into my lip. "Consider it a favor."

My cheeks redden, and I bite into his finger with my top teeth. He doesn't flinch, only presses his finger in harder, and I sink my teeth onto it.

One of us will kill the other before the sham of this marriage even begins.

His eyes pierce mine, almost in challenge of who will concede first.

Who will submit to the other over something so small.

It's not about the touching. It's the push, the pull, the I won't let you step all over me even though I need you to stay alive.

"I can sit here all fucking day, Natalia," Cristian says, challenge dancing in his eyes, as if he can read my mind.

I slacken my jaw. He smirks before moving his thumb to skate over my top lip and then opening his palm, clasping my face in his hand. Holding in a breath, I wait for his next move.

He has me nearly trapped, and he pets my cheek. "That's my good girl."

I release the breath when he withdraws, turns his back on me, and opens the door. My heart whips in my chest, and I place my hand over the same spot where his just was. I stare at his back, watching him step out of the car, but then he abruptly stops.

"Oh, one more thing." Turning to face me, he dips his hand into his jacket pocket, pulls out an object, and carelessly tosses it at me.

It falls into my lap with a *thump*.

It's a black velvet jewelry box.

I'm terrified to open it.

What kind of ring could the most powerful man in the city choose for his fake wife?

Hell, I didn't even know I'd get a ring. I shake my head and verbally smack myself. I don't know if there's a ring in there.

"I picked up your ring today." He meets my stare, answering my question. "Put it on."

I grab the box and play with it in my hands. "Cristian Marchetti, such a romantic. You couldn't even get down on one knee?"

"I got down on two knees for you last night," Cristian replies smugly. "I'd say that's worthier."

I scoff.

The nerve of this man.

He dips his head back into the SUV, and the smell of him revisits my senses. "I'll do it again if it atones for my lack of romance." That deep voice of his somehow intensifies, and he snatches the box from my hand, his two thick fingers playing with it how I had. "You won't find love with me, Natalia, but when you're mine, I will pleasure you and always make you feel untouchable."

That much is obvious.

"Like I said earlier, that is never happening again."

"Then, don't expect to see me on my knees again." He drops the box back into my lap. "Open it."

We're silent. My eyes latch on to the box as I slowly open it. I gasp at the sparkling diamond resting on a simple diamond band.

The stone is transparent. Flawless. Breathtaking.

It's simplistic but extravagant.

Expensive but not tasteless.

It's perfection.

"Who even just *picks up* a ring like this?" My fingers shake. I'm nervous to even take the ring out of the box.

"Put the ring on and get the fuck out of the car, Natalia," Cristian demands.

And I slip it onto my finger—because what girl doesn't want to don an expensive diamond on her finger before possibly dying?

The right size too.

How does this man seem to know everything about me?

And why do I want to know everything about him?

14

CRISTIAN

"Cut the bullshit," my cousin Dino states, standing across from me at the bar. "You're not marrying that woman for love. You don't have a heart, you cold bastard."

We're in a private back room at L'ultima Cena. It might be noon on a Thursday, but there's always business to attend to—and what better way than with a glass of bourbon and good food?

Natalia and I need to start making appearances together to convince my family that I truly have feelings for her in the end. I also want to watch her with the other women in the family, see how compatible she is with them. Not that it'd be a make-or-break situation if she wasn't. They'd be obligated to like her, no matter what. But it says a lot about a woman—how she interacts with other women.

Take Carmela, for instance. She's in the corner, speaking with her cousin and shooting glares at Natalia with every word that leaves her mouth. Carmela is bitter, so it's obvious she'll hate Natalia. Natalia is taking the man Carmela so desperately wants.

Carmela was never anything more than a fuck to me. She's

desperate and whiny, and even though she's a bitch to others, she submits to every demand I give her.

Obedience is nice and all. It's a requirement to work for me and live.

But it doesn't always make my dick hard.

I love a woman who challenges me. Benita was the last woman who had the guts to speak back to me.

I haven't fucked Carmela in months. She was starting to get needy, too attached, assuming we'd be anything more than fuck buddies.

Plus, I've witnessed how Carmela is with the other women. Helena loathes her. Celine, my half-sister, threw a drink at her once. One of my cousins attempted to fight her.

But Carmela's family has been on the Marchetti payroll for decades, starting with Rocky's great-grandfather. They've been loyal to us, and we've been generous to them. No matter how much of a bitch Carmela is to them, Carmela will always have a seat at the table because of her last name.

That is, if she doesn't piss me off too much. If that happens, then shit will start to change.

So far, Natalia seems to be hitting it off with the women better than Carmela. Not surprising. Even though she has shit taste in men and is a pain in my ass, there's no reason not to like Natalia. It's why I allowed Gigi to be friends with her. She's a good woman, intelligent—apart from the Vinny bullshit.

Ignoring Dino, I stand at the bar and watch Natalia, the bourbon in my glass swishing against the rim. Dino has a big mouth, and I tend to tune him out half the time. I wouldn't even speak to the idiot if he wasn't one of the best snipers in the city.

Not once have I told these stupid motherfuckers I'm marrying Natalia for love. Like Dino said, I don't have a heart. For some stupid reason, people think marriage and love are synonymous.

Roman, my nephew and Helena's youngest son, scoffs. "Who marries for love?"

Helena is at least teaching her kids to have some goddamn brains.

"I love my wife," Lorenzo, my brother-in-law and Helena's husband, answers and holds up his glass in pride.

I shoot him a threatening look. "You'd better fucking say that."

Other men in this lifestyle wouldn't bat an eye at their brother-in-law's adultery, but not me. My father arranged their marriage, but I made it clear to Lorenzo that he'd better learn to love my sister and treat her right. Unless she decided to leave him, he was with her until he was in the ground. Lucky for me, he hasn't crossed me.

"Everyone knows the Lombardi nitwit wants her," Dino says, pouring himself a glass of straight vodka. "You're being dumb and marrying the broad as a favor to your daughter."

I down my drink.

I'll do what I want, when I want.

The same with killing someone.

My mom once told me, "You're lucky you're the boss, Cristian. Otherwise, I'd have already attended your funeral."

I'll die before I allow someone to order me around.

Roman steps forward. "If you need someone for her to marry, I'll volunteer as tribute."

Of course he'd *volunteer*.

As soon as I walked in with Natalia, every pair of eyes went straight to her. They took her in, sizing her up in all different ways. It fucking pissed me off, and I wanted to kill every single one of them.

Natalia is a new face—a rarity among us. Most of our relationships are planned before we hit puberty, so we bring few outsiders in who aren't Mafia-related. It's the code of conduct. We know how to react, to keep our mouths shut, and live this life. We know the process if detectives show up at our door or if we need to stash guns or money.

This is a lifestyle, a life we're born into, and not many can handle it.

I always told Gigi no when she asked to invite Natalia to parties. Natalia wasn't part of our life. But then Natalia turned dumb and thrust herself right into this insufferable world.

"I'll take her as my *goomah*." Dino's nasally-ass voice interrupts my thoughts, suggesting Natalia be his side chick. "The Lombardis know who I am." He whistles. "That woman has a body like the ones I watch in porn when my wife reads my kids their bedtime stories. I'd love to see those titties—"

Dino doesn't get the opportunity to finish that sentence. I slam my drink into the bar, shattering the glass, and punch Dino in the face. My fist burns. I hit the fucker so hard. He stumbles back, grunting, and I snatch a shard of glass. I don't even give a shit if I cut myself while punching him again before holding the fragment to his throat.

"Say something like that about my future wife again, and I'll slit your fucking throat and watch you bleed out." I push the glass harder into his neck, not being cautious like I was with Natalia. "I won't leave until every ounce of your blood is gone from your lifeless body. Then, I'll find your wife a new husband who isn't a pathetic lowlife."

I can feel the pulse thrumming in his neck, his Adam's apple bobbing against the glass.

I do have to give the motherfucker credit for keeping his head held high and his voice controlled when he finally says, "Sorry, Cristian. It won't happen again."

I dig the sharp glass into the hollow of his chubby neck, drawing out a flash of blood. The sound of him hissing through his teeth at the sting delivers a sense of satisfaction, atoning *somewhat* for his disrespect.

Not one person in the room is stupid enough to defend him.

Not even his wife.

I release Dino, retreat a step, and then spit on his feet before speaking to the room. "Let that be a lesson to all of you. Disrespecting Natalia is disrespecting me. And everyone knows what happens if you do that."

Everyone silently nods, and the door opens as if with perfect timing. Servers file into the dining room, and those who aren't already sitting take their seats. I stalk across the room before Natalia makes herself comfortable, grab her waist, and lead her to the chair next to mine at the head of the table. A server stops behind her and pours a glass of red wine into her glass while another drops an unbroken and fresh glass of bourbon in front of me.

This is a small luncheon with no more than fifteen people. I like to keep a small circle. I learned that years ago after too many men before me made too many mistakes and trusted too many people. That's why I have to watch every move Natalia makes.

Natalia was unaware that others knew about the engagement until we walked in. I'd dropped the news to Helena this morning, knowing that was all I needed to do to get the word out. My sister is loyal, but if it's gossip she can spread, she will scatter that shit every-fucking-where.

At first, she cursed me out, telling me, "Leave the poor girl alone." Once I explained the situation, her words then changed to, "You'd better protect her, Cristian."

The first course is delivered—a caprese salad—and before taking a bite, Helena asks, "So … have you settled on a wedding date yet?"

Natalia grips her fork and refuses to look at me. "We're thinking a long engagement."

We're?

Where the fuck did she come up with we're?

We haven't discussed anything yet.

"We're working on those details." My gaze locks on Natalia, but she's still not looking at me.

This won't be a long engagement.

I need to work out the details and figure out my game plan.

But the sooner we marry, the faster I get what I want.

Time to play house, Natalia.

15

NATALIA

I'd have given anything for Cristian to let me stay at the gallery. The anxiety from the car ride *and* from being in this room has knots twisting in my insides.

I'm surprised I can stomach eating.

I probably wouldn't if the food wasn't delicious.

The bistecca alla fiorentina is to die for.

Ugh, not *die for*. The reason I'm here is to *prevent* myself from dying.

Everyone gawked at me when I walked into the dining room with Cristian. Their gazes were intense, but nowhere near as intense as my future husband's.

Something about Cristian's stare sends shivers down your spine.

It's dark and soulless.

Burning with a certainty that he can either protect or destroy you.

There's no in-between.

I quietly eat my food, listen to their small conversation, and am thankful when talks of our wedding details stop. Cristian has hardly spoken to me after I proclaimed we'd have a long engagement.

But how was I supposed to know how to answer?

This all has happened so fast, and we've yet to discuss anything wedding-related other than that it *would* happen.

Cristian thinks it's okay to screw other women if I'm not a dutiful wife.

Yes, that entices me to want to skip right down the aisle with him.

I can't stop from staring at my sparkling ring every few minutes. Cristian spared no expense when buying a dream engagement ring—a solitaire pear cut diamond that glistens even when I don't move my hand. Everyone admired my ring when we walked in ... except for Carmela, who seemed disgusted that Cristian would gift me—a random woman he hardly knows—a ring so extravagant.

But modesty and Cristian don't go hand in hand. The monster might hide in the shadows, but when he creeps out, his wealth, power, and superiority are undisputable. His wife should fit the look, and the queen can't have a mediocre engagement ring.

At least no one else has almost died since we sat down.

Anger poured through Cristian, every muscle in his strong body tense, when he pinned Dino to the wall earlier. I was the only person who seemed surprised at the possibility of Cristian slitting Dino's throat. Not even Dino's wife, who honestly seemed a bit tired of his shit anyway, batted an eye.

I don't know *what* started their argument, but I have a feeling it was related to me since every man directed their gaze to me when Dino was released.

"More wine, ma'am?" The server's voice behind me snaps me from my thoughts.

I glance over my shoulder and offer a friendly smile to the woman. "Yes, please."

She pours my second glass of wine. It's a stupid move on my part since I plan on returning to the gallery, but I'm attending a

Mafia luncheon. All a regular person can do is drink to loosen their nerves.

Helena clears her throat when the servers begin clearing our dishes from the table. "Cristian, Natalia, I know you said you're working on wedding details, but I'd love to help in any way I can."

Cristian's tense arm rubs against mine at his sister's words, and I'm sure anyone else but his sister would have been terrified to bring up a subject he already closed.

Helena casts a quick glance from Cristian to me. "Italian engagements are short. People will wonder why it's taking so long."

"Yes," Margaret, Cristian's aunt, adds. "The men don't like waiting to get their women in bed."

She winks at Cristian, and my cheeks burn.

Carmela snorts. "Men don't like waiting because they want to fuck their *virginal* wives." She shoots me an icy stare, relaxes in her chair, and lifts her glass in my direction. Her words are slurred from the endless glasses of wine she's had to wash down her bitterness. "But we all know Natalia has spread her legs for Vinny. Cristian is getting his leftovers, and Natalia is getting mine. Not that he'll stop sleeping with me."

The room falls silent.

My face and neck burn, and I draw my shoulders back, straightening my posture. I've played the bigger person all day and ignored her, but that decency stops now. I won't allow her to speak to me or about me that way.

Not only am I humiliated by Carmela's comment, but a fire of jealousy burns in my stomach.

"Excuse me—" I start, preparing my rant, proud of how strong my voice is.

Cristian raises his hand to stop me from continuing. My gaze skates to him, and he's staring Carmela down—his gaze a mixture of anger and disgust, as if she's his next victim. My skin crawls in fear of him ever looking at me like that.

His anger circulates the room, but he's quiet, contemplating Carmela's punishment. Carmela stares at me in fear before sliding her gaze to Cristian. Her hand trembles as she lowers her glass back onto the table, spilling it in the process. No one cleans it up.

Cristian nearly killed his cousin earlier, and she thought it'd be a peachy idea to poke the Mafia king?

I guess that little outburst wasn't planned, and she's realized her mistake.

I don't blame her fear. There's this thing I've noticed about Cristian. It's what makes him scarier than Vinny. He's a psychopath, but there's a restraint to his madness. He's level-headed in his viciousness. The beautiful, terrifying man beside me can have fury storming through him, but he remains controlled in his own way. He was calm while holding Dino to the wall and in charge of every emotion flowing through him. His every move was methodical.

We silently await the punishment Monster Marchetti will give the daughter of his right-hand man for disrespecting his future wife.

Cristian, slow and composed, drops his napkin onto the table, slides out of his chair, and rises to his feet. I hold in a breath, and a rapid expulsion of air escapes Carmela. She squeezes her eyes shut. Cristian brushes his hand along my shoulder before moving toward Carmela. When he stops behind her, she twitches, as if sensing his presence.

Carmela hisses, her eyes shooting open, when Cristian digs his fingers into her hair. He fists the strands at the roots and forcefully jerks her head back until she's looking up at him.

"Boss," Rocky speaks out, but Cristian raises his hand, stopping him how he had done me.

"Carmela was bold enough to disrespect Natalia," Cristian says. "She needs to suffer the consequences of doing so."

Rocky's face turns slack, but he shuts his mouth, like a toddler who'd been told not to speak.

Carmela winces in pain, but you can tell she's struggling to stay calm.

Cristian's gaze cuts to me as he speaks to Carmela. "Let's talk about you, Carmela." He stabs his fingers deeper into her hair, creating more pain, and her eyes water. "How do you think your future husband—that is, if you find one pathetic enough to marry a disgrace like you—will feel, learning all you're valued for is sucking dick and letting men degrade you?"

Carmela cries out as he yanks her back harder, but he doesn't part his gaze from mine, as if gauging my reaction and not caring about anyone else's.

"And don't think you're anything special," Cristian says through clenched teeth. "I'd never marry a bitch who can't deep-throat."

My heart races, and I can't seem to break our eye contact. I match his penetrating stare, our eyes burning with desire.

In one way, this is disturbing as hell.

In another, it's the hottest thing I've seen in my life.

For a man to defend my honor like this.

Maybe that makes me just as fucked up, but it also makes me horny as hell.

My breathing is heavy, and I hope people believe it's from fear, not lust.

Cristian licks his lips and continues his insults. "How tragic it is for your father to know his daughter is a whore." He snaps Carmela's head back down and turns it so she's facing me. "Now, I'll leave it up to *my fiancée* to decide how she'd like you to be punished for your smart mouth." He smirks at me in amusement. "My sweet Natalia, how do you want me to deal with Carmela's disrespect?"

The room seems to close in as everyone stares at me.

I've never felt so awkward.

My heart was pounding before, but now, it's thrashing against my ribs so fast that I'm waiting for it to land on the table. I'm terrified … but also soaked between my legs.

I stare at my husband-to-be, struggling to appear mortified. Everyone waits for me to answer—to decide Carmela's fate. I might be engaged to a monster, but I can't become one myself.

I clear my throat and direct my gaze to a terrified Carmela. "This is your only warning. If you disrespect me again, I'll let my future *husband* handle you in whatever way he sees fit."

Those words. That tone.

None of them are me.

I shiver.

Cristian is rubbing his craziness off on me.

"Today is your lucky day." Cristian frees Carmela so suddenly that her head snaps forward, her face smacking into the table. He then makes a show of eyeing everyone in the room. "Now, does anyone else have something to say about my future wife?"

There are shakes of the heads, *no*es, and *of course not*s in response as Cristian stalks back toward me.

My skin flushes when he pauses behind my chair. He gently grabs the back of my neck, cupping it with a softness I've never had from him, and kisses me. His mouth lingers on mine as he slides his tongue between my lips before slowly pulling away and sitting back down.

The only noise in the room is Carmela sobbing.

Until, as if on the worst cue ever, the servers enter the room with dessert trays. Without a lingering glance at a crying Carmela, a server sets the dessert in front of her.

"None for her," Cristian directs him.

The server nods, snatches her plate, and hands it to Margaret.

🌹

Even if I were to return to the gallery, my brain would be mush.

Thanks to Cristian, I already sold more today than I had in

the past two weeks. So, I text Bonnie, asking for the day off, and she replies yes with at least fifteen exclamation marks.

This day feels like it's lasting forever.

I'm sure to everyone else, it's just another lunch.

But for me, it's overwhelming.

I dated Vinny for years but never attended a family event with him. We tried keeping our relationship separate from that part of his life. It was stupid and should've told me we had no future. Vinny said we'd marry one day, but that was *only* if his father agreed. Which, thinking about it now, I was stupid to believe that. I had no connections, didn't come with a business deal, so to Vincent Lombardi, I was useless. Vinny stupidly assumed I'd be okay with being a side chick and was shocked when I refused. I broke up with him, and his ego got hurt, so now, he doesn't want anyone else to have me.

At least with Cristian, we don't have to seek permission for our marriage.

Cristian doesn't ask for permission.

He gives it.

Now, the others have left, and Cristian is huddled in the corner, speaking with Dino, Roman, Lorenzo, and Rocky while I wait for him.

I should've asked for a to-go wine.

"Don't fuck it up," Cristian tells them before they break away.

The men shuffle out of the room, and Cristian stalks toward me. I bite into my lip and shift from one foot to the other. I hate how much his man affects me and how my mouth waters at the sight of him scrubbing a hand over his mouth.

The same mouth that pleasured me last night.

The same hand that touched me like I'd never been touched.

I frown at the realization—that's all I want from him right now. He could push me up against the wall, pull my skirt up, and I wouldn't dispute it.

No, bad Natalia.

No dirty thoughts of your best friend's dad, who's a legit madman.

His brooding gaze latches on to mine, and my stomach flutters when he reaches me. "Ready to go?"

I nod. "Yes, unless you plan to pour me another glass of wine."

A smirk plays at his lips, and he motions for me to start walking. I head toward the door. Cristian's chest brushes my back as he trails me, the heat and protection of him like my personal bodyguard.

"Can you tell me your plan?" I ask as we walk down the hall. "One minute, you're ready to hand me over to the Lombardis like I'm chopped liver. The next, you're giving me an engagement ring and defending me in front of your fuck buddy."

He's so close that he can whisper in my ear. "I never allow anyone to know my plans."

The heat and sticky air slap me in the face when we step outside, and I shuffle toward the Escalade. Cristian screams my name at the same time I'm tackled to the ground. I gasp, air leaving my lungs, and my ears ring.

Gunshots.

My heart pounds.

My life flashes before my eyes, deeper than it did with Vinny.

A heavy weight—*Cristian's* weight—covers my body like a shelter from a storm. I shut my eyes, screaming each time a bullet hits the Escalade, certain that the next one will strike me. I can't breathe—from both the fear and Cristian's heaviness—and I can't speak as tears fall down my face.

A window shatters, fragments of glass hitting Cristian's back and the ground, and I hear a gentle, "Shh," from him.

When I open my eyes, my face is shoved into Cristian's chest, so I see nothing. Cristian shields me the way a man would do with a woman he never wants to lose.

I thought I'd die at the hands of Cristian.

Not be protected by his body.

16

CRISTIAN

I'll never forget the first time I heard gunshots.

I was five, bored at my aunt's wedding reception, and asked my dad, "Can I go watch the fireworks too?"

It was right after the Fourth, so fireworks were the first thought that came to mind.

My father cocked his head to the side at my out-of-the-blue question. Then, reality dawned on him when he noticed the black car slowly approaching.

"Spari! Spari! Scendere!"

Shooting, shooting. Get down!

I'll never forget the *boom-bang-boom* of the gunfire as I crawled underneath the table. Other kids cried out for their moms, but not me. Not one tear slipped down my cheek when I poked my head out from under the tablecloth.

I wasn't allowed to cry.

It was a rule of my father's.

Some kids got spankings for cursing.

I got them for crying.

"You want men to think you're weak, Cristian?"

I shook my head.

"Then, don't ever show someone your weakness. Marchetti men

don't cry. We leave the crying to our enemies before we take their last breath."

People called my father a cruel man and claimed I had no hope since he'd trained me to be exactly like him. They were right. He taught me to be merciless, to make others fear me. It was Marchettis first, no matter the cost.

Even at that age, I was intoxicated from that adrenaline. I wanted to climb out from under the table and protect my family like the other men. The shots didn't last long. They never do.

My aunt Ada died on her wedding day. She was the first person I watched die. My mother cried, begging with God not to take her sister, all while blood gushed from my aunt's chest and mouth. My father stopped her when my mother tried to block me from watching.

I needed to become familiar with death. To witness firsthand what happens when our guards are down for even one second.

They say men like me—those who take over their families—die within twenty years of assuming control. I've surpassed that statistic, but I know death is always knocking on my door. Well, my gate. Motherfuckers will have to fight the devil before they make it to my doorstep.

Now, I can sense gunshots from miles away.

But today, my guard was down. All my thoughts were on Natalia as I watched her walk to the car. She wasn't attempting to strut, to appear sexy, but the ass on her made her sexy without trying.

How is one woman consuming me?

Making me cause scenes at lunches to prove no one disrespects her?

My mind was distracted by all the filthy ways I wanted to touch her, to pleasure her, to fuck her.

Natalia squirms underneath me, but I don't move. The thought of a bullet tearing through my flesh doesn't scare me, but my blood runs cold at the thought of it happening to the woman beneath me.

My men return gunfire, but I don't move from Natalia until the gunshots fade and all violence ceases. Until my future wife is safe. I gulp in deep breaths as I withdraw from her body, and she chokes out coughs.

I kneel next to her as she cries out in panic. She flinches when I rest my palm along her chest, over her heart, and feel her heartbeat. It's beating faster than the bullets shot at us, but it's beating. I quickly run my hands along her body, frantically searching for any injuries. She doesn't have pain, just shock.

Vinny protected her from the ugly side of this world. I won't do that. She will acclimate to this life. I can't tackle her to the ground again.

The realization of my mistake crashes into me.

Marchetti men always worry about killing the enemy first.

Then, they check on others.

I went against the very code I'd punished others for breaking.

Natalia isn't supposed to be my weakness.

Weaknesses are what get men killed.

I glare down at Natalia in frustration and scorn. "We're getting married ASAP."

17

NATALIA

I'm in a real-life *Final Destination* movie.

Death is determined to get me, and I can only escape it so many times.

I walk into the mansion in what seems like slow motion, with Cristian following. He hasn't muttered a word to me since our drive from the restaurant.

His attention stayed on his phone as he screamed, "Gut every motherfucker who had the balls to shoot at me."

My soon-to-be husband exists in a constant state of anger, as if he knows nothing else, but tonight, he's carrying an intense rage unlike anything I've seen.

This is Monster Marchetti.

The man everyone fears more than the boogeyman.

"Bedroom, Natalia," Cristian orders, his command thundering through the foyer like a storm.

Terror balls into my stomach in warning, but arguing with him would be a death wish. There are already too many death threats knocking on my door. No need to add another. So, I do as I'm told.

Some of that terror unravels when Cristian makes a right

into his office, leaving me to go upstairs alone. When I reach the bedroom door, it's locked.

My only options are to wait for Cristian or go to his office and ask for the code. As much as I'd like to avoid him, I don't want to wait in the hallway. With a sense of dread, I whip around to find him already stalking in my direction.

I didn't hear him—didn't *feel* him, as I normally do. That further proves how dangerous Cristian is. If he wants his presence known, if he wants to intimidate you, he will. But he can just as easily hide in the shadows, waiting for the perfect opportunity to rise from the pits of hell and ruin you.

A bottle of whiskey is clutched in his hand. His glossy eyes and the scent of liquor tells me he's already made use of the alcohol. I flatten my back against the wall when he reaches me, giving him space to key in the passcode. When the lock clicks free, he steps to the side and uses the bottle to usher me inside.

I gulp as I walk into the room.

I'm either stepping into the safety of the bedroom or the danger of the monster's den.

How stupid of me.

Agreeing to marry a man I'm constantly worried might kill me.

Cristian slams the door with so much force that it rattles against the hinges. I wince but refuse to turn and face him.

"Strip," he demands to my back.

I don't move.

"I said, strip, Natalia. I don't like repeating myself."

I'm quiet, searching for the safest words to tell him he's batshit crazy without getting myself murdered.

"Natalia." His tone is impatient, louder, angrier.

Fear crushes through me as I work up the nerve to turn around. When I do, my panic-stricken eyes meet his sinister ones. I cast a quick glance at the door when he advances a step toward me, as if escaping is an option.

Cristian would stop me. Overpower me. Force me to do whatever he wants.

He thrums his fingers along the glass and glowers at me as if I'm the cause of every one of his problems. As if he wants to get rid of me yet also keep me.

When I gain the courage to speak, I say, "I'm not sleeping with you."

"Didn't say I needed or wanted you to." He takes a swig of the whiskey. "Now, take off your clothes before I do it for you. And trust me, I won't be as gentle."

"I was just shot at. Give me a sec." I wipe my sweaty hands down my dress and hold back the urge to ask him to share the whiskey.

If anyone needs liquid courage, it's me.

Cristian works his jaw, his grip tightening so firmly on the glass that I'm waiting for it to crush in his hand. My stare penetrates his. I study his eyes, his face, his stance.

The anger is clear, but tonight, there's something more.

Something different.

He downs the whiskey before violently shaking his head, as if wanting to throw any emotions off his face. I jump when he hurls the bottle across the room. The glass shatters as it smacks into a wall, and liquor pours down the white paint onto the floor.

"I shouldn't be worried about you dying," he hisses through clenched teeth, his lips wet from the whiskey.

I stay quiet, uncertain of how to reply to that. Or if I even should.

"You're making me break my rules, Natalia." His tone is accusatory, as if *I* were the one to break whatever rule he's referring to.

Nausea swirls in my stomach as he circles me, as if he were a shark, ready to attack. I bite into my lip, trembling, awaiting and dreading his next move. I gasp when he suddenly stops in front of me, curls his hands around my waist, and squeezes me so tight that I'm sure there will be bruises in the morning.

"Cristian," I whisper.

His frame towers over me, blocking me from moving or looking around him. When he tips his head down to look at me, his face is darkened with frustration, his eyes burning with sin.

He bares his teeth. "Making me do things I normally don't."

I stare down at the floor. "Then, stop doing them."

A cold laugh escapes him, and he jerks me closer.

My chest to his.

My breathing mixed with his.

Mine frantic.

His controlled.

He reaches down, edging his hand between us, and knots the hem of my dress in his fist. In one swift motion, he whips the dress over my head and tosses it across the room. The dress lands on top of the whiskey mess.

Even though he's seen me naked, I cross my arms to cover myself.

The last time he saw me this exposed was different.

It was intense, but nothing like this.

Cristian grabs my elbows, tugging them away from each other, and pins my arms to my sides. "Don't move them."

I whimper when he releases them, only to slip a hand up my stomach. He slides a finger beneath my bra strap, tracing it back and forth before snapping it back. As soon as it hits my skin, he skillfully unhooks it. The bra drops to our feet, and he kicks it away. He takes a step back, and his gaze hardens while traveling down my body. Goose bumps crawl over my skin when he reaches out and rubs his palms over my breasts. I blush, my skin warming as he smooths his hands over them, his thumbs brushing my nipples.

But his touch doesn't linger.

His hand splays over my collarbone, and he snarls as his finger grazes a scratch on my skin from when he tackled me.

"It's just a scratch," I whisper, wincing. "I'll be fine."

He curves a hand around my throat, his grasp loose, and circles behind me. I shiver when he pushes my hair away with his knuckles and explores my skin. He presses his lips to the back of my shoulder when he finds another scratch.

"Cristian," I say.

"Shut up."

The tiny gentleness he had evaporates when he scrapes his teeth into my neck. Shivers trickle down my spine when he drops my hair and lowers his touch down the contour of my back, and then he studies my body for any more harm done. My skin is on fire at his touch.

Then, Cristian lowers himself to one knee, places a single kiss on each one of my ass cheeks, and smooths his hands down the backs of my thighs.

"Turn," he demands.

I turn, and he guides me to where he wants.

Where his face is only inches from my thighs.

"Why did you save me, Cristian?" I stare down at him, seeing only his hair, and wish I could run my hand through it. I don't have the guts to, though.

He doesn't reply, only continues to touch—to *inspect*—every inch of my body.

Those rough, crime-stained hands caress my skin in a way I never thought possible. And when he's finished, I expect him to stand.

He doesn't.

Instead, he settles himself on both knees. My heart races, and my throat dries as I wait for his next move. Groaning, he winds the strings of my panties between his fingers before slowly sliding them down my legs. As if on instinct, I kick them off and slide out of my sandals.

My legs tremble, and I moan when he licks the inside of my thigh.

Oh my freaking God.

My heart races so fast that I can feel my pulse in my neck.

"Fuck," he hisses, pushing my legs farther apart, giving him more room to make himself comfortable.

I gasp when he separates my folds and slides his finger through my wetness.

I'm soaked for him.

He lowers his head and dips his tongue between my slit. My knees wobble, and I struggle to hold myself up. He pauses to rest one of my legs over his shoulder to balance me and then settles his hand on my stomach to keep me in place.

Then, he pleasures me in ways I never thought possible from his position.

His fingers thrust in and out of me.

So good, so perfect.

His tongue sucks on my clit.

Slides through my folds.

His sharp teeth bite into my thigh.

I stare down, watching this powerful man at my feet.

My striking soon-to-be husband.

It's intoxicating, as if I'd been the one drinking the whiskey.

A high only Cristian can give.

He doesn't slow until my body shakes above him, my back arching, and I moan, "Cristian … fuck … Cristian … I'm almost there. Don't you dare fucking stop."

I ride his face, nearly suffocating him.

Anything to get closer.

"Let go, sweet Natalia."

And just like always, I do what he said.

I moan, my body shaking, and fall limp. He catches me, gathers me into his arms, and walks me to bed. My head spins as he settles me in bed and throws the comforter over my naked body. I'm catching my breath when the door opens, and he leaves the room.

18

CRISTIAN

A man like me doesn't have weaknesses.
But today, I showed one—Natalia.

I should've handed her over to the Lombardis.

Had I done that, I'd have a clearer head.

She was disposable, nothing to me, but then I had to go and touch her.

I wouldn't be thinking about how she tasted or how good it felt when her plump lips were wrapped around my cock.

I walk downstairs, licking the sweet taste of Natalia on my lips, and find Benny and Rocky waiting for me. Benny is pacing the foyer like he's a man who impregnated his mistress, his shoes creating an ear-grating squeak that echoes through the house.

Rocky is perched against the wall, his back stiff and his hands shoved in his pockets.

Benny stops when he sees me. "What the fuck happened?"

"We were shot at." I stretch my tense neck from side to side. "Not the first time it's happened, and unless our enemies fall off the face of the earth, which would make life tragically boring, it won't be the last."

I won't die of old age or cancer.

None of us do.

It'll be murder.

My grandfather was the victim of a blown-up car.

My father, a gunshot, execution-style.

I snap my fingers and gesture to my office. They follow me inside. Benny shuts the door and clicks the lock. No one mutters a word as I walk to the bar cart and pour myself a glass of Pappy Van Winkle. I drain it in one swig, which unfortunately washes down the taste of Natalia, and refill the glass. The liquor tastes nowhere as delicious as Natalia's pussy.

Fuck.

My daughter's best friend has consumed me.

She's fucking tormenting me.

Her information has been close to useless.

She's getting my men—getting *me*—shot at.

She isn't worth the trouble, but giving her up is becoming harder.

I need to change that.

Benny returns to his goddamn pacing as I take a seat behind my desk. Rocky returns to the same stance he had in the foyer.

I sink into the leather chair, lift my glass, and say, "Benny, sit the fuck down before I throw this glass at your fucking head."

Benny freezes and takes a seat.

"You think it was the Lombardis?" he asks, rubbing his forehead.

Rocky snorts. "Of fucking course it was the Lombardis."

I wish Vinny's dumbass had chosen a subtler retaliation. Public shoot-outs are bad for press. There might be word on the street of our illicit businesses, of our crimes, but we provide no evidence to back up their claims. We're careful, logical, and we keep our corruption in the shadows. We sure as fuck don't shoot people in public in the middle of the goddamn day.

Fucking amateurs.

Vincent should have Vinny by the balls just for that. Benny frustrates me sometimes, but at least he has some goddamn brains. Like me, my children learned the rules of this life at an early age. There will be no fucking up the Marchetti legacy.

I scrub a hand over my jaw. "How's Lorenzo?"

Lorenzo was hit in the shoulder during the shoot-out. He laughed it off and said Helena would be sending me his dry-cleaning bill. She's tired of cleaning bloody shirts. Yet another reason to shoot Vinny in the head.

You don't threaten or harm our family and get away with it. Lorenzo will want his head just as much now. Same with Helena. I already expect a call from her in the morning, demanding I make sure the man who shot her husband dies.

"Spencer fixed him right up," Rocky replies. "He's as good as new."

Dr. Spencer Ashford is New York's finest ER doctor, a pillar in the community, and the man who provides all medical care for the men in the Marchetti family.

All medical care resulting from illegal activities, that is.

I nod and point at Rocky. "Tell Helena to send Vincent Lombardi the bill."

Benny chuckles. "Send him a bomb with the bill to save us the trouble of dealing with him."

Rocky cracks his knuckles. "You want Vinny? I can get him for you."

I narrow my eyes at him. "What I want *from you* is to keep Natalia protected and your daughter to keep her fucking mouth shut."

Benny blows out a breath, shaking his head, aware of Carmela giving Natalia trouble.

Rocky's back straightens along the wall. "She's upset, is all, boss."

"She's becoming a liability." I relax in my chair and lean back.

Even if she's sucked my dick, I have no problem getting rid of Carmela. She means nothing to me.

"I'll speak with her." His forehead wrinkles in worry. "It won't happen again. Carmela knows her place."

Benny scoffs. "Her place is the fuck away from here."

Rocky shoots Benny a murderous glare, but he'd never. Everyone knows they'd die in a second if they touched one of my heirs. Not that Benny can't protect himself. I taught him just as young as my father taught me.

Since I have better things to do than talk about Carmela, I snap my fingers toward Rocky. "In the next twenty-four hours, I'd better know the names of every man sent to kill me, their addresses, and every person on their goddamn family tree."

Rocky pushes off the wall. "Yes, sir." He keeps his head down as he leaves the office and shuts the door behind him.

"I vote Carmela dies," Benny says. "I can't stand the bitch."

Benny has hated Carmela since she tried to fuck him when he was drunk one night. If you can't snag the king, might as well try for the prince. That's when I was done with Carmela.

"I vote you shut the fuck up," I reply.

"She'll only cause issues with you and Natalia. She needs to go."

"Let me worry about Carmela."

He drags his hands through his hair. "What's the deal with Vinny?"

Benny stands, strolls to the bar cart, and pours bourbon from a decanter into a glass. He's the only one allowed to make a drink in my office. My father would've slit my throat had I made myself a drink from his bar cart, but I'm not that big of a bastard. If my kid wants a drink while we talk about murdering someone, let him drink.

"I never knew he was on our radar before the Natalia situation," he continues.

I rub my eyebrow. "The kid is a fucking idiot."

He blinks. "He do something to you?"

"Did you forget he's suspect number one of shooting at us earlier?"

"*Before* that," he stresses, sitting down and balancing the drink on his knee.

I jerk my head toward his glass. "You spill that, and I will shoot the hand holding it."

He tightens his hold on the glass.

"If I had an issue with Vinny before, he'd already be dead."

"Do you want to kill him because he wants Natalia?"

I stay quiet and start shuffling through bullshit paperwork.

"Are you marrying Natalia to keep her safe from Vinny or because you want her?"

"Get the fuck out of my office." I point at the door.

He nods, finishes off his glass, and stands. "I'll make sure to get the video footage of the parking lot."

When he disappears from the office, I drop my head back.

The Marchettis have rules to live by.

One of them is to shoot before saving.

Whatever came over me—the need to save Natalia—needs to stop.

She's nothing but a pawn.

Never give a fuck about your collateral.

19

NATALIA

I'm woken by my stomach growling, as if I hadn't gorged myself with enough pasta and dessert at lunch.

I guess being shot at makes you starved.

That, along with being pleasured by a Mafia king who also happens to be my best friend's father.

What is my life anymore?

I must've fallen asleep after Cristian disposed of me in bed and left. I flip off the comforter, turn on a lamp, and dress in the softest silk pajamas I've ever touched. Then, I venture downstairs, on the hunt for a snack.

It's when I hit the last stair that I hear it.

Moaning and grunting.

Skin smacking against skin.

Sex.

My blood boils.

How dare he.

Cristian was intimate with me earlier, and now, he's screwing another woman? Infidelity is why I left Vinny, and I don't know if I can tolerate it with Cristian—saving my life or not.

And I swear to God, if it's Carmela, all hell will break loose.

My gut tightens—no longer hungry and now nauseated—as

I tiptoe toward the noise. Settling one hand on the wall, I peek around the corner and into the dining room. Relief swallows me when I see Gretchen bent over the table, her dress shoved up to her waist, as Benny thrusts inside her.

"Take that dick, baby," Benny hisses around a loud groan. "And don't you dare fucking stop."

Really, Benny?

This place has ten bedrooms, and *this* is where he chose?

Where the family eats.

At least it's where he sits.

Fab news for Cristian: I'll no longer attempt to sit next to Benny.

I'm still for a moment, and as I'm about to walk away, Gretchen's eyes meet mine, and she gasps.

"Benny," she says, slapping his arm.

He stops at the same time I spin around, ready to dash upstairs so I don't look like a damn voyeur, but Benny's voice stops me.

"Stay, Natalia," he says. "We need to chat."

I keep my back to him. "We can do this another time … when you're not—"

"You ruined that already."

I ruined it?

There are whispers and shuffling behind me, but I still don't turn. I could easily ignore Benny's request and walk away, but I'm curious about why *we need to chat*.

"You can turn around now," Benny says.

I count to five, turn, and see Gretchen dashing out of the dining room through the kitchen door.

"I thought you were sleeping." Benny runs a hand through his hair. "My bad."

I wave my hand in the air. "It's fine." I move into the dining room. "Does your dad care that you …?" I gesture to the door Gretchen disappeared into.

"Fuck Gretchen?" He shrugs. "He doesn't like it, but I don't like being married off for some bullshit contract."

"You're going to break her heart, Benny." My comment is blunt, but I've seen how Gretchen stares at Benny. She's in love with him.

Benny blows out a stressed breath. "I don't want to talk about it."

"Do you like her more than just sex?"

He scratches the back of his neck, pulls out a chair, and sits. "I heard what happened today. How are you doing?"

"Okay ... given the situation. A little shook up, but it's not to be surprised," I reply, allowing him to deflect my question about Gretchen. "Is that something that happens on the regular?"

"It happens, but not what I'd consider on the regular. I guess it was Vinny, so technically, it wouldn't have happened if my father hadn't decided to marry you."

"Great," I grumble. "It's my fault."

"It's my *father's* fault." He grabs a half-full glass of amber liquid from the table and points at me while gripping it. "Don't tell him I said that."

I make a zip motion across my lips. "Thank God your dad jumped on top of me. I guess he does have a little humanity behind that evil exterior."

Benny chokes on his drink and pounds on his chest to catch his breath. "He ..." Another cough and chest hit. "He what?"

"He saved me."

His shoulders tighten. "What do you mean, *saved you*?"

"He tackled me to the ground until the shooting stopped."

Something flashes in his eyes, and he shakes his head. "He wasn't supposed to do that."

"Do what?"

"Protect you."

"What ..." I stutter. "What do you mean?"

He grimaces. "We shoot back at the enemy first. Then, we worry about others. It's the Marchetti way."

"Oh …" My voice trails off because I have no other words.

Benny is quiet for a moment before saying, "That's how my mom died."

My voice softens. "She was shot?"

"A drive-by shooting." He slams his eyes shut before slowly opening them. "My father shot back instead of protecting her because that's the code. She was struck by a bullet and bled out before even making it to the hospital."

My stomach clenches. I knew their mother had died, but Gigi never shared how. As someone who lost a parent, I knew the pain of enduring people asking too many questions about their death, so I never pushed Gigi. If she wanted to share with me, I was there. She was the same. But now, I know that both of our mothers were murdered. I wish Gigi were here right now, so I could wrap her in my arms and hug her tight.

When he stands, I see the pain in his eyes, and he walks toward the doorway.

"I hear you'll officially be my stepmother. I'd say welcome to the chaos, but it seems you're at the center of it right now."

"Benny?" I call to his back.

He glances at me over his shoulder and raises a brow.

"Did your father love your mother?"

It takes him a moment to reply. "I think so."

I slowly nod.

"Don't tell my father about this conversation."

And he leaves the room.

My stomach growling reminds me of why I originally came downstairs. The massive kitchen—a space that'd put Martha Stewart's to shame—is empty when I walk in. I make a beeline to the pantry, collecting a handful of Oreos from the package, and leave the kitchen. Cristian's office door is shut when I pass, and I contemplate knocking but chicken out.

I slip back into bed and eat my Oreos. Hopefully, Cristian

doesn't have an issue with eating in bed. Late-night snacks in bed are a must in my life. Benny's words stay with me as I lick the cream filling from one.

"That's how my mom died."

Is that why Cristian was so different earlier?

Why he wanted to make sure I wasn't hurt?

It's late when the door opens, and Cristian enters the bedroom.

I feign sleep.

The shower turns on, and when he joins me in bed, he settles on his back.

His body is tense, and his breaths are stressed.

My fiancé.

My monster.

Maybe he isn't as heartless as I thought.

Cristian is gone from our bed the next morning.

It seems my husband-to-be isn't a fan of sleeping.

His hobbies only seem to include bossing me—and everyone else—around, murdering people, and having his tongue between my legs.

I hate the first two.

The last I'll take at any time, all day, every day.

It'd keep him from murdering people, so call me a humanitarian.

I step out of bed, undress on my walk to the bathroom, and turn on the shower. As I wait for the water to warm, I drop my engagement ring onto the vanity. The diamond most likely cost more than my car. Cristian had better get an insurance policy on it. I'm the queen of losing things.

My car in parking lots.

Hair ties.

Louie, my pet hamster, when I was ten. *God rest his soul, MC Hamster.*

When I step into the shower, I drop my head back, and the hot water feels like bliss against my sore body. Cristian's tackle had done a number on me, but his rough touch last night added to the ache. A bruise is already forming on my hips from where he gripped them.

I shriek when the glass door swings open. A draft of cold air hits my body, and a naked Cristian joins me. I blink through the blurriness, adjusting my eyes through the water to see him.

He stands underneath the second showerhead, looking gorgeous as water pours down his body, but the stern expression on his face cancels out that gorgeousness. He's holding something in the air.

I squint.

My ring.

I stumble forward into his space when he captures my wrist.

"Why isn't this on your finger?"

"I'm in the shower."

I attempt to yank away, but he overpowers me, holding me in place. My nipples harden, the cold air hitting them, as I'm now standing halfway under his showerhead.

"Doesn't answer my question."

I swallow. "I don't wear engagement rings in the shower."

His face hardens. "What other engagement rings have you worn?"

Even though the answer is zero, I don't appreciate his attitude.

So, I don't reply.

He forcefully shoves the ring onto my finger. "Put it on."

I ignore him.

He stares at me, out of patience, but releases me now that I'm wearing the ring. "Take it off again, and I'll have it sewn on to your finger."

"Why?" I raise my voice. "Will you wear yours twenty-four fucking seven?" I scoff. "Or will you wear one at all?"

Ignoring me, he grabs the shampoo bottle and pours some into his hand.

I stare at this infuriating man.

Appraising his body as if it were a one-of-a-kind structure in a museum.

His face, hard yet handsome.

His chest, muscular, zero body fat, six-pack.

Impressive for his age.

My eye-fucking is obvious, but he pays me no attention.

As if he forgot I was here.

I bite into my lip when my gaze drops to his thick cock. It's hard, throbbing, and pointing toward me. The tip of it is purple and aching.

Oh, his cock definitely knows I'm here.

I run my tongue over my lips, remembering how it felt in my mouth.

How he tasted as he choked me with it.

My fingers ache to touch him again. Indecision thrashes through me. Shaking my head, I return to our earlier conversation, so I don't drop to my knees and beg him to let me suck him.

"Cristian," I say, my gaze returning to his face, "Did you hear what I said?"

He scrubs a hand through his hair, as if I hadn't said a word.

I grab my washcloth and throw it at him. "God, I want to kill you."

My words startle me, and my eyes widen in regret.

Thou shall not threaten a murderer, Natalia.

I never seem to learn.

Cristian catches the washcloth and plays with it in his hand. "Do you know what I do to those who threaten violence against me?"

I can't stop myself from scoffing. "I hardly think I'm much of a threat to you."

"Everything is a threat to me."

"Screw you, Cristian." Anger jolts through me, and I attempt to edge past him to leave the shower.

He grabs my arm, pulling me back into the space, and I almost fall on the slippery tiles. I know I'm in trouble when I'm thrust forward and the side of my face is shoved against the tiled wall. Cristian's large hand covers nearly my entire cheek as he pins me in place.

You don't talk to the king like that and get away with it.

Just because he's had his tongue between my legs doesn't mean I'm awarded the freedom to smart-mouth him.

I gasp for air, pain spreading through my face when his hand digs into my cheek harder. His thumb tightly presses into my jaw, making it impossible for me to speak. My heart rumbles in my chest, and I shake when his chest flattens against me.

His wet skin against mine.

The wild beating of his heart against my back.

I shiver when he dips his head, the stubble of his facial hair scraping roughly against my neck as his lips go to my ear.

"Did you give me this for a reason, sweet Natalia?"

Given I can't move my head to find what he's referring to, I don't understand his question. Until his free hand slips between my legs, holding something, and my hips buck forward when he slides the washcloth between them.

He holds me in place, gripping the washcloth, and cups my pussy with it. He slides it back and forth, and my legs shake every time the soft texture of the towel brushes my clit. I pant, flattening my hands on the wall as he pleasures me. I move with his touch, rotating my hips, and forget the pain in my face. All my thoughts are on the washcloth and the feel of his erection sliding against my ass with every move he makes.

When he releases my face, I gasp, pulling in deep breaths of air. I don't get a chance to ask him, *What the fuck*, before he snatches my ring hand and slams it to the wall like he did my face. He holds my arm above my head, as if he needs the view of me wearing the ring from behind me.

Steam surrounds us as he drops the washcloth and replaces it with his hand. He cups me like he did with the washcloth before thrusting one … two … three fingers inside me.

"Oh my God," I moan, my back arching.

He positions his fingers perfectly, curving them at an angle and hitting my G-spot each time. I never knew my G-spot existed until Cristian.

A wave of warmth rolls through me as I repeat, "I'm there. Don't stop. Don't stop."

Just as I'm about to collapse onto the floor, Cristian's fingers are gone.

Without warning, he uses his ankle to nudge my legs farther apart and shoves his cock inside me. Then, he starts fucking me exactly how I imagined Cristian would fuck a woman.

Unrestrained.

His thrusts are as powerful as he is.

Deep moans come from him.

His grip is tight as he slams inside me. My hand on the wall drops, too sore to stay in place, and Cristian smacks my ass.

"Put your fucking hand back, Natalia," he demands, bowing his head and sinking his teeth into my neck.

I slam it against the wall, my head falling back as water slips over my lips. Cristian places his hand over mine, interlocking our fingers, and spreads them so my ring is fully displayed.

I whimper beneath him as he fucks me with no inhibition.

It's not romantic.

Or comfortable.

"You take me so well, sweet Natalia," Cristian groans into my ear. "It's like my cock was made for you."

I throw my head back, moaning, and he fucks me harder.

"Will you throw things at me again?"

I fuck him back just as rough while sharply panting. "Depends on if you make me mad."

He smacks my ass—harder this time.

That will definitely leave a mark.

It's like he's marking me as his.

"Wrong answer." He slaps my ass again, pushing me forward, and I whimper when I smack my head into the wall.

He roughly chuckles. "Let that be a lesson to reel in the attitude. Now, shut up and take my dick. Don't stop until I'm coming inside you."

My knees go weak as he thumbs my clit. My pussy tightens around his length as my moans grow louder. I tell him I'm close, and he gives it to me harder.

I fall apart first, and he holds me in place while pounding inside me.

The water turns cold as our moans falter, and he steps back, pulling his cock out of me. His cum slides down my legs alongside the water, and he reaches out, spreading it across my skin.

He whips me around and gets in my face, and his voice is thick with arrogance. "Make no mistake, sweet Natalia, I love my cock inside you." He snags my hand and licks my ring finger, sucking it into his mouth. "That ring doesn't leave your finger again."

20

CRISTIAN

I'm picky with my pussy.
 I've fucked only a short list of women.
But I've never had pussy like Natalia's.
Her body, olive skin with curves in all the right places.
Her round ass is enough to fill my palm.
Her hair, easy for me to wrap around my wrist and yank on.
Her pussy.
Tight. Wet. *Mine.*
Fucking perfection.
Other than that smart mouth of hers.
But why does her attitude always make my dick hard?
I've never been one to tolerate disrespect, yet I'm letting her give me lip and punishing her by fucking her senseless.
I planned to wait to fuck her until we were married, but that plan went to hell when I walked into the shower and saw her naked, and she started talking shit. She needed to be taught a lesson.
Not that she didn't want it just as bad. She licked her lips, staring at my cock as it grew harder and harder. Then, she had to throw the washcloth at me. That was my breaking point. I was only going to use my fingers, but as my body moved against

hers, as my cock slid along her ass crack, I could no longer restrain myself. That ass was in the air, begging for my cock, so I gave in.

I throw my head back, remembering how I feasted my eyes on the view of my cock sliding in and out of her pussy. She took my cock as if it had been made for her.

I didn't wear a condom. Other than with Benita, I've always wrapped up. But the thought didn't even cross my mind with Natalia.

If I get her pregnant, then oh well.

I'll get another heir to my empire.

Nothing will ever be as sweet as Natalia.

She's ruined me for any other woman.

I'm so fucked.

My sacrifice is becoming harder to give up.

When Natalia walks downstairs into the dining room, my dick stirs as I follow her every move. I want to smack my son for doing the same.

Instead of focusing on business, thoughts of this woman consume me. Thoughts of how and when I'll fuck her next.

She's becoming damn addictive—the taste of her, the smell of her, the sight of her.

"Where are you going?" I ask when she drops her phone into her bag.

"Work," she replies as if I'd asked the stupidest question of the century.

"Why?" I raise a brow. "You sold plenty yesterday. You deserve a day off after your sales."

I bought that art for good reason—so I wouldn't have to bother having one of my men babysit her there. A small price for not having the headache. I might keep a few pieces to myself and then either give away or donate the rest.

"*Deserving* a day off isn't a valid excuse to call in. For those of us who aren't bosses, this is how real-life jobs work, Cristian."

I gesture toward the chair next to me—*her* chair. "Sit for a sec."

As she walks farther into the room, I inhale the sweet scent of her perfume. That smell—with hints of vanilla and some type of flower—has become my favorite as it lingers in our bedroom, on our sheets, in the shower.

I grab my phone as she sits, Google a number, and listen to the ringing on the other end.

"Hello?" a woman answers.

"Bonnie," I say into the speaker, "it's Cristian Marchetti."

Natalia reaches forward, attempting to snatch the phone, but I pull away.

"Hi, Cristian darling," Bonnie cheerfully replies.

"Natalia is taking the day off." I disregard Natalia's attempts to kick my shin.

She's growing braver and braver. I'll need to teach my little pawn a lesson. Even though I've eaten her pussy, I still have no problem being the monster I am.

"That's no problem at all," Bonnie chirps. "You spend the day together and celebrate your new art."

"Thanks." I end the call and pin my stare on Natalia as I drop the phone. "You have the day off, sweetheart."

She narrows her eyes at me. "You can't make those decisions for me, Cristian."

I shrug. "Just did."

"What do you suppose I do then?" She raises her arms before dramatically dropping them to her sides. "This is a nice home—don't get me wrong. The problem is, it's bore city, hanging out here alone."

My home has been referred to as many things.

An architect's dream.

Immaculate.

Castle-like.

Bore city was never one of them.

"What about hanging out at Seven Seconds?" Benny suggests before I immediately cut my idiot son off.

"Not happening."

Seven Seconds is the club we co-own, which Benny suggested I invest in. I put the money up, earn half the profit, and Benny runs the day-to-day operations. When it was time to name the club, I chose Seven Seconds in honor of my favorite game.

Natalia perks up in her chair. "Sounds good to me."

I look back and forth between the two. "Am I the only one who remembers you have an angry ex after you?"

"I'll mind my business and stay out of harm's way," Natalia says.

I shake my head. "No. You already have a busy schedule today."

"Doing what?"

"Dress shopping and wedding planning with Helena and Celine."

She frowns. "I planned to wait until Gigi came home to do that."

"You won't have time. FaceTime her while you're there or something. Luca will accompany you."

"Luca won't like that."

"Do you think I give a fuck what Luca will or won't like?"

Benny snorts. "Better Luca than me."

I glower at my son. "Keep suggesting idiotic ideas, and that will become your job."

Luca walks in, interrupting our conversation, and just as Natalia said, he looks irritated at his job assignment.

Like Benny, Luca was born into this life. Marchetti blood flows through his veins. No man in this business—especially one of our pedigree—appreciates babysitting duty. After what happened with Dario, I need to be careful. Sticking her with inexperienced soldiers will only cost me men.

Helena told Luca of his duties before I had the chance to. He looks as if I'd asked him to quit this life, but he doesn't argue. Surprisingly, Natalia doesn't either. A flicker of excitement flashes across her face.

Natalia slides out of her chair and waves at Benny and me. Luca follows her out of the room.

As soon as they're out of earshot, I glare at Benny. "Keep your mouth shut when it comes to ideas for Natalia."

Benny runs a hand along his jaw. "She's bored here."

"Have Gretchen hang out with her. She sure seems to keep you entertained."

A smile plays on Benny's lips. "You're marrying Natalia. Get to know her."

When did my son assume he could give me advice?

Let alone relationship advice.

The kid has never had a serious relationship in his life.

"I'm marrying her as a favor." I wipe my mouth with my napkin. "I don't care to get to know her."

At least, that's what I'm trying to tell myself.

21

NATALIA

I've never been a girl who daydreamed about having a perfect wedding.

Sure, I figured I'd marry someday.

Just not to a man I hardly knew.

To my best friend's father, who's twenty-three years older than me.

Or who didn't love me.

None of those were on my vision board.

It's a quick ride to the bridal shop, and Luca parks at the rear entrance. When we step inside the shop, Helena and Celine are browsing dresses, glasses of champagne in hand. As I survey the room, seeing all the dresses, reality slams into me.

I'm marrying Cristian Marchetti.

Soon, I will be Natalia Marchetti.

Celine smiles while waving me over. "Are you ready for this?"

I accept a glass of champagne from Helena. "As ready as I'll ever be."

It's either I dress shop or my father casket shops for my dead body.

Dress shopping it is.

I choke on my champagne when Cici Lamole—an A-list

wedding designer—strolls into the showroom with an armful of dresses and fabric and a measuring tape thrown over her shoulder.

"You will be a beautiful bride," Cici squeals. "Let's get to work on making sure you have the perfect dress for Mr. Marchetti."

Three hours, four glasses of champagne down, and ten dress try-ons later, I find *the one*. I smile as I stare at my reflection, skating my hands down the lace as they tremble.

The girl who never dreamed of the perfect wedding dress has found hers.

After Cici measures every inch of my body, we leave the shop, and Helena becomes Wedding Planner 2.0. We hop from one place to another, making selections. Flower arrangements—black and burgundy roses to fit the mood. Cake flavors—Bavarian with raspberry. Catering menu—one that I have to confirm five times to make sure the price is okay. Helena takes full advantage of Cristian telling her we had no budget.

Our last stop is dinner. We're exhausted as we collapse into our chairs, order our food, and share a bottle of wine—Luca included. If I were Luca, I'd prefer doing this to Cristian's crime bidding anytime.

"Oh, I just love planning weddings," Helena says before reaching across the table and tapping Luca's hand. "I can't wait to plan yours."

Luca scratches the back of his neck and fails to meet his mother's eyes.

"We need to find you a wife first," Helena adds.

Luca grabs his drink and motions toward me. "Have that fun with hers." He lowers his tone. "Arranged marriages are such bullshit."

I point at Helena and then Celine. "Did both of you have arranged marriages?"

Helena nods. "My parents knew who I'd marry as soon as I left the womb. Not that I had a problem with marrying Lorenzo." Her face lights up when she says her husband's name. "I love that man."

Celine finishes off her wine. "Mine was different. I'm not married to a *Mafia man*. Santos is their attorney. The daughter of the mistress has slimmer options."

"Oh, don't let her fib you." Helena swats Celine. "She loved Santos long before they married."

"Did either of you refuse?" I lean in closer and show my impeccable manners by resting my elbow on the table.

"I tried," Celine answers. "When my father died, he put a clause in his will that Santos and I had to marry." She puckers her full pink lips. "Cristian refused to let us out of it."

I shake my head. "Sounds like my future husband."

"Welcome to the arranged marriage club," Celine says, pouring herself another glass.

I'll take being tipsy to drunk any day.

Tipsy is so superior.

You get the benefits of that buzz, but your brain still functions. I can count to one hundred, spell Mississippi, and walk in a straight line.

"Off to Seven Seconds we go," I singsong to Luca, swooping my arm through his as we return to the SUV after dinner.

Luca snorts but doesn't unwind us. "Off to bed in your dungeon or wherever Cristian keeps you hostage."

"Seriously," I say around a bubbly laugh. "They said I could after we finished."

Technically, that's a lie.

The topic was brought up, *somewhat* shut down by Cristian, so my tipsy self doesn't consider the case closed.

Luca assists me into the passenger seat before joining me.

I dig my phone from my bag and text Benny.

Me: Tell Luca I'm allowed at Seven Seconds.

Moments later, Luca's phone rings.

He eases his phone from his pocket, checks the caller, and glares at me. "You need to stop doing that."

I innocently shrug.

"Yeah?" Luca asks, answering the call, and then goes quiet as he listens. "Bye." Side-eyeing me, he tosses the phone into the cupholder. "You do know Benny isn't my boss, right?"

I flick my hand through the air and relax in the leather seat. "Same last name. Say we got Cristian and him confused."

He stares at me with unease. "Swear to God, the longer I watch over your ass, the higher the chance of being murdered—by either Vinny *or* Cristian."

"I promise not to let that happen. The last thing I need is Cristian sticking me with Rocky. Hard pass on hanging out with that crazy pants."

"Crazy or not, Rocky is loyal to Cristian."

"He hates me."

"Rocky hates *everyone*."

As we grow closer to Seven Seconds, Cristian texts me.

Cristian: Where are you?

Either Benny or Luca most definitely snitched on my going there.

I text him back.

Me: On my way to come see you, my hubby.

Cristian: Don't call me that.

Me: What would you rather I call you? Daddy? Psychopath?

Cristian: You're pushing it, Natalia.

Me: See you soon, hubs.

Seven Seconds is an upscale club that attracts partiers in their early-to-late twenties. Trust fund babies, influencers, and celebrities are okay with being overcharged for alcohol because sexy girls bring out the bottles with sparklers, and they can tag their location on Instagram. It was voted the best up-and-coming club in five magazines and on fourteen websites.

Like it seems with everywhere we go, Luca makes a left into a private drive that leads to the club's back entrance.

Cristian is waiting for me as soon as I step out of the car. It's dark, so I can't see his face, but I'm sure it's not bright and cheerful.

"What do you think you're doing?" he hisses.

"Coming to see you, like I said," I answer as innocently as I can.

I yelp when he snatches my elbow, drags me inside and down a hallway, and then pushes me into a room. He suddenly releases me, causing me to stumble forward, and slams the door shut. It's just the two of us in what appears to be an office.

I frown and rub at my wrist.

He walks around me and stands in front of the desk, crossing his arms. "Did you find your dress?"

Not the question I expected him to ask.

I rock back on my heels. "Our holy matrimony dress?"

He nods.

"I did." I drawl out the two words.

"Let me see."

"You're not allowed to see until I walk down the aisle."

"Says who?"

"Uh, tradition."

He rolls his sleeves to his elbows before performing a *come here* gesture. As if caught under his spell and unable to say no to his commands, I shuffle toward him. Spreading his legs, he settles me between them. I shudder, my skin prickling, when he skims his hand along my collarbone.

"Sweetheart, do you think I give a fuck about tradition?" He clasps his hand around the back of my neck. "We're already past traditions, are we not?"

"You'll see the dress when I walk down the aisle." I settle my hand on his chest, and even though the weight in the room is heavy, I can't stop myself from smiling up at him. "And you'd better cry tears of love."

He chuckles.

Swear to God, he *chuckles*.

If I wasn't in his arms, I'd pinch myself to make sure I wasn't dreaming.

"You and your smart mouth will be the death of you." He nips at my lips.

His sternness has faded into playfulness—so unlike Cristian. I pull away to get a better look at him. His shoulders are relaxed, his jaw unclenched, and his face doesn't contain a murderous expression.

Is he on the tipsy train too?

I take two whiffs to detect alcohol on this breath, but nothing.

"Oh my God." I dramatically gasp and place my hand over my chest, similar to how Helena did in the living room. "Did I just make *the* Cristian Marchetti laugh?"

He digs a finger into my neck. "No."

I nudge his shoulder. "You laughed ... and it wasn't your classic psychopath laugh. It was a regular person laugh. That gives me hope about the wedding-day tears."

I'd expect meatballs to drop from the sky before Cristian shed tears of love for me.

His dark eyes lower to mine. "I've never shed a tear in my life, so don't get your hopes up, sweetheart."

I raise a brow. "Never?"

He shakes his head.

"Not even as a kid?"

"We lived in a cry-free home—unless we wanted my father's wrath."

"A baby ... surely, you cried as a baby."

His face is indifferent, like his father's actions didn't affect him. "*For as long as I can recall*, I've yet to shed a tear."

How sad.

For your father to forbid you from expressing your emotions.

He slides his hand from my neck before shoving his face into my shoulder, raining kisses along my neck. "Now, back to the dress. Let me see."

I tilt my head to the side, providing easier access, and I'm thankful I pulled my hair into a ponytail earlier. "It's being altered at the bridal shop."

"Show me a picture." He licks down my neck.

I shiver, my knees feeling weak. "I don't have one."

"Guess I'll have to settle for you describing it to me then."

He grips my waist and picks me up, and I wrap my legs around him. He returns to the other side of the desk and settles me on it. I whimper when he eases his hands up my thighs.

"How long is the dress?"

"To my ankles."

Even with the simple touches he's giving me, my body is already aching for him.

His touch drops to my ankles, and I groan, wishing he'd gone in the other direction. He raises my legs, pressing them to his thighs, and stands between my legs, the same way I did with him earlier.

"And will you be wearing panties?" He stares between my legs and licks his lips.

I groan when he rubs his erection against me. "Undecided."

He flips my dress up. "I want this pussy to be covered and for my eyes only." He pulls at my hair. "No other man will ever see, touch, or even think about what's mine."

The urge to tell him I'm not *anyone's* is on the tip of my tongue, but it stays there. I don't want him to stop touching me. Hell, right now, he could tell me I belonged to aliens, and I'd agree so long as he kept touching me.

I stare at him in anticipation, in need, in everything as he skates his fingers back up my thighs.

Higher and higher.

Underneath my dress.

Right where I need him.

But he brushes both thumbs over my pantie-covered clit before pulling at the hem of my dress and saying, "Take this off."

I undress for him.

He roughly shoves his hands down my panties. "God, you're so fucking sexy, Natalia."

I grind into him and spread my legs wider.

"That," I whisper. "Keep doing that."

Holding one hand shoved down my panties, he moves his other to my chest, cupping my breast before lowering my bra to expose my nipple.

"And what will be here?" He feathers his palm over a nipple, and I arch my back off the desk.

"Scoop neckline. Thick straps. Simple."

"Simple? There will never be anything simple about you."

And in one swift motion, he tears my panties off and shoves them into a drawer. He plunges one … two … three fingers inside me, stretching me so wide I can feel my pussy expanding with each thrust into me.

He lowers his head to suck on my clit with his fingers still at work until I fall apart.

He wastes no time unbuttoning his pants and shoving them down to free his thick cock. And with one thrust, he's inside me, and it feels like everything I've ever needed.

As Cristian fucks me, there are no wedding thoughts.

No Vinny thoughts.

Just us.

Him inside me.

Pleasuring me.

Two people who aren't supposed to be touching each other.

I stare up at him, soaking in the vision and beauty that's Cristian Marchetti as he wildly fucks me. His head thrown back, his eyes squeezed shut while he bites into his lower lip.

He bows his head, as if he senses my stare, and our eyes meet—his on fire.

"You look so fucking sexy like this."

He's thrusting inside me so hard that my ass slips off the desk with each stroke. If anyone is outside this office, they're getting a free vocal sex show.

I moan, and he cups his hand over my mouth to mask the sound.

"Do you want everyone to hear you?" His voice is low. "To know I have you spread open for me in here?"

I smirk. "We're simply discussing wedding plans."

A wicked smile spreads along his face. "We do need to go deep"—he withdraws before slamming back into me—"into wedding planning."

I gasp when he loosens his tie, slides it off, and shoves it into my mouth. Rotating his hips, he hits my G-spot, and it's over. I cry out his name, nearly gagging on the tie, and my body shakes beneath him as I come undone.

My orgasmed-out body fights for the strength to keep watching him until he finishes.

Two more strokes, three more moans, and Cristian pulls out. Releasing his cum over my clit. My breathing hitches when he slips a finger between my legs, coating it with our pleasure, and smooths it over his lips before running his tongue over them.

"We have a lot of nights to go over wedding plans," he says between heavy pants.

22

CRISTIAN

I've been called a monster for years.

That's why I carry no guilt for fucking my daughter's best friend. Just like there was no regret when I almost traded her to the Lombardis. Remorse isn't in my vocabulary.

I hadn't planned on fucking Natalia in this office. But Helena called, eager to inform me that Natalia had found the perfect dress, awakening my curiosity. That curiosity became full-blown need when Benny told me Natalia was coming to Seven Seconds. I allowed it because I wanted to see her.

That's rare—me wanting to see a woman.

I was younger than Benny when I married Benita. My father had passed, so I could've pulled out of the agreement. But I chose to honor my father's contract with hers a decade prior. Plus, marrying her came with valuable real estate and connections. We had few conversations—from which I found her weird—but we created a decent marriage. She became the perfect wife, and while I became the not-so-perfect husband, I respected her. It wasn't until she was dying in my arms that I realized how deeply I cared for her.

Natalia is catching her breath when she says, "We have to stop doing this before Gigi finds out. She'll be home soon."

I stare at her. *She's such a fucking sight.*

I can smell our sex in the room, and I want it to soak into these walls, so every time I step into this room, I think of her.

In my office, her pussy dripping with my cum.

"Stop what?" I clear my throat.

She gestures back and forth between us.

"Fucking each other?"

She pinches her lips and attempts to straighten her lopsided ponytail. "You say it so crudely."

"How else should I say it?" I walk to the bar cart and pour myself a drink while waiting for a response that doesn't come.

As I've spent time with Natalia, I've picked up on her traits, her response to certain situations, and I know she's resisting the urge to make a smart-mouthed response.

I motion toward her with my glass. "You'd better straighten yourself up then because you look thoroughly *fucked*."

"If you weren't *you*, I'd be flipping you off right now."

"Do it. I'll just pin you down and make you fuck yourself with that finger in front of me."

My cock stirs when she fights back a smile.

"Where are your thoughts about flipping me off now?"

She narrows her eyes, and just as she opens her mouth to reply, there's a knock on the door.

"Just in case you didn't know, you're loud as fuck," Benny calls from the other side.

Natalia covers her face with her hands. "I'm never showing my face here again."

I lick my lips. "I enjoyed our wedding chat. Now, I have business to attend to. You were supposed to stay at the mansion, so I wouldn't have to worry about you."

"I decided against that."

"Looks like you'll sit in here then. Trust me when I say, this room is more … what'd you call it? Bores town?"

She glares at me. "How about I go hang out in the club … grab myself a drink?"

"How about I fuck some sense into you?"

It's like she lives to push my buttons.

She frowns.

"I'll be back." I do a circle gesture of the room. "Watch TV. No more alcohol. Stay out of trouble."

"I always stay out of trouble."

I scoff before leaving the room and find Luca and Benny talking in a corner.

"Why the fuck did you bring Natalia here?" I shove Luca into the wall and bare my teeth.

Luca points at Benny.

Benny shrugs. "Didn't seem like you had an issue with her presence a few moments ago." He spreads his hand along his jaw to hide his smirk. "FYI, one of Vinny's men tried sneaking into the club. We caught him, of fucking course, and he's tied up in the Northern Room."

The Northern Room is a room in the back, where we take men to interrogate them. It's soundproofed, not on the blueprints, and away from clubbers and employees.

I nod. "Give whoever spotted him a raise."

Vinny sending men here means he's up to something.

"I want you watching over Natalia." I snap my fingers at Benny before turning my glare to Luca. "It seems this one allows her to boss him around."

23

NATALIA

This office—whoever's it is—has no personality whatsoever. White walls, black and blue-gray granite tiles, and framed newspaper covers and article clippings praising the club hang on the walls. It's nothing as extravagant as Cristian's office at the mansion. Then again, not many could compete with the space there.

Conversation passes through the door from the hallway, and I stroll to the desk. I open the top drawer and snatch my panties from it. If this is some rando's desk, my panties aren't staying there. After casting a quick glance at the door, I take the opportunity to rifle through the drawers.

In the drawer he shoved my panties into is a gun, knife, loose sticks of wrapped gum, and condoms. In the one below it are random office supplies. The tall one on the left is locked.

Is this Benny's office?

Did Cristian dick me down on his son's desk?

My cheeks redden in embarrassment.

I've never been one for public sex, but Cristian Marchetti's charm had me spread eagle on the desk.

Gripping the edge of the desk to balance myself, I slide my panties back on before strolling to the bar cart.

These men and their bar carts.

Skimming my fingers along the bottles—most of them full or half-empty—I snag one with a pretty label even though I can't pronounce the name. I twist off the lid, grab a glass, and pour it to the brim. Just as I'm returning the bottle, the door opens, and Benny walks in.

I swing my arm toward the desk. "Is that yours?"

Benny shakes his head. "My dad's, though he hardly comes here." A sly smile spreads over his handsome face. "Don't worry, Natalia. You didn't just fuck my dad on my desk."

I pluck the liquor bottle from the cart in case I want another drink, and I struggle to clutch that and my glass as I walk over to the couch. I'm proud of myself for not spilling anything as I collapse onto it. "Why does your dad own a club he's never at?"

"My dad has plenty of businesses he's not involved in daily." He unbuttons his black blazer—one so similar to what his father wears—and slips his hands into his pockets. "I proposed the idea of a club, asked him to invest, and now, we're here."

Benny confiscates the bottle from me faster than I can stop him. "This shit will fuck you up with one shot. My father will kill me if he comes in here and you can't walk."

"Your father is always going to kill someone," I grumble before taking a sip of my drink and cringing at the taste.

Benny might've taken the bottle, but I still have a full glass of the *shit that will fuck me up with one shot*. And from the drink I just took, I believe him.

He returns to the cart, puts the bottle back, and grabs another before handing it to me. "It's part of the lifestyle."

I shift on the couch and make myself comfortable, sitting cross-legged. "Will you be the same when you take over?"

His face is unreadable. "I don't know how I'll be if I ever take over."

"You've never thought about it … since you'll be the one to do so?"

He scratches his unshaven cheek. "The only reason I'll ever take over is if my father dies. So yeah, not aiming for that."

"Vinny always said he couldn't wait to take over." I wince, now realizing what that meant. He was counting down the days until his father died.

"Vinny has no respect for his father, his family, anyone. He's a selfish motherfucker who stupidly thinks when he takes over, he'll be king of New York."

"King? Like the strongest family?"

He nods and sits on the other end of the couch. "Which is why any of us—other families included—would be fine with him dead. The guy is a goddamn liability. I'm surprised he hasn't figured out a way for his father to be killed, so he can take over the family and run it into the gutter."

"He wasn't always like that …" My voice trails off.

"We never are. Well, most of us. My dad and I were raised differently. We were taught to be this way from a young age. Vinny's dad was stupid enough to baby him, let him be normal, and it fucked him up when he got a sliver of power."

"Power changes people." I play with the glass in my hand. "Do you think it's weird that I'm marrying your dad?"

"Yes, but who am I to talk about weird? I offered to marry you for the same reason."

"And your dad said no." I sigh. "Who's this girl you're marrying?"

"Neomi." He snarls his upper lip. "She's the fucking devil."

I laugh. "That's a great way to describe your wife-to-be. Bad blood?"

"We've only been around each other a few times. Each time, we've wanted to kill each other."

"Does Neomi know about Gretchen?"

"Nah, we don't talk. She's out living her life too. Neomi isn't one of those Italian girls who sits at home and knits." He shuts his eyes and shakes his head. "The woman is wild."

"Sounds like maybe what you need." I smirk. "A girl to put you in your place."

He snorts. "For sex maybe."

"Do you plan to be faithful to her?" I tap my fingers against the glass. "To give up Gretchen?"

He runs a hand through his hair. "Who knows when we're getting married? Gretchen and I could be done by then, but Gretchen knows Neomi is my future."

I feel stupid for responding with, "Do you think your father will be faithful to me?"

He shrugs. "That's not my answer to give. But I will tell you one thing: my father is picky about the women he sleeps with. He doesn't trust people. Unlike many of these Mafia men who have women everywhere, he's never been one of them."

"He sure seemed to like Carmela." I gulp down the remainder of my drink, stand, and walk to the bar cart to refill my glass with the liquor Benny warned me about.

Benny shakes his head but doesn't try to confiscate it again. "Yes, because Carmela is obsessed with him, is in this world, and Rocky is her father. My dad knew he didn't have to worry about her turning on him or selling information. She's as loyal as Rocky is."

I take a long swallow of the drink as I go back to the couch and plop down. "Not loyal to me."

"She will be. My dad will find her someone else to marry."

"Maybe Luca?"

"Luca would rather chop his dick off than marry Carmela. He knows she's slept with my father and then tried fucking me—"

"Wait." I hold up a hand and raise my voice. "Carmela tried sleeping with you?"

"If you can't have the king, might as well go for the prince."

"I mean, that does have a nice ring to it."

He chuckles, and we glance at the door when someone jiggles the knob.

24

CRISTIAN

Benny and Natalia are on the couch when I return to my office.

Natalia's eyes are glossy, and my gaze drifts to the glass in her hand. The only beverage options in this room are alcohol, so there's no doubt that's what's in my little troublemaker's glass.

"I told you to watch her," I snarl at Benny, rubbing at my temples.

Benny holds up his hands. "Technically, she was already drinking when I walked in." He motions toward Natalia. "She doesn't listen."

"I'm beginning to learn that." I take three long strides to Natalia, pluck the drink from her hand, and down the rest without a flinch.

Rocky enters the office, shaking his head, and I hold out my hand toward Natalia.

"Come on, drunkie." I wiggle my fingers. "I can't take you anywhere."

"Except the bedroom," she says, her tone flirty as a flush sweeps up her face.

"Jesus," Benny hisses. "I regret not taking that drink now."

I help Natalia off the couch, gripping her elbow, and escort her outside, where Francis is waiting for us with Rocky behind us. As we make our way to the SUV, I look from each angle to make sure the coast is clear. If Vinny had one of his men sneak into the club, who knows what else the idiot would try to pull.

"Francis," Natalia says when we reach him. "I sure have missed your driving. Luca doesn't stop at red lights and texts while behind the wheel." She whirls around, a bit wobbly in the process, and smiles. "Don't tell him I said that."

I don't pay Luca to obey traffic laws.

Realistically, I pay him to break laws.

Natalia climbs into the back seat, me behind her, and my cock thickens when her dress slides up, showing me a glimpse of her ass cheek. Francis and Rocky take the front seats.

"I am *starving*," Natalia says. "Let's get tacos."

I ignore her.

"Have you ever had drunk night tacos?"

"No."

I have too many responsibilities to have *drunk night tacos*. I've never been one to have guys' nights or party—luxuries I give my children. My dad insisted I spend all my free time with him, learning about the business. After his death, there was even less time for me to do anything that wasn't business-related. It's difficult, being a don, and I had to work extra hard to prove myself because of my age.

Living this life has its pros and cons.

Pros being money, power, and carrying on your family's legacy.

Cons being that the pros become your life.

Natalia slaps the back of Rocky's chair, and he jerks forward. "What about you, Rocky?"

"No," he grunts, holding in the restraint to lash out at Natalia.

"I request you take a right, Francis," Natalia says as if we take orders from her. "There's a to-die-for taco joint around the corner. Paco's."

"No one wants tacos," Rocky barks.

"Wrong. *I* do." Natalia leans forward, sticking her head between Francis and Rocky. "Do you want tacos, Francis? You look like you could go for a good taco."

Francis laughs, shaking his head. "I could go for one."

This is why Francis is my driver and not one of my men. Yes, he'll shoot a guy if his life is in danger, but he's more laid-back than us.

I reach out, grab the back of Natalia's dress, and yank her away from them, so her back is against the seat. "I'm beginning to question why I allowed my daughter to befriend you."

"Boss?" Francis asks, looking at me through the rearview mirror.

I wave my hand through the air. "Fine. But make it quick."

Natalia squeals at her win.

Not exactly a win.

If she wants tacos, she can have fucking tacos.

I'd have had them brought to the mansion if that was what she wanted.

But I suppose this is more convenient.

"Give Rocky your order," I tell Natalia when we pull up to the no-parking curb in front of Paco's Taquerias.

"No, I'll go get them. I'm picky about my tacos." She swings the door open and jumps out—nearly face-planting—before I can stop her.

"I'm going to strangle this woman," I mutter.

"Cristian—" Rocky starts, but I tune him out, step out of the car, and follow Natalia before she gets herself killed.

Protecting her seems to have become my full-time job, of which I'm also working overtime.

I grab her arm, jerking her toward me, and her back hits my chest. "If we're doing this, you walk with me and don't leave my fucking side."

With her back still against me, she tips her head up and smiles. "Aye aye, hubby."

"I'm never letting you drink again."

From my research on her, she's never been much of a drinker. Her newfound attraction might be my fault. I've been known to drive people to drink—as well as throw themselves off buildings and disappear from their families.

I flinch when she slides her hand into mine, threading our fingers, and steps toward the taqueria. Her hand is warm, soft, and I can't stop myself from squeezing it.

When was the last time I held hands with someone?

Benita. And that was a rarity.

All eyes are on us when we step inside the cramped taqueria. Every table is full of people talking, yelling, and shoving food into their mouths. I've had Paco's plenty of times, but this is my first time being inside. I'm a takeout guy.

Tonight is also the first time I've stood in line for tacos.

For anything really.

There are many luxuries of being a monster people fear—one being, you're always taken care of. Normally, I wouldn't stand in line. I'd either go straight to the front, ignoring those waiting, or have someone else do the waiting for me.

As much as I want to skip right to the front, something tells me Natalia would bitch about cutting in line. I keep aware of my surroundings as we wait.

"Shoot," Natalia says. "I forgot my wallet." She slips me a guarded look. "Can you spare your fiancée some taco change?"

I force myself not to crack a smile. No one has ever talked to me, defied me, the way she does.

I pat her shoulder. "I can pay for your tacos, sweetheart."

She grins, tapping my chest before shoving her face into it, surprising the shit out of me.

"Mr. Marchetti!"

My attention flies to the front counter at the sound of my name to find Paco, the taqueria's owner, waving his hands in the air. "I didn't know you were in line. I'm so sorry. We would've helped you right away."

The one time I want to remain in incognito, and someone calls out my name.

"Keep your head down and stay close to me," I whisper to Natalia before leading us toward the front, where Paco is waiting.

Natalia recites her order—a large one, so I'm sure she plans to share with everyone.

"Nuh-uh," Paco shouts when I go to pay. "On the house! A Marchetti never pays here."

Businesses yearn for my family to frequent them. It shows it's a place we respect and is protected. But I don't like my name being yelled when I'm with a woman with a damn bounty on her head.

With my hand still in Natalia's, I use the free one to grab my wallet and shove two hundreds into the tip jar. "Can you just make it quick?"

Paco nods, grinning from ear to ear. "Of course, of course."

Minutes later, Paco hands over a bag of tacos.

"Let's get out of here," I tell Natalia, speed-walking us out of the taqueria.

Just because I'm protecting her doesn't mean she can act so reckless. She's not safe any longer. I'm sure with Vinny, getting tacos wasn't a big deal. It's different now.

Natalia eats her tacos in the SUV and sips on her soda.

Francis saves his for later.

Rocky and I decline.

When we return to the mansion, I tell Rocky I'll chat with him in a minute and take Natalia upstairs to our bedroom.

"I don't know if it's the liquor, but I've never had tacos so delicious," she says around a hum before sinking back onto the bed, taking off her shoes, and tossing them onto the floor.

When I stand in front of her, she pulls herself up, bringing her hands to my pants and attempting to unbuckle them.

I retreat a step. "You're drunk."

"And you are very smart for noticing that." She reaches

forward again, but I stop her. "I'm not fucking you while you're drunk."

Her shoulders slump. "What happened to all the *behave or I'll fuck your face* Cristian? In times like these, he's more fun."

"I'll fuck your face in the morning." I blow out a breath, and my cock hates me for turning her down. "Don't you dare get sick in our bed."

And as much as I'd love to fuck her face now, especially with the carefree mood she's in, I leave the bedroom.

"I like her, Cristian," Francis says when I walk downstairs to find him eating his tacos. "She's good for you."

Francis and Benita formed a friendship during our marriage. As her driver, he became one of her closest confidantes.

This is the first time he's approved of any woman he's driven for me.

"Don't let the tacos bribe you," I say, running a hand through my hair. "She's a pain in the ass."

He waggles his finger toward me. "But she's also … fun—something you need to learn to have."

If this were anyone other than my loyal-as-fuck senior driver, I'd have already kicked him out of my home. Francis will most likely work for me until he can no longer drive. Then, I'll take care of him and his wife so they can live the rest of their lives comfortably. He's a good man.

"I need to learn how to have fun like I need a bullet to the brain."

"She also has great taste in tacos." He drops the bag onto the foyer table. "I saved you two, *but* do you mind if I bring some to Quinn?"

"Take all the tacos to your wife. She deserves them for you having to put up with us."

I snap my fingers, interrupting the guys gossiping in the

corner of the room like a damn boy band, and whistle toward my office.

Rocky, Lorenzo, Benny, and Luca situate themselves in my office.

"First off," I say, pinning my glare to Luca, "anything Natalia-related goes through me."

Lorenzo shoots his son a hard look for his disobedience. Just like Francis, my brother-in-law is a good and loyal man to his family.

Luca firmly nods. "Got it. My apologies, and it won't happen again."

I glance at Lorenzo. "Did you get rid of the body?"

Lorenzo nods, a hint of a smile on his face. "Sure did."

Vinny's guy was a lackey with the brains of a worm. With two punches and a promise to spare his life, he blew the whistle on everything he knew about the Lombardi family. Not that we kept our promise in the end. His body has now been laid to rest, buried with the worms.

And right before I blew his brains out, I learned Vinny had offered five hundred thousand dollars to anyone who brought him Natalia—dead or alive. And a million to anyone who brought her to him alive.

Surprisingly, Natalia is awake when I come to bed.

"Do you ever sleep?" she asks, pausing the TV.

I start unbuttoning my shirt. "That's what I'm about to do now."

"And then wake up in what, three hours?"

I shrug. "Probably four."

"Lack of sleep is unhealthy."

"Lack of sleep being healthy is the least of my problems, sweetheart."

Not going to lie, I like that she's worried about my health.

I've never had anyone question me about my choices like that.

"If you're so worried about sleep, why are you awake?" I add. "I expected to find you passed out in your drool."

"Ew, gross." She scrunches up her nose. "I waited up for you."

"Why?"

She shifts, bringing her knees to her chest. "Benny said you want Vinny dead."

Why do my men keep opening their mouths up to this woman?

"I do want him dead. Do you have an issue with that?"

She hesitates, squeezing her eyes shut, and then nods … and then shakes her head … then nods … then shakes her head … then nods.

Natalia has a good heart, and even with Vinny wanting to murder her, she's not cruel like me. She needs to learn that if a man is a murderous sociopath who wants you dead, you'd better shake your head when asked if you have a problem with him being killed. Otherwise, you might be the one dead. I can only protect Natalia if she protects herself as well.

"What will happen after you kill him?" she asks. "Do we divorce?"

I snarl at her last word. "Divorces don't happen in this family."

"Don't you make the rules?" Her words come out strained, her face mortified, as if she thought this would be an easy arrangement to leave.

"I do make the rules."

She releases a breath of relief—a sound that makes my blood boil.

"That's not a rule I'll break," I continue, bursting her bubble. "There hasn't been a divorce in our family in ninety years. I won't be the man to break that streak."

Natalia stares at me, horrified, and holds up a finger. "To clarify, divorce isn't an option once we get married?"

I nod. "Till death do we part."

25

NATALIA

I search the house until I find Gretchen in the kitchen, restocking drinks in the refrigerator.

"Grab your bathing suit and meet me by the pool," I say, plucking a can of sparkling water from her.

Gretchen turns and runs her gaze over the kitchen, unsure if I'm speaking to her.

I poke her shoulder. "We're hanging out today."

"Oh no." She shakes her head and returns to the fridge. "I have to work."

"Your workday is over." I wave toward her clothes. "Now, go change."

She clutches a can to her chest. "But Mr. Marchetti—"

"I'll tell him it was my idea, and I insisted," I interrupt.

"Okay." She offers a dimpled smile before sliding the can into the fridge and shutting it. "I'll meet you outside."

After she leaves the kitchen, I finish stocking the fridge in case anyone tries giving her shit. I scoop up my bag from the floor by the patio doors and walk outside.

The mansion's backyard is one of my favorite spots at the estate. It's massive—sprawling acres of green grass, a guesthouse, an infinity pool, and a tennis court. A stone perimeter wall does its best at protecting us while not appearing too prison-like.

I inhale the fresh air as I pass wild rose bushes, peonies, and red tulips.

My sanity *and* my hangover can use a relaxing pool day.

I have my sunglasses to block out the bright sun and plan to nap the day off until Cristian comes home. I don't know when that'll be since it seems my future husband is always on the move and hardly sleeps. We need to improve on communication since I have no idea where he is.

I wave Gretchen over from the stone pathway and tap the lounger next to me. She's changed into a white cherry-print bikini that shows off her suntanned skin and tiny waist.

"I grabbed these since it's hot as sin out here." She holds up two bottles of water.

"Thank you." I take one from her.

She spreads out the towel I tossed onto her chair before sitting and making herself comfortable. I take a long drink, stretch my legs, and tilt my head back.

The pool and wall fountains create a serene environment, and I start nodding off until Gretchen makes conversation.

"Did you tell Mr. Marchetti about Benny and me?"

I shake my head. "And I won't."

I decide against informing her that Cristian already knows. The poor girl doesn't need more anxiety.

"Thank you." Her voice is soft-spoken. "My mom would kill me if we lost this job. If I get fired, they'll most likely let her go too."

"Cristian won't fire you even if he finds out."

"That's what Benny said, but Benny is … well, Benny."

I turn my head to look at her. "Are you in love with him?"

She hesitates before answering, "Yes … which makes me foolish."

"It makes you human."

"A stupid human."

"Human nonetheless."

She sighs.

"We're not the first to fall in love with the wrong people, nor will we be the last. Just because we have a brain doesn't mean we always use it. Sometimes, our heart beats louder than our brain and drowns out reality ... drowns out the truth."

"Are you still in love with your ex?"

I bite into my nail. "Do we ever fall out of love with anyone?"

It's a question I've asked myself many times. Vinny was my first love, and I imagined spending the rest of my life with him. And then everything changed. I'll never know if it changed because it was an act he put on for me or because his father finally allowed him to be more involved in the family business. Either way, he became hotheaded and cheated like it was his duty in the world to sleep with as many women as possible, and eventually, I'd had enough.

I was so blinded by my hurt that when I ended it with him, I didn't think about *who* I was breaking up with. Vinny didn't take the rejection well. At first, he begged, apologized, and promised he'd change. When that didn't work, he moved on to threats.

So, the answer is, I don't know.

Are there takebacks with love?

Can you love someone and then, one day, wipe your heart clean of those feelings?

If you're angry with someone and forgive them, you don't forget what they've done. That anger is still harbored inside you, no matter how much you try to tell yourself otherwise. You'll never forget.

Is it the same with love?

That it stays, still harbored inside you?

Vinny showed me what love was, then what love wasn't, and both experiences will forever stay with me. I don't care what anyone says. Those you love always leave pieces of themselves behind.

But just because I love Vinny doesn't mean I love him more than myself—more than *my life*. That's why I nodded when Cristian asked me if I had an issue with Vinny's death. I want to be that good person who doesn't stoop to their levels, but in that same heart that fell for him, I know he won't stop until he has me in his grip or kills me.

Vinny can die, and I'll bury that love and guilt to stay alive.

But will I find love again?

Once I say *I do* to Cristian, we'll forever be tied to each other until one of us says our good-bye to this world.

Is Cristian capable of loving?

Deep down, beneath the layers of trauma and darkness, something beats in Cristian's chest. I need to figure out how to bring it into the light.

There's nothing like a good poolside nap.

The sun on your skin.

Getting your vitamin D.

Forgetting people want to murder you.

"My men are staring at you."

I jerk forward when my sunglasses are ripped off my face. Adjusting my eyes, I find Cristian standing at my side. His head is bowed as he icily stares at me, as if I'd dropped all his bar carts off at Goodwill.

"So are you." I retrieve my sunglasses, shove them back onto my face, and dramatically recline back into the lounge chair.

Cristian, wearing a complete suit like it isn't summer in New York, points his chin toward a nervous Gretchen. "I take it, her not working is your doing?"

"You take it right."

"My office—*now*."

I shift so I'm sitting and reverse to glance back at Gretchen. "BRB."

Her eyes are wide, and she nods. Cristian grips my elbow and tugs me from the lounger before I have the chance to bring myself up. When he releases me, I grab my phone, and he whips around toward the house. I trail him and run my tongue along the back of my teeth. We're rarely in this position—me behind him. He's usually at my back, guiding and protecting me from harm.

I've never *checked out* a man's ass before, but with Cristian, every inch of him is desirable. From the way he talks to how he walks—long, fast strides—and how his back muscles tense with each step he takes.

This man—sexy and powerful—will soon be my husband.

The reality sends chills through me. When Vinny and I were together, I never thought I'd be attracted to anyone else, but he has nothing on Cristian.

I nearly trip on my feet and stop when my phone rings.

Gigi's name lights up on the screen.

This phone call might keep me out of trouble.

"Hold on a sec! It's Gigi," I call out to Cristian before answering the call. "Hello?"

"Hey, babe," Gigi says on the other end. "Sorry I didn't text back. This time difference thing is a bitch."

No matter what I'm going through, Gigi's voice always delivers a sense of comfort.

When I peek forward, I find Cristian stopped, staring at me, and a smirk plays on his lips. I eye him suspiciously.

The monster looks like he's up to no good.

"Totally fine," I croak when Cristian begins tapping his foot.

"*One sec*," I mouth to him, holding up a finger.

Cristian, out of patience, takes one long stride to grip my free hand and drags me down the hallway so fast that I nearly drop my phone. I suck in a breath to stop myself from yelling at him and attempt to listen to Gigi.

I'm a terrible friend, though, because I'm not comprehending anything she's saying. I yelp when he shoves me into his office, and as soon as the door shuts, he whips me around. I don't get a chance to tell him to wait a minute before he tugs on the string of my bikini bottom, undoing it, and then does the same to the other side. The sliver of fabric falls to my feet, and before I get a chance to stop him, he does the same with my bikini top. My breasts burst free, and he tosses the top onto the floor.

"What the hell?" I whisper, shoving his shoulder but not moving away from him.

I balance the phone between my shoulder and ear as he pulls me around the desk. Without warning, he moves and bends me over it. A low moan escapes the back of his throat as he uses his feet to spread my legs. I hiss between my teeth when he presses his palm against my back, flattening me against the desk, and arches my ass into the air. Without warning, he thrusts two long fingers inside me.

"Oh my God," I gasp, and my knees buckle.

"What?" Gigi asks.

I'm a sucky friend since I forgot she was on the phone.

I lift my head to glare back at Cristian, and he gives me a *pleased with himself* smile.

"I just ..." I bite my tongue when he thumbs my clit, and heat creeps up my face. "I saw a spider."

"A spider?"

"Yes." I close my legs, caging his hand in to give myself a break to think. "And now, he's running away."

"Okay ..." She drawls the word out. "Call me back when you're done dealing with Charlotte and her web."

I end the call and glare at him over my shoulder before tossing my phone at him. It smacks into his shoulder and drops to the floor.

"Gigi doesn't think we're actually hooking up and doing the

husband-wife screwing part," I croak out. "Do you want us to get caught?"

He uses his knee to open my legs back up. "That might be the worst excuse I've ever heard." He deviously smirks. "We both know Gigi will find out about our intimate relationship."

I don't fight when his fingers slip back inside me. "It's not exactly easy to come up with a good excuse when someone is fingering you."

"Not someone. The man you're marrying." He hums. "And so wet for me too."

His chest brushes my back, and his breath tickles my ear when he leans forward to whisper in my ear, "I'm going to fuck you so good on this desk that it'll be all you think about."

I swallow. "And I'm going to fuck you back so good that every time you sit here, it'll be all *you* think about."

He shudders above me as he rises, and his breaths are rapid. I frown when he withdraws his fingers, but that excitement is restored at the sound of him unbuckling his belt and pants.

He grips my waist and shoves his cock inside me, and there's never been a more perfect feeling. I draw in a sharp breath, relishing in how he stretches me yet fits me, as if we were made for each other.

I immediately push into him.

He grabs my ponytail by the base and pulls it as he fucks me. "Give me that sweet pussy, Natalia."

"Take it," I moan, hissing when he smacks my ass. "It's all yours, Cristian."

"Fuck yeah, it is." He pumps in and out of me, circling his arm around my waist, so he can control our pace.

"You fuck me so good, sweet Natalia," he groans. "Take this cock like it was made for you." He kneads my ass before loudly smacking it.

The office is consumed with our heavy breathing, moaning, and the sound of our bodies smacking together. Desire sparks through me, loving the noise, the feel, *us*.

I whimper when he suddenly pulls out, turns me around, and then pushes his cock back into me. I swivel my hips to grind into him. His hand lowers to my clit, and his thumb plays with it, massaging and then flicking it. I'm soaked, the evidence of that smearing against his desk, and if Cristian wasn't fucking me so hard that I could hardly think, I'd be mortified.

I tilt my head to stare down at our connection, at his cock sliding in and out of me. He does the same, and pleasure burns on his face.

"Fuck yes, Natalia," he hisses, biting into his bottom lip. "Spread your pussy juices onto my desk, so every time I walk in, I smell it."

My eyes widen at his dirty mouth, and then he bends his neck forward to kiss me. He slides his tongue into my mouth and teases mine with it.

I love the taste of him.

Everything that is him.

The room feels like it's on fire.

"Give it to me. Tell me how you like to be fucked," he groans into my mouth while slamming into me harder.

"Don't stop," I beg. "I'm almost there."

"Fuck me back until you come," he growls. "Feed my cock that pussy until you're falling apart underneath me, and then I'll fill you with my cum."

Those words set me off. My legs shake, my back arching, and I stop fucking him back because my body feels as if it were now made of jelly. Luckily, Cristian does the job for me. He holds me in place, thrusting, before his arms fall forward. His hands slam to each side of me on the desk, his chest brushing mine as we catch our breaths. His eyes are hooded as he stares down at me, captures a loose strand of my air, and then slides it off my sticky cheek.

The king and his sacrifice.

No, the king and his soon-to-be wife.

26

CRISTIAN

I've never fucked a woman in my office before.
 My office is my sacred space, my church, where I make hard decisions and clear my head. I could've dragged Natalia to our bedroom, but I wanted to see her spread open on my desk as I pleasured her. I wanted to commit the sight of fucking my future wife on that desk in my memory.

"You like her, don't you?" Benny asks when I return to Seven Seconds.

This is where I've spent most of my day, but when I saw Natalia on our home security footage on my phone in that black bikini, I needed to touch her.

To take that bikini off.

And because I'm a responsible man, I told everyone we were taking a break. Unfortunately, since I trained my son to think like me, he knew *exactly* why I was running home for a quick errand.

I didn't plan to come back, but Santos, our attorney and Celine's husband, said it was urgent we meet with him.

I shove my phone into the pocket of my blazer. "Who?"

"Natalia."

I ignore him.

"You do."

I continue ignoring him.

"Of course"—he chuckles—"I won't get an answer out of you."

"Stop wasting both of our time trying then."

My feelings toward Natalia are complicated. I'm picky with those I care about—*genuinely* care about. It's a small list, but Natalia is squirming her way onto it.

We look up when Santos enters Benny's office.

My son put more effort into his office here than I have. It's his main office, so understandable. I'd describe my office at home as old money with its dark furnishings and rich wood paneling. Benita called my style as medieval and romantic when we built our home.

Benny's office, on the other hand—which he refers to as *modern*—reminds me of a damn doctor's office. The walls are alabaster white, the lights bright, three computer screens take up the entire space of his desk—so I don't know how he gets shit done—and the furniture looks about as comfortable as sitting in a church pew while the priest preaches about murder after you killed three men the night before.

"I heard you're engaged," Santos says, smirking while drawing his shoulders back. "And that you've known the girl for quite a while."

Fuckers must be growing balls if they want to make *fucking your daughter's best friend* jokes. Santos had better watch out before I leave her e and fuck his mom for his smart mouth.

I pin my glare on him. "Change the subject and tell me what's important before I have to call my sister and inform her it's time to plan your funeral."

Santos shakes off my threat. "It's been brought to my attention that you have a rat in your inner circle."

My blood turns hot.

Benny steps forward. "What the fuck does that mean?"

He shouldn't ask that question because we know what it

means. I grind my teeth. For years, I've done my best to keep a loyal family, and I can count the snakes in the grass I've had to kill on one hand.

Santos opens the folder in his hand and slaps a newspaper onto Benny's desk. "Someone leaked the real blueprints of the club—ones that differ from the prints we submitted to the city. The room that isn't on the blueprint? The *New York Teller* and people online have referred to it as a—and I quote—'crazy torture room.'"

"Torture room?" Benny stifles a laugh. "It's called an interrogation room."

"Semantics," Santos replies. "They know what you do in there."

"Both of you idiots are wrong. It's the supply closet, where we keep the cleaning supplies. The city must not have received the final blueprints. Call the *New York Teller*, demand they to retract their statement unless they want their business destroyed, and leak *our* prints online, which'll make them look stupid." I shrug. "Easy fix."

Santos holds up a finger. "Moving on to problem two: they're also accusing you of laundering money through the club. I haven't received all the information on what they have—"

"If they even have anything," I interrupt. This isn't the first time we've had stories leaked about us that we've fixed with a simple phone call.

"This is serious." Santos shakes his head. "Someone in your family is turning on you. You need to find out who."

My stomach curls.

"I hate to ask this, Cristian," Santos says, his tone turning lawyer-like. "I know the girl is Gigi's friend, but she dated a Lombardi—"

"Then, don't ask it," I snap, taking a step toward Santos and staring him down.

The thought of Natalia leaking information and putting my

family in harm's way makes me want to destroy everything in my path.

Benny shakes his head. "Natalia never snitched on Vinny."

"She told you everything about him, Cristian," Santos points out.

I swipe the papers he placed on the desk, throw them onto the floor, and dig my foot against them. "You find out this source."

"It has to be those Lombardi cunts," Benny says. "That's probably why he's having his guys sneak in. Natalia stayed in the office the entire time she was here. There's no way she even knows about that room."

"Look, Celine said the girl is nice," Santos continues. "All I'm saying is, watch your back and be careful."

"I'm always watching my back," I snarl.

"Apparently not well enough." He holds up his hands when I pin a death stare on him. "Don't kill the man who ensures your ass stays out of prison."

It's late when I enter our bedroom.

I've gone from screwing my fiancée in my office to questioning if she's double-crossing me. I wasn't there when Vinny killed Dario. It could've gone down differently, and she could've been in on his death.

Natalia is in bed, wearing silky black pajamas and eating a goddamn Oreo cookie … on sheets I had imported from Italy. As I stalk into the room, she eyeballs me, opening and then shutting her mouth. It's as if words are on the tip of her tongue, but she doesn't know how to say them. Usually, I wouldn't care, but everything about this woman arouses my interest.

"Spill it, Natalia," I say, stopping at the edge of the bed.

"Spill what?" She looks away and separates a cookie before licking off the frosting.

Fuck. My cock grows hard as I watch her drop crumbs in our goddamn bed. *What is this woman doing to me?*

"Whatever it is you want to ask or say."

She dismissively waves her hand into the air. "It's nothing."

"Say it," I grind out.

"Will you …" Her voice trails off.

I crouch down so we're at eye-level and adjust my dark gaze on her. "Will I what?"

"Will you be a good husband?" she finally asks, her question taking me off guard.

"That depends on what your definition of a good husband is."

She breaks eye contact and runs her fingers along the bed. "My father was a good husband."

Why would she bring up her father while half-naked in our bed?

Not that it'll stop me from corrupting her body in it tonight.

Reaching forward, I use my thumb to wipe frosting off her top lip, and goose bumps form on her arms. "If there's anything I can guarantee, it's that I'm nothing like your father."

She frowns. "You don't know my father."

"I know enough." I draw back and unbutton my pants. "Whether or not I'll be a good husband is an opinion you'll need to form on your own."

"So far, with half of your behavior, I'm worried and thinking not so good."

"Most of that behavior was pre-engagement, Natalia."

"That doesn't excuse your actions."

"You're right. Now that we've discussed what's on your mind, let's move on to what's on mine."

"Okay." She elongates the word.

I harden my voice so that my frustration is clear. "Are you feeding anyone information?"

"What?" Her mouth falls open, and she draws herself back. "What are you talking about?"

"Someone leaked information about the club and my finances."

She presses her hand to her chest. "And you think that someone was me?"

"If there's one thing I hate, it's a rat."

"Do you consider me a rat for telling you Vinny's secrets?"

"No, I consider you smart." I crouch down again, smack my palms down to each side of her, and invade her space. "But crossing me? That's not smart."

Her breaths quicken, and she attempts to keep her words steady. "I could've gone to the police instead of you, Cristian. They'd have also offered me protection."

"You know they could never offer the extent of protection I can." I inch closer to her space, inhaling her sweet scent, and can't stop myself from brushing a hand along her thigh. I love that she shivers at my touch.

"Yes, but I had that option." She chews on her lower lip and stares down at my hand massaging her leg. "I had someone approach me months ago, asking about Vinny, and I told them nothing. I swear, I'd never put you guys in harm's way. I care too much about Gigi, Benny … and *you*."

I lift my other hand to stop her chewing and trace a finger along the seam of her plump lips. "I had to make sure."

I read people well—most likely *why* we haven't had many traitor problems—and I'd bet my entire empire that Natalia has said nothing. And as Benny noted, she hasn't had access to anything that was leaked.

She opens her mouth to drag her tongue across my finger. "Anything else?"

I disengage from her, standing and straightening my shoulders. "Yes. Don't eat fucking Oreos in our bed."

She grins before rolling over, her ass cheeks peeking out of her shorts, and grabs a handful of cookies before making herself comfortable.

I rub my forehead. "Who would've guessed our downfall would be fucking cookies?"

She laughs. "Lighten up some, Monster."

I cock my head to the side. It's the first time she's referred to me by my nickname.

"A monster never lightens up," I say. "But you know what I do?"

"What?"

I latch my hands around her ankles and drag her across the bed to me. "Eat my future wife until she orgasms on my tongue, and I taste her all night."

27

NATALIA

"I have to go back to work today, Cristian." I tell him this as we're drying off post-shower and post-orgasm.

Post-orgasm is always the best time to bring up stuff he'd typically say no to. The shower is my favorite space to share with Cristian. I love the view of his wet, naked body and the smell of his shampoo and body wash. Plus, he can't keep his hands off me.

"No, you don't," he says, his voice stern as he knots a plush towel around his waist.

"Yes, I do." I pinch my lips together. "I can't do that to Bonnie, and she only needs me for a few hours."

"I'll go with you then."

I freeze mid drying off. "Go with me to work?"

"Yes."

"As in sit there and hang out?"

"Why not?"

"You'll scare people."

"Scare them into buying art from you." He smirks. "Bonnie won't mind."

"You'll make *me* nervous."

"Act like I'm not there." He drops his towel, and I can't stop my gaze from dropping to his erect cock. "I need a birthday gift for Helena. I'll find one there."

"You told me your last purchase at the gallery was for Helena's birthday. The one you didn't even look at before purchasing?"

"She has a few more birthdays coming up." He picks up another towel and runs it through his hair. "I like to be prepared."

"Fine, but don't say I didn't warn you. It won't be fun."

"Sweetheart, do I ever have fun?"

"You do when you're with me."

"Fucking pain in my ass." He kisses my forehead.

"From now on, if I can't accompany you to work, Rocky will," Cristian says as Francis parks in front of the gallery. He ducks out of the SUV and then helps me out.

Rocky?

I'd rather be unemployed or take part-time hours before spending time with Rocky.

Is that harsh? Possibly.

But the man hates me.

His daughter hates me.

"Cristian!" Bonnie calls out, rushing over to us when we walk through the glass door into the gallery.

I motion toward him. "Do you mind if he sticks around during my shift?"

Not that he'd take no for an answer. Cristian makes the rules everywhere he goes even if he doesn't own the business.

Also, not that Bonnie would say no either.

"Not at all, honey," Bonnie replies. "Cristian is always welcome here."

Cristian strolls over to one of the velour couches in the corner and sits.

I inhale a few breaths, gathering my thoughts, and then get to work. Cristian watches my every move while I do so.

He doesn't sit on his phone or keep himself preoccupied with another task. It's as if he can't take his eyes off me. He stares at me the same way he did the first night I walked into his office.

When customers walk in, their attention immediately swings to Cristian. He does his best to steer them to us and then assists us with sales in a Cristian-like fashion.

"Buy that," Cristian tells a man who's practically drooling at the mouth at the sight of him.

"That'll look nice in your home," he suggests to another woman, and she purchases it without asking the price.

Whatever he suggests to a customer, they buy.

Bonnie eats up the attention and attempts to high-five him with each recommended sale, but he doesn't high-five her back. Cristian might help her with sales, but the man is definitely not a high-fiver.

Four hours later, my shift is over. I can tell Bonnie wants me to stay, but Cristian promised lunch. And your girl is starved.

"Select something for yourself," Cristian tells me before we leave.

I blink at him. "What?"

"Choose something for our home. The queen needs to add her special touch to our castle."

28

CRISTIAN

I drop my pen onto my desk when there's a knock on my office door. Before I get the chance to speak, Natalia walks in.

There's no stopping myself from licking my lips at the sight of her. And she didn't walk down in sexy lingerie. She's wearing one of my tees that she stole without asking. *Shocker.* The black shirt reaches her knees, so I don't know what she's wearing underneath. I wouldn't be surprised if she thieved a pair of my boxer briefs along with the shirt. The woman loves getting into my personal space.

She bumps her hip against the door. "Want to watch a movie with me?"

I'm quiet.

"Friday night movie night."

Movie night?

I've never had a movie night in my life.

Not even with my children when they were younger. When they hit their teens, they'd ask to watch movies they thought I'd be interested in, like *Goodfellas* and *The Godfather*, but I was too busy with work.

"Please," she says in a begging voice.

A begging voice that nearly kills me.

"I'll grab some snacks and popcorn. It'll be fun."

I rub my hands together, as if I just finished the last of my work. "I'll watch a movie with you *in bed* until I fall asleep."

Compromise.

I don't have to participate in this ridiculous movie night idea. But I get to spend the rest of the night in bed with Natalia.

A win for both of us.

She grins in victory. "I'll grab all the snacks and meet you in the bedroom. Get your sugar tooth ready."

"Don't bring fucking Oreos," I call out to her back as she leaves the office.

When did we start being okay with eating in bed?

My mother would've had my ass if I'd so much as had a cracker in my bed while growing up. If we wanted food, we had to sit at the table. Anywhere else wasn't an option.

I wait until I hear her shuffle upstairs before shutting down my office and walking upstairs. She left the door open, and the only light comes from the lamp on her nightstand. I'm already removing my cuff links as I enter the room but halt when my gaze hits the bed.

She wasn't bullshitting about the snacks.

Oreos—four varieties.

Popcorn—two varieties.

Sodas and bottles of water.

And a shit ton of boxed candy, like you'd see at a movie theater.

All of which are either on the bed or her nightstand.

"I had no idea they made so many different Oreos," I comment.

I told Natalia to give Gretchen any grocery requests, and it seems she had Gretchen buy out the Oreo aisle.

She pats the open space next to her, where I sleep. "The more you hang out with me, the more random knowledge you'll learn, Marchetti."

Her gaze locks on me, and she snacks on a cookie while I undress to only my boxer briefs before joining her in bed.

"I have narrowed down a selection of movies so as not to overwhelm you," she explains, holding up the remote. "You make the final decision."

I rest my back against the headboard. "Choose whichever you want."

I'll wait until she falls asleep to return to my office and finish my work. Surely, she's bound to have a sugar crash.

"I've never done this before," I say when she plays the movie.

"Done what?"

"Watched a movie like this."

Her shoulders slump, and her voice fills with sorrow. "You had no childhood … or teenagerhood, did you?"

I pop my knuckles. "We grow up differently in my world."

"Gigi and Benny did this stuff." She gestures to the TV. "We watched plenty of movies together. You have a movie theater in your home."

"In *our* home," I correct, ignoring the movie. "And I wanted my children to have a better childhood, *teenagerhood*, than I had."

I've lived my life knowing and not caring that people will never understand me. I am Monster Marchetti—a man with a void in his chest that should forever be empty. People fear me, but here this woman is, asking me to have a movie night with her. Even after I made her life hell in the beginning.

She gave me forgiveness for the mistakes I'd made.

Honesty is what I can do to make up for it.

I clear my throat. "I didn't want my children growing up miserable."

"Did you grow up miserable?"

"I was forced to grow up before I knew what growing up meant."

She stares at me, her gaze comforting, and brushes her finger over my forearm. "I'm sorry, Cristian."

"Benny and Gigi were lucky." I pinch at the skin of my throat to level my voice. "Their mother was nothing like mine. Benita grew up in a softer family, which gave her a kinder heart."

"Did you love Benita?" she whispers.

"I don't know," I answer honestly.

"Did you tackle me during the shoot-out because of how she died?"

"How did …?" I pause. "Fucking Benny."

I should've deprived him of a childhood. Maybe he'd have learned how to keep his mouth shut.

She strokes my arm. "I'm sorry you had to go through that."

"There are few times I've ever felt weak, like I didn't have control over something." A pain forms in the back of my throat, and I attempt to swallow it down. "The first time I felt powerless was when my father was murdered. The second was watching my wife die in my arms." I reach around her to smooth my hand over her hair. "You asked me if I'd be a good husband. Probably not."

Her shoulders tighten.

"I have flaws, Natalia. A lot of them. I learned a lesson when I chose to put the rules over my wife. I swear to you, I won't be that husband again."

"I know you'll always keep me safe, Cristian."

I bow my head to kiss the top of hers.

She reaches across the bed, pulls an Oreo from the container, and holds it out for me.

I shake my head.

"Have you ever had an Oreo, Cristian?"

I glare at her.

"Seriously." She groans, throwing her head back. "Were you deprived of tears *and* Oreos growing up? Now, I understand why you're so damn cranky all the time."

"I doubt the lack of Oreos affected my childhood much."

"It definitely did." She separates the two cookies. "First, you have to lick the frosting off."

"Just give me the damn cookie." I snatch it from her and shove it into my mouth.

Natalia is teaching me there's more to life than being the head of the Marchetti family.

I am a father, a son, and soon, a husband.

And an Oreo fan, goddammit.

29

NATALIA

I grab my phone when it rings.

Bonnie's name flashes across the screen.

"Natalia, is there any way you can come into the gallery?" she asks when I answer, her tone frantic. "My granddaughter is ill, and I need to pick her up from school. No one else can cover for me."

"Of course," I reply. "I'll call Cristian for a ride and be there as soon as possible."

The line goes silent for a moment before she says, "See you soon." Her three words are rushed out as one.

Cristian answers my call in two rings. "Kind of busy right now, sweet Natalia."

"Bonnie's granddaughter is sick, and she asked me to cover the gallery for her," I tell him. "Can you take me?"

"I'm stuck in an important meeting."

"Totally fine. I'll just drive."

"What did I tell you?"

Shit. Fuck. Dammit.

"Um … I don't remember." I hold in a breath.

"Rocky or I take you, Natalia. You're not driving."

"I think Rocky is busy."

Before Cristian left, he told me Rocky was staying behind in case I needed anything. So, I'm sure the sociopath is wandering around here, plotting a murder—possibly mine. From what I've learned, the man eats, sleeps, and breathes homicide.

"I'll call him."

"What about Benny?" I ask.

"He's out."

"Francis?"

"Took the day off for his wife's retirement party."

I groan.

"You don't have to hang out with him, sweetheart. I'll tell him to sit in the car until you're finished. Have a good day at work."

"Ugh, fine."

We end the call.

I collapse onto the couch, drop my phone, take a long sip of my lemonade, and slump my shoulders in dread. I've never been alone with Rocky before, but he makes my blood run cold.

When they almost handed me over to the Lombardis, Rocky made his hatred for me clear, hissing in my ear all the ways he hoped Vinny would carve my body up, while Cristian poked Vinny the bear.

I don't get much time to put on my *avoid Rocky* thinking cap because he walks into the living room and says, "Cristian said you need a ride to the gallery?"

Dammit, Cristian.

I gulp. "Yes."

He attempts to smile, but the man has so much anger that it looks more serial killer–like than friendly.

He jerks his head toward the door. "Come on."

I flinch before standing, my movements slow and cautious, to the point where I probably look overdramatic. If Rocky notices, he doesn't comment on it.

When we get to the car, I take the back seat.

"I think we got off on the wrong foot," Rocky says, peering

at me through the rearview mirror and bobbing his bald head to the music.

There are scars on that head, and I always want to question him about them.

One doesn't easily get a scarred head.

There have to be stories.

"It's okay," I croak. "I'm not one to hold grudges."

"It isn't. I was upset because Carmela and Cristian had a relationship."

I scrunch up my nose at him saying their names in the same sentence.

"But Cristian made no commitment to Carmela. I promised Cristian that Carmela and I would behave around you, and I give you my word as well."

"Thank you, Rocky."

I run my hands up and down my arms before deciding to send a quick text to Benny, Cristian, and Gigi, letting them know I'm on my way to work. The more people who know where I am, the better.

"Shoot." I frantically pat my pockets and frown. "I forgot my phone."

"We're about to be at the gallery," Rocky says. "I can drop you off, grab it, and then bring it back to you."

After Vinny attacked me in my apartment and I realized I was phoneless, I swore that'd never happen again. I haven't forgotten to take it with me anywhere. But it's either have Rocky turn around, spend more time with him, and make Bonnie wait longer, or agree to his plan.

His plan means less Rocky time, so sold.

Rocky kills the engine when we park in front of the gallery. "I'll walk you in and then grab your phone."

I wave a hand in the air. "You don't have to walk me in."

"Cristian's orders."

I nod and slide out of the SUV.

He jumps out of the car, surprisingly following me, and the gallery is empty when we walk in.

The classical music that typically flows through the speakers is off.

"Bonnie!" I call out, making my way toward the back room. "Are you here?"

"Natalia."

I sprint to the back at the sound of Bonnie yelling my name.

"Natalia, I am so sorry," Bonnie says in hysterics as I turn the corner. "They said if I didn't call you, they'd hurt my grandchildren. I didn't know what to do."

Strong hands wrap around my waist, pulling me back, and I scream when something is shoved against my face.

Then, everything goes black.

30

CRISTIAN

"Make this deal, and we'll give you rights to this entire block," Severino Cavallaro says, pushing his chubby thumb onto an outlined map placed on the table in front of us. He draws a line within a larger radius. "There are twenty businesses within these limits. You take half, we take half, and all is good between us, Marchetti."

It's a profitable deal.

Will double my income.

The agreement will also tighten the relationship I have with the Cavallaros.

Most consider the Cavallaros a notch down from us regarding influence, fear, and authority within New York crime families. It's wise to have these men on my side—especially after I execute Vinny. The Lombardis won't be happy about their idiot son's death and could create war. I need as many bodies on my side as I can get.

My phone rings just as I'm about to throw out my final questions.

I tend to ignore calls when I'm in meetings. People become skeptical of phones during these meetings to begin with. You can easily record conversations with them.

But I don't snub this call.

It could be Natalia again. Rocky said he was taking her to the gallery, but I haven't heard from her since.

Benny's name flashes across the screen instead.

I hit the Ignore button and shove the phone back into my pocket.

It rings again moments later.

Benny.

Ignore.

Again, this time Santos.

Ignore.

Benny once more.

I hold up my hand. "Give me a sec."

They nod and start a new conversation as I stalk to the corner of the room.

"What?" I snap, answering the call. "I told you I was meeting with Severino today."

"Where's Natalia?" he barks.

"The gallery."

He releases a long breath. "She drove?"

"No, Rocky took her."

"Fuck!" he yells, and I hear him hit something.

My blood pressure elevates at his response. "What?"

"Santos had his PI working on finding the rat. He checked everyone's phone history, and Rocky had a few calls with numbers linked to men in the Lombardi family. That doesn't confirm he's our rat, but it damn sure looks suspicious. Until we figure out why he's calling them—and not smart enough to use a burner, fucking idiot—we need to keep him away from Natalia."

I clench my jaw. "Meet me at the mansion right now." After ending the call, I turn to the men. "I need to go. We'll reconvene later."

"What the hell, Marchetti?" Severino shouts. "We're trying to close a deal here."

"We'll close it later. I need to murder a traitor first."

"Ah." Severino grins, showing off his gold tooth. "One of my favorite parts of the job. Have fun and let me know when you're finished. Take pics of your work if you have them. That shit is like porn to me."

Of course the fucker would request pictures of dead bodies.

Severino will soon be Benny's father-in-law.

Good luck, Benny.

31

NATALIA

My head is dizzy, and my throat burns from whatever they soaked the rag in before they shoved it into my mouth.

It was something chemical. Since I've watched enough true crime, I'd bet chloroform.

I blink before slowly opening my eyes, one by one.

"Natalia, baby."

His voice grows deeper with each word.

A manic voice.

A familiar one.

Vinny steps in front of me, his back straight, and his lips are curled into a perverse smile.

Panic clutches at my stomach, but I will myself to stay calm.

Or at least pretend to appear calm.

I don't realize I'm zip-tied to a chair until I jerk forward to flee. Panic consumes me, but I inhale deep breaths. I need to have a clear head to handle whatever torment Vinny has planned for me.

"Vinny, what the hell?" I say. "Untie me right now."

I don't think he'll listen, but it's worth a try.

"No way," he says, chewing on a toothpick. "I'm not risking

you escaping me again." He signals to his eyes. "You had my vision fucked up for days with your little pepper spray trick."

I scan the room but recognize nothing.

This isn't some dirty warehouse where people are killed or a bachelor pad. There's a white velour couch, leopard-print pillows, and canvas paintings of Chanel and Louis Vuitton logos.

"Are you ready to have some fun now?"

The question is asked by a feminine voice. I hear heels clicking against the floor. My back straightens, panic crackling through me, when Carmela steps to Vinny's side. A vile smile is smeared across her face as she eyes me with pleasure. She's been waiting for this moment.

Oh no.

"Not so smug without Cristian, are you, bitch?" Carmela asks, her face burning. Sweat trickles down her forehead, causing her self-tanner to bleed.

Stay calm, Natalia.

Carmela wants to see me squirm.

I refuse to give that to her.

"Vinny, you couldn't have done any better?" I ask, keeping my eyes on him and not paying her a glance.

My question is risky, but it'll show me what Vinny's play with Carmela is.

If he sticks up for her, I'm in deep shit.

If he doesn't, I'll need to figure out a way to charm Vinny into untying me.

"You stupid whore," Carmela yells, falling right into my trap as she charges toward me with her hand in the air.

I shut my eyes and wait for the blow. When it doesn't come, I open them to find Vinny gripping a fistful of Carmela's hair. He aggressively yanks her back, and she topples in her heels, catching her balance before she falls on her ass.

"Don't you dare put your hands on her," Vinny roars, his face on fire.

"What the hell, baby?" Carmela's voice turns into a whine, and she approaches Vinny, attempting to kiss him.

He shakes his head, flattens his hand against her forehead, and shoves her back.

Carmela releases a string of curses, and spittle forms in the corners of her mouth, but she doesn't try attacking me again. She still maintains that murderous glare pinned on me, though.

"Vinny and I are getting married," she says, thrusting her chest out and smiling in satisfaction, as if she'd hit the husband lottery.

Does she think I'll be jealous of that?

Let the two crazies be together.

No doubt Carmela will soon be filling out conjugal visit forms to visit her prized hubby in prison.

"Congrats to the bride and groom," I say, rubbing my wrists together against the ties. I pretend smile. "And good news: I'm also getting married."

This time, Carmela falls back a step on her own. "Stupid slut," she hisses. "You think Cristian will keep you around for long? He told my father his plan with you. You're nothing but bait to draw Vinny in. He wanted Vinny to do this, so he would have the opportunity to kill him." She cackles. "Little does Cristian know, his days of being *king* are quickly coming to an end. Vinny and I will become the king and queen of this city."

"You can kill me, but make no mistake, Cristian will come for you both. When he finds you, expect his wrath." I stare them down. "He has men everywhere. You won't stay alive much longer."

"Men like me?"

I wince and nearly fall over in my chair when Rocky steps into my view.

"I'll be so happy to get rid of you." He shakes his head, and his voice is so monotone, it's terrifying. "You made me defy my loyalty to Cristian and lose our friendship."

"*You're* the rat?" I ask in a disbelieving tone.

Rocky flinches at the word, as if it's the worst name he's ever been called. "I'm no rat. Cristian disrespected my daughter. I had to stick up for her, and this is how she wanted it done."

"How could you do that to him?" I ask. "He trusted you."

Rocky looks away with a pained expression on his face.

"How do you want to do it, baby?" Carmela asks, needing the attention back on her. "Let's tape killing her and send the video to Cristian. I don't want her death to be fast, either. No bullet to the head. I want to watch the stupid bitch suffer." She's jumping up and down, her words coming out quickly, and I'm positive an illegal substance is flowing through her bloodstream.

This is when shit starts getting real.

There are spots in my vision as I stare at the three of them, knowing they have my murder planned. My heart twinges. I feel just as powerless as Cristian said he felt when his wife died in his arms. There might be no way out of this, but that doesn't mean I won't try.

"No, let's make it quick," Rocky argues sternly. "And no video. That's evidence."

I've never seen Rocky nervous.

He clearly isn't the man in charge of this plan.

"Why?" Carmela whines. "I thought this would be entertaining when we finally got her." She stomps her foot. "Cristian will be looking for her soon. I don't want her alive to escape or possibly be rescued."

"Give me a minute, Carmela," Vinny snaps.

The room is quiet for a moment … until Vinny draws out a gun, and I scream.

Loud as hell.

Then, I follow up with, "Somebody, help me!"

I don't know if anyone can hear me, but I might as well give it a shot.

"Natalia, shut the fuck up," Vinny says, rushing over to me and slapping his hand over my mouth.

Rocky, as if knowing what to do, hands Vinny a roll of tape, and I violently shake my head as he presses the tape over my mouth. He pats it a few times to be sure it's snug and tight.

"Jesus, I'm done waiting for you guys to man up and kill her." Carmela stomps across the room, opens a drawer, and withdraws a gun. "Time to go, bitch."

A grin is on her face as she points the gun at me. I attempt to scream, but the tape muffles me.

I say a silent prayer, shut my eyes, apologize for my sins, and wait for my death.

Ringing explodes through my ears at the sound of a gunshot, but I feel nothing. I open my eyes to find blood spurting from Carmela's forehead. Her body falls back and she collapses onto the floor.

"God, I couldn't wait to get rid of that cunt," Vinny mutters with annoyance, gripping his gun. "The bitch would never stop talking."

I gulp and try to scream again, but I can't.

"What the fuck?" Rocky yells, puffing out his chest and drawing out his weapon.

Vinny leaves my side to approach Rocky, and before Rocky pulls the trigger on him, Vinny shoots Rocky's kneecap.

Rocky grunts before falling onto the floor.

Man, this is not going how those two expected it to go.

They made a deal with the wrong man.

Vinny is as loyal as a Zeus in pretty much every Greek myth.

"Stupid geriatric motherfucker," Vinny says around a laugh as he kicks Rocky's gun away from him. "You think I'd ever let a rat in my family?" He bends to capture Rocky's gun, plays with it in his hand, and then shoots Rocky's other kneecap with it. "Or marry his whore daughter?"

Rocky cries out in agony, screaming like a baby, and can't move. His eyes are consumed with regret when he looks away from Vinny to me.

My head spins.

Carmela didn't get out of this.

Neither did Rocky.

I'm starting to think I won't either.

Vinny seems particularly trigger-happy today.

"Looks like it's just you and me, baby." Vinny twirls the gun in his hand, and every move he makes is erratic. "I missed you, and we have so much to catch up on."

My body trembles, and I try to suppress my tears, but I don't have the energy.

Vinny cracks his neck from side to side before crouching down so that he's in my face. He smiles—a smile leaking with intimidation—before harshly kissing my lips over the tape.

He smacks me across the face. "That's for being a cunt and threatening Cristian's wrath against me." He rises and punches his puffed-up chest. "Cristian had better hope he doesn't run across me. I will kill that motherfucker. He won't even know what hit him. Now, it's time to have some fun with you."

32

CRISTIAN

"Natalia's phone GPS says she's at the mansion," Benny tells me. "We checked the cameras, and I talked to Gretchen. She left willingly with Rocky."

Francis is speeding and weaving through traffic toward the mansion. I've lost count of the number of times I've called Rocky. My chest tightens. There are only two reasons he isn't answering: he's in trouble or he turned on me.

I bounce my foot and shut my eyes, not wanting to consider the second one.

Rocky has been at my side for decades. That'll fucking hurt.

"Did you call the gallery?" I ask.

"Ten times," Benny replies. "No answer."

I look up at Francis and tap his shoulder. "Go to the gallery."

"Got it, boss." Francis whips the steering wheel around, and I fly forward when he makes a quick U-turn.

As Francis approaches the curb in front of the gallery, I swing the door open and jump out of the SUV. My heart is on fire as I sprint to the door and then curse at it for being locked. Rearing my fist back, I ram it through the glass, and it shatters. Blood trickles from my knuckles as I reach through the broken shards, unlock the door from the inside, and walk in.

The gallery is quiet.

Not one employee or customer in sight.

A Starbucks cup and a half-eaten breakfast sandwich are at the front counter. I tip my head forward at the sound of rustling from the back. Francis walks in behind me as I follow the noise. I find Bonnie tied up to a chair when I walk into what appears to be a break room. Tape is over her mouth, and she's swinging her body side to side, moving the chair, as if trying to make as much noise as possible.

She winces when I rip the tape from her mouth and blows out a series of breaths.

"Bonnie," I yell. "What the hell happened?"

She bows her head, and tears stream down her cheeks. "I don't know. They were wearing masks."

"Who was wearing masks?"

"The people who took Natalia." Her tears fall faster. "They threatened to hurt my grandchildren if I didn't call and ask her to come into work. I did … and they took her." Her words turn into sobs. "I'm so sorry! I'm a horrible person."

I snap my fingers, trying to keep her attention. "Did you catch any names?"

She shakes her head.

"Male? Female?"

"Both."

Francis starts untying Bonnie as I retrieve my phone from my pocket to update Benny on the situation. *We need to find them.*

My phone rings before I get the chance to hit his name.

Rocky.

I answer on the first ring. "Where the fuck are you, Rocky?"

"Hello, Cristian."

My temples pulse, my nostrils flare, and the need for violence possesses me at the sound of the recognizable voice.

"Rocky is currently … incapacitated," Vinny says with a deep chuckle. "You get to speak with me instead."

"You motherfucker," I bark, ignoring the stares coming from Francis and Bonnie.

Vinny snorts.

"Where's Natalia?"

"With me."

"You touch her, and I will kill you, slow and vicious." Spit flies from my mouth with every word.

Bonnie whimpers as she listens.

"Natalia is mine," Vinny says.

"Be a man and tell me where you are. Prove you're tough. Let me come to you."

He scoffs. "You think I'd do something so stupid, Marchetti?"

"Don't be a fucking pussy. You want to be king?" My voice rises until I'm nearly screaming. "You have to take the king down."

"I'll take you down on my own terms. The first of which is taking Natalia." He tsks me. "What I can give you, though, is the location of your rat. You can pick him up at Carmela's and do as you please with him. I suggest you do so rather quickly—before he bleeds out."

My mouth turns dry, and my pulse speeds. "I will grant you a faster death if you release her now."

"Natalia is mine, Cristian." He scoffs. "You think she'd want to go back to you after she learned you'd planned to use her to get to me? She wants nothing to do with you."

"I will gut you, make you eat your own fucking flesh, and then put a bullet through your head."

Vinny's laughter is like one you'd hear from a villain in a damn comic book movie. "I have your girl. Prepare for me to take over your empire."

33

NATALIA

Dr. Jekyll and Mr. Hyde.
It's the best way to describe Vinny.

When we first met, he had me fooled. He was charming, showering me with what I blindly believed was love. I knew he was trouble. The problem was, I was clueless on how deep his derangement was.

What I know now is that Vinny isn't to be underestimated. If I want to make it out alive, I need to be smart about my approach with him.

"Consider this a message to Cristian that it's never a good idea to fuck with me," Vinny tells Rocky as he writhes on the floor in pain. "His men—and cunts he used to fuck—will die."

He slaps tape on my mouth again, forces me toward his car right outside the home, and shoves me in the trunk of his BMW.

While in the trunk, I prayed I wouldn't run out of oxygen. Thankfully, it wasn't long until the car came to a full stop, and I was dragged out of the trunk and into another home.

Bad, bad, bad.

Everyone knows that once you're moved to a second location, your chance of survival decreases drastically.

A sliver of my tension releases when I realize we aren't in some dingy warehouse or somewhere he could easily bury my body. It's the Lombardis' two-story Cape home. Vinny's mother will kill him if he gets blood on anything. The woman is a clean freak.

Vinny captures my elbow, holds a gun to my head with his free hand, and then guides me into the house. He shoves me into the living room, pushes me onto the leather sofa, and tears the tape off my mouth.

I cringe at the sting, twitching my lips, and then fuss with the zip ties around my sore wrists. "Vinny, these ties are hurting me. Will you please cut them off?"

Vinny's face is filled with conflict as he stares down at me. "I don't trust you, Nat."

Now that we're alone and we don't have Rocky or Carmela with us, he's calmed some.

"There isn't much around us." I tip my chin toward the front door. "It's not like I can run off."

His eyes bunch up. "Like I said, I don't trust you."

"You did once. Remember?" I lower my voice. "We trusted each other more than anyone."

He drops his gun on the coffee table and retrieves a pocketknife from his jeans. "Then, you left me."

During my time with Vinny, I learned his weaknesses. I need him to remember our good times, for him to believe that I love him and that he means everything to me. Vinny loves being loved and revered.

"I didn't end things because I no longer loved you. I did it because you were breaking my heart." I force my voice to crack. "I wanted you to only be mine, but you were with other women." I squeeze my eyes shut and shake my head. "Because of how much I loved you, I refused to share you."

"You don't think you broke my heart when you ran to Cristian Marchetti?" He slams his hand against his chest over his heart. "Him out of all people!"

"I didn't know where else to go!" I cry out. "I was alone, and he's Gigi's father. She's the only reason I went to him. The whole marriage thing came out of nowhere after he almost handed me over. By that time, your father had made it clear that your family would kill me. I was backed into a corner of life or death."

He reaches down, picks up the crystal coffee table bowl, and hurls it across the room.

"Vinny," I whisper, my body shaking, "you're scaring me."

The desperation in my voice strikes him, and he drops his head.

"Nat, baby," he says, his voice softening, "I'm sorry."

My shoulders curl forward when he steps to me, gripping the knife, but I rasp out a breath when he shifts me and cuts off the ties.

I rub at my sore wrists. "I'm sorry too. I should've tried to talk to you."

He sits on the edge of the couch cushion next to me, his gaze cautious. "But the pepper spray—"

"Shh." I press a finger over his lips. "Let's start fresh and put that behind us."

"Has he touched you?" The vein in his forehead protrudes, and his face tics.

"Of course not." I shake my head and frown. "I slept in the guest room. Everything he said was to get underneath your skin."

"That motherfucker." He tugs on his earlobe and jumps up from his seat. The man is at war with himself, his mix of feelings puzzling him. "But you still told him information. Otherwise, he wouldn't have known all the shit he told my father."

Vinny is reckless. As much as he thrives on being like Cristian, it'll never happen. Cristian is even-tempered and calculated in every move he makes. Vinny's sloppiness and uncontrolled rage will stop him from ever being the monarch of the Lombardi family, let alone the ruler of New York City.

"I had to tell him enough to keep myself alive." I press my

hand over my chest. "Promise me, no more women, and I'm all yours, Vinny. I've always been yours. Cristian—*no one* has ever held my heart but you."

He warily sits back down, and I scoot in closer to him.

"I'll prove my love to you, Vinny." I hesitate before reaching down and grabbing his hand in mine. "I want us to get married. I want to be your wife. No one else's."

Vinny flexes his chest. "We'll get married and take over the world."

I want to vomit when his lips press into mine.

34

CRISTIAN

Carmela's front door is unlocked, and I don't hesitate before gripping my Glock and walking in.

Muffled groans are the only sound inside. My mouth turns dry when I see a body on the floor with blood puddled around it. I make three long strides and focus on the woman. My head clears at the leopard-print dress and curly hair.

Not Natalia.

Carmela.

Thank God.

A shot to the forehead.

At least Vinny awarded her a quick death.

I spit on her body and step over it without an ounce of remorse. I've always known Carmela wasn't the brightest, but I didn't think she was stupid enough to get wrapped up in Vinny's game and double-cross me.

She got what she deserved.

The same punishment any person receives for fucking with me.

"Jesus," Francis says behind me, holding his gun with both hands.

When we arrived here, I instructed him to stay in the SUV,

but he wouldn't allow me to go into Carmela's alone. I talked to Benny on the ride, and he said he'd meet me here. I refused to wait. Finding Natalia is the only thought in my brain.

I follow the groans to find Rocky on the floor of the living room. As I grow closer, I see his kneecaps are shot and shattered. He's coughing up blood and cursing as blood trickles down his cheek. A heaviness sinks onto my shoulders.

Had this been yesterday, I'd already be saving his life.

Now, I can't.

He's a traitor, a rat, and his actions are how Vinny has Natalia.

I'm called Monster Marchetti for a reason.

A heartless bastard.

But that doesn't mean I don't give a shit about my men. I wouldn't be where I am today if I didn't have loyal and good men at my side. I'm proud of my men and trust them with my life. I never second-guessed Rocky's loyalty. He'd never given me grounds to.

This man has killed for me. I've killed for him.

And now, I must kill him.

His eyes droop when I stand over him and bow my head. He cries out in pain when I kick him in the stomach.

A snake deserves to be kicked when he's down.

"What the fuck did you do, Rocky?" I snap, striking him again.

His eyes open and close.

He's slipping in and out of consciousness.

He attempts to shift into the fetal position, but his body has lost all power.

Rocky thought Vinny would treat him better than me?
Provide better protection?

Within hours, all Vinny provided him was death.

His daughter's and now his own.

"I'm sorry, Cristian!" he says, choking out blood.

I kneel, snatch him by the collar, and drag him up to the

couch. Blood spreads along the white cushions, but it's not like Carmela will use it again.

"Why am I not surprised?"

I whip around to find Benny strolling into the living room, baring his teeth. His face is red, and he's clenching his fists. Luca, Roman, and Lorenzo are behind him. All of them have murderous expressions on their faces.

They know why we're here.

I ignore them and get in Rocky's face.

My body shakes with fury.

"Decades, Rocky." I punch him in the face. "We've worked together for decades, and you do this?"

I shove my hand into my pocket, extract my brass knuckles, and slide them on. Rocky screams when I punch him again, and even though it's what has to be done, it fucking hurts. But then I remember Natalia might die because of him, so I give him another punch, this one with more fury.

"Sorry," he yells, raising his hands to block another blow. "I never wanted to betray you, but you were hurting Carmela's feelings. Your actions were hurting my daughter."

"I disrespected her for years," I say, staring down at his face gushing with blood. Unless you knew it was him, he's unrecognizable.

"Hell, I also disrespected her," Benny chimes in.

"What you did at lunch at L'ultima Cena crossed a line, even for you. She's my daughter, and you humiliated her." Rocky coughs up blood. "You broke her heart, so I did it for her."

"Rocky, you know there are no lines when it comes to me. I do what I want. Say what I want. Fuck who I want. And fucking kill who I want. Your whore daughter thought she could cross me. Then, *you* thought you could cross me. And now, you'll join her in death."

I should've grabbed her knife and slit her throat when she talked shit at the luncheon. That would've saved me from all this trouble.

"Desperate motherfuckers will do anything for money," Lorenzo says, stepping around Benny. "Fucking pathetic disgrace."

"It wasn't about the money," Rocky argues. "It was about my daughter."

"I don't give a fuck what it was about," I roar.

"He won't let her go," Rocky tells me, and with each word, his voice grows weaker. "Vinny is obsessed with Natalia. He approached Carmela with the plan, and she begged me to go along with it."

"Where are they?" I need to get answers before the bastard dies on me.

"I don't know."

I raise my Glock and point it at him. "I'll give you the same opportunity as I do others. Seven seconds, motherfucker. Drag your rat ass up and try to flee and dodge my bullet."

This fucking hurts.

I never thought I'd have to kill him.

Benny steps to my side. "Dad, let me do this."

He reaches for my gun, but I stop him.

I shake my head. "This is my job."

Rocky doesn't argue, nor does he try to stand.

He knows his fate. He knows he can beg all he wants, but he'll still be dead before I leave.

And it fucking kills me, but I pull the trigger and shoot Rocky in the head, leaving him in a pool of his own blood.

"Gigi is on the phone," Benny tells me as we stand in Carmela's living room and brainstorm on how to figure out where the hell Natalia is.

We went through Carmela's phone.

She'd fallen right into Vinny's trap.

He used her to get to Natalia.

"You told your sister?" I ask, seeing red.

"Yes, to see if she had any idea where Vinny could've taken her."

"And?"

He holds up the phone, and Gigi's voice comes through the speaker.

"You need to find her, Dad."

"What do you think I'm trying to do?" I snap.

"I'm calling Antonio," Gigi says.

"Why the fuck would you call Vinny's brother?" Benny yells, inching closer to the phone.

Gigi ends the call.

Later, I'll question why my daughter has contact with anyone having the Lombardi name. It's normal for men from families to attempt to use women as pawns to get to rivals—just like Vinny did with Carmela … and me also with Natalia. Over my dead motherfucking body will that ever happen with my daughter.

"All right, let's clear our heads and think about where he could've taken her," Benny says.

Clear our heads.

It's where Vinny goes to clear his head.

"I know where she is." I hold my hand out to Francis. "Keys."

"Where are we going?"

I shake my head. "I'm going alone. If Vinny is there and sees us, he might kill her. I'll let you know if I need backup."

"Dad—"

"I will call you."

Benny sighs. "Here lies the war of Natalia."

"A war we're about to win."

35

NATALIA

Vinny is calm.

Well, calm for Vinny.

His hands are knife- and gun-free.

But his weapons are still within reach, just in case he needs to use them on me—per his words. I need to be smart with every move I make. Like I told him, escaping won't be easy.

I've run several strategies through my head. I settle on convincing him to drink with me. I'll get him drunk and steal his car. *Easier said than done.* Vinny's known for his high alcohol tolerance.

He's next to me—too close for my liking—with his feet kicked up on the coffee table as we watch TV. After kissing me, he attempted some groping, but I stopped him and complained of a headache from the chloroform. His not disputing that it was chloroform answered my question on what was on the rag that'd been shoved against my face.

I smile when my stomach growls. "I'm starving."

He pauses the show. "I had Greta stock the kitchen yesterday. Anything sound good?"

"What are my options?" I start to stand but pause. "Am I allowed in the kitchen?"

"Yeah, but I need to go everywhere with you until you prove you can be trusted." He draws himself to his feet before holding out his hand and helping me up.

"You had Greta stock the kitchen … had you planned on bringing me here all along?"

He nods and leads me into the kitchen. "I told Rocky he had three days to bring you to me unless he wanted trouble."

"How did that come about? You, Carmela, and Rocky?"

"Do you really want to hear that?"

Quick breaths leave me. "Do I *want* to hear it? No. But I feel like I need to." I squeeze his arm and lean into him. "I was open and honest with what happened with Cristian. Will you please do the same with me?" I pout my lower lip.

Do I care what he did with Carmela? Hell no.

He could've married Carmela and had twenty babies, and there wouldn't have been an ounce of jealousy in my bones.

What is in my bones? Curiosity.

How this came to be.

Rocky deserves an Emmy for his false allegiance to Cristian.

Vinny leans against a cabinet and smirks. "Everyone knows Carmela was Cristian's fuck buddy, but she wanted more. I used his rejection of her to my advantage. I contacted her, asked her out, and she fed me information. Eventually, I convinced her that we'd marry, *but* to do that, we needed to get rid of you. In doing so, we needed Rocky's help. He was the key to getting what I wanted."

I stare at him, speechless, and digest his words.

Yep, Vinny is calculated as hell—maybe a little underestimated.

"The plan was always to get you here," he continues, crossing his ankles. "I needed to spend time with you to talk things over. We had too much miscommunication."

"But I thought you wanted me dead?"

"Dead or mine."

I recoil, and a shiver runs over my arm. "I'm sorry I put you through that."

There's nothing harder than apologizing to a man who just admitted he wants you dead if you don't stay with him. But for my life, that's what I have to do.

I hook a thumb toward the refrigerator. "I'm thirsty. Can I grab something?"

"Make yourself at home, baby."

I rush to the fridge as repulsion slithers up my throat and grab a bottle of water. My hands tremble as I untwist the cap and take a long gulp.

That repulsion intensifies when he comes up behind me, wraps his insincere arms around my waist, and digs his chin into my shoulder.

"How about we open a bottle of wine?" His mouth goes to my ear, and he grins as I shiver—although for a different reason than what he thinks. "For old times' sake."

"I like the sound of that."

"Anything in particular?"

I tap my finger along the side of my lip. "What was that bottle we drank when we came here for the first time?"

He wiggles his fingers at me. "Ah, you want the good stuff."

I soften my gaze. "I like the memories of it."

"That's in the wine cellar." He pulls away but freezes. "Are you going to pull something tricky?"

"Of course not." I brush my hand along his arm. "I can go with you. *Or* I can make grilled cheese—your favorite."

"With bacon?"

"With bacon. Extra crispy."

He smacks a kiss on my cheek. "You're the best, baby. Be right back."

"I'll be right here," I call to his back.

As soon as he turns the corner, I open a drawer, snatch a knife, and shove it into my back pocket. *This dummy is making it easier than I thought.* He'd never make it as the boss of his family.

He's bringing his guard down, so now, I'll wait for the perfect time to escape.

My heart thunders when I hurriedly open the refrigerator and gather grilled cheese ingredients.

Vinny returns and holds up a wine bottle. "Found it. It's a different year, but close enough."

I grin. "Close enough."

He settles the wine onto the marble countertop while I open the pantry for bread.

"Are you okay with me grabbing a butter knife?" I toss the loaf next to the cheese and bacon.

"I doubt you can do much damage with a butter knife, baby."

I playfully poke his shoulder before opening the drawer.

He uncorks the wine, pours two glasses, and hands me one. I make a *cheers* motion before taking a tiny sip. He brings the glass to his lips, downs the contents, and pours himself another.

I fake another drink, and he freezes mid-swallow when an alarm sound blares from his phone.

"What's that?" I chew on my lower lip and rest my glass on the counter.

Vinny picks up his phone. "The alarm. It alerts when someone comes in the vicinity of the house."

"Could it be your parents?" I refrain from chugging the wine. "Do you think Cristian called your father?"

Vinny retreats a step and eyes me suspiciously. "Did you tell Cristian this address?"

"Of course not." My voice quivers. "This is our private place, Vinny. I'd never share that with anyone." I sweep my hand over his shoulder. "Plus, you know how terrible I am with directions. I couldn't tell him how to get here without a GPS even if he held a gun to my head and made me try."

The alarm blares from his phone again.

My heart booms in my chest.

Please be Cristian.

"Someone is here." Vinny slams his phone down, opens a cabinet, and extracts a gun.

I tiptoe away, but he stops me.

"What are you doing?"

"I …" My voice is toneless. "If I look out the window, I can see if someone is here."

"I don't fucking think so."

I spin to face him, and he cups my cheeks in my hands. "It's you and me, okay?" I run my thumb over his cheek. "We don't need anyone else. I'll kill Cristian myself if I have to. I'll never let anyone hurt you."

He bows his head and rests his forehead against mine. "I knew you still loved me."

I have to get out of here.

Vincent said he wanted me dead, so if it's him, I'm done for.

It's now or never, Natalia.

I kiss him, slip the knife from my back pocket, and use all my power to impale the blade into Vinny's chest. He groans, his body going stiff, and I jerk the knife out as fast as I can. I snap around, clutching the knife, and run.

"You stupid bitch." Vinny tackles me to the floor and pins me down, facing him. "You think I haven't been stabbed before?"

I struggle underneath him while crying out in hysterics.

He shifts so his knee is against my neck and wrenches the knife out of my hand. In one hand is his gun, and the other now has my knife.

He plays with both in his hand while glaring down at me. "You thought you were being so smooth, didn't you? That you'd outsmart me?"

"Vinny," I gasp as his knee presses harder into my throat and cuts off my air supply.

"Here I thought, you weren't a whore." He presses the gun against my forehead. "I'll give you the same good-bye I gave Carmela."

I shut my eyes and tremble while waiting for my life to end.

"Get off her before I give you that good-bye."

Vinny's body turns rigid at the sound of Cristian's voice, and he laughs. "Fuck off, Marchetti. If you shoot me, I shoot her. Do you really want to hurt her?" He snorts before snatching a handful of my hair.

He returns the gun to me—this time between my eyes—and plays with the trigger with his thumb.

I squeeze my eyes shut and scream at the sound of a gunshot. Something wet splatters over my face. One by one, I open my eyes at the feel of a heavy weight collapsing on top of me.

Blood.

A dead Vinny.

There's a bleeding dead body on top of me.

Seconds pass, as if the world stopped, and I scream before pushing at Vinny's body. Cristian rushes to my side, shoving Vinny off, and Vinny falls with a *thud* next to me. I scoot back, placing as much space between his body and mine, and then scramble to my feet with Cristian's assistance. He sweeps me into his arms, holding me tight, and repeatedly whispers that I'm safe.

When he pulls away, he tips his head down, and his stormy gaze pierces mine. He closes his strong hand around my face, cupping it like I'm a precious stone he's been hunting for years.

His hand is rough, but his touch is gentle, calming me instantly.

My personal sedative.

With him, I'll always feel safe.

My breaths are rushed.

His are ragged.

He rubs his thumb over my bottom lip.

I want this man so much.

Need him.

He found me, risked his life for me, *killed* for me.

I'm crying, nearly on the verge of hyperventilating, but I need him. My face is red and tearstained. My body weak, as if it'd been running a marathon all day.

I'm exhausted and have gone through hell, but it's as if he hit a switch and I suddenly feel protected.

A breathless whisper of his name escapes my mouth before I press it to his. I shove my tongue into his mouth and kiss him brutally.

He kisses me back possessively, his hand moving from my face to grip the back of my head. My body throbs for him. Pictures fall from the walls, shattering, when he slams me into it. I moan as he rains kisses down my neck and unzips my shorts. My body is on fire as he slides down the zipper, and I help him shove my shorts down my legs before I kick them off.

Deviousness swirls in his eyes as a slow smirk builds along his lips. I'm catching my breath as he slips off his blazer, unbuckles his pants, and frees his cock.

My body shakes.

Waiting for him.

Needing him.

I rotate my hips, a silent beg for more.

I cry out his name when he slides his cock between my folds, feeling how wet I am, and he thrusts into me as he shoots Vinny again.

Another thrust, another shot at Vinny.

Another thrust, another gunshot.

With each stroke, he shoots my ex-boyfriend.

Over and over again.

Adrenaline pours through me as I fuck him back.

This is deranged.

Hot as fuck.

My monster is screwing me against the wall, next to my dead ex-boyfriend.

My monster, who's become my savior.

36

CRISTIAN

"Marchetti, we have a problem," Antonio Lombardi says over the phone.

I kick my feet onto my desk while in my chair, resting the phone against my shoulder. "And what would that be?"

"Cut the shit." I hear the snarl in his voice. "You murdered my brother."

"Are you sure about that?"

"Yes."

I inspect my fingernails and chuckle. "You have the wrong man."

"Christ," he hisses. "This is why people hate talking to you." He blows out a long breath. "We know you wanted him dead, *and* we also found out about his little kidnapping plan with Carmela and Rocky. We found his body, and all the cameras have been wiped clean. We're not stupid."

The Lombardis have no proof that we killed Vinny. Santos and his men cleared the security cameras. The place was wiped clean of prints. Not that the Lombardis would involve the police. They deal with situations like this on their own.

"My father wants you to hand Natalia over." Antonio's tone is controlled, but there's a hint of wavering in his voice.

His hesitation reveals he doesn't want Natalia dead as much as his father, but he'd never rebel against him.

I raise my voice. "No."

"Cristian, you don't want a war."

"I will kill every man, *including you*, who tries to hurt her," I sneer. "Do you understand me?"

"He was my brother."

"And she *is* my wife. I care about her more than you did him."

"That makes you weak."

I scoff. "No, Antonio. That makes me crueler. Something to make sure I live for, and I'll kill every motherfucker who threatens that."

"Look at it from my father's point of view. What if someone killed Benny?"

"Vinny would've ruined your family's legacy. Be happy, Antonio. You're next in line now *and* better suited for the job. Now, are you done wasting my time?"

Antonio is the mild version of Vinny.

The more rational one.

Most prefer handling business with Antonio over Vinny. Not that they have much choice now.

"I'm done," Antonio says in annoyance. "Watch your back, Marchetti."

He ends the call.

Stupid motherfucker.

Luca and Benny went back and cut off three of Vinny's fingers in case they piss me off enough, and I'll mail one to them. For Antonio's attitude, maybe I'll frame one of Vinny's fingers and mail it to him.

The Marchettis are known for retaliating ten times worse than we're hit. That's why so many families don't fuck with us.

I call for Benny. He strolls into my office and raises a brow.

"It's time we set your engagement in motion." I drop my phone and settle my gaze on him. "We've waited too long."

He leans back in his chair and shakes his head. "We can handle the Lombardis without the Cavallaros. We can convince them it was the Corobras who killed Vinny. It'll be a good way to rid of the Corobras anyway."

"I spoke with Severino. Prepare to marry Neomi."

37

NATALIA

Sunlight spills through the curtains of our bedroom. The warmth of Cristian's body against mine is a comfort.

I prop my head on his bare chest and gaze up at him. "Thank you for saving me."

Cristian runs his hand through my bedhead and plays with the strands between his fingers. "You don't have to thank me every day."

"Yes, I do." I sigh, relax into his touch, and press my lips to his chest. "I'd be dead if it wasn't for you."

Dead or Vinny's prisoner.

I shudder, not sure which would be worse.

After Cristian killed Vinny … and sex, he carried me out of the house to the SUV—sans driver—and held my hand the entire drive home. When I walked into the mansion, everyone was waiting for us.

Helena cried.

Gigi did the same over FaceTime.

Benny wrapped me in a hug.

Gretchen squealed that I was okay.

Their affection warmed my soul.

Growing up in such a small family, endearments like this

never happened. I had my father, who showed me love, but never a room full of people who cared.

So much had changed.

That first night I'd walked into Cristian's office, terrified for my life, I'd encountered nothing but a coldhearted man. Then, I realized how cruel he was when he almost handed me over to Vinny. As Cristian and I grew closer, that coldness began to thaw.

The Lombardi family wanted—or possibly still wants—Cristian to hand me over for killing Vinny. But Cristian refuses to turn me over to them.

I learned this from Benny after I asked. I was too nervous to ask Cristian about Rocky. My heart dropped when he said Cristian was the one who had killed his friend.

Not because I was sorry for Rocky.

I hated that Cristian had had to endure that with someone he cared for.

The mood shifts, and Cristian stares down at me in silence.

He clears his throat. "Do you still want to marry me, Natalia?"

My mind goes blank, an answer taking forever to come to me.

Is he about to kick me out of his bed now that Vinny is dead?

It's a valid question really.

I'm not worried about Vinny, but that doesn't mean I'm not concerned about the Lombardi family taking their revenge out on me. Even though I wasn't the one who killed Vinny, I played a large part in his death.

Oh, and I did stab him.

"Do you still want to marry me, Cristian?" I whisper, my mouth turning dry.

"I'd marry you this second."

I can't help from grinning as I slide my bare legs against the sheets. "Are you saying I'm no longer your pawn?"

He settles his hands into the cradle of my hips to lift me

until I'm straddling him, and he situates his back against the headboard. "I don't know if you were ever my pawn, even when I swore you were, Natalia."

I circle my arms around his neck. "What am I now?"

"My weakness," he answers in seconds.

I gulp and bow my head. "That sounds bad."

He snaps his fingers before lowering one to the bottom of my chin and lifting it. "Being someone's weakness isn't always bad, sweetheart. You being my weakness proves that no matter how hard I fight, I want you. *I need* you. There'd be no stopping my need for you, even if I killed myself trying. When I wake up in the morning, you're my first thought. Not my business, or trouble, or who I need to kill. It's you."

"Weaknesses get people killed," I whisper.

"You being my weakness doesn't mean I'm weak everywhere. I will kill anyone who threatens my weakness because I can't go without it."

"Is that your way of saying you like me?" As soon as those words leave my mouth, I feel immature.

He smooths his hand over my jaw as his free hand travels up my thigh. "That's my way of saying I breathe for you."

I cup my hand over his on my thigh. "What does that even mean?"

"It means, sweet Natalia, that even though you've done nothing but create chaos in my world, within that chaos, you've stolen my soul with those delicate yet reckless hands of yours." He slides his hand out to lace our fingers together before pressing them against his chest, over his heart. "As long as this black heart of mine beats, it is yours." He releases a low chuckle. "And quite frankly, you might be the only person who can handle me."

I move our hands from his chest to mine. "I'd marry you this second."

He swallows, and his Adam's apple bobs. "I can't promise to

be perfect. I'm a man who sins for a living. But I will be a husband who fights to prove I deserve you."

"Cristian …" My voice shakes. "I have to marry you. I ordered our Mr. and Mrs. Marchetti monogrammed towels the other day."

He chuckles. "Ah, yes. A very important reason to marry me."

"You wanted me, so you could get to Vinny … but why?" I sigh. "Your plan was for him to hurt me, so you could kill him in revenge?"

He nods and looks away from me. "He wanted to be king, and it was the easiest way to rid of him, so I wouldn't have to worry about dealing with him when his father is gone."

"It's fine. Things were different then." I squeeze his hand. "Nothing will change how I feel for you. You could've just killed Vinny and handed me over to the Lombardis."

"I will make it my life's mission to make that up to you."

"I want to be your wife." I stroke his skin. "I think I'm falling in love with you."

Those green eyes of his turn gentle. "I can't wait to marry you, so you'll forever be mine."

"Do you …" I swallow. "Do you love me too?"

"I'm still trying to figure out what love is." He shuts his eyes. "But I feel for you, and if I had to guess what love is, it's how I'm feeling for you."

A mixture of comfort and desire fires through me. His breathing hitches when I brush my lips over his.

Softly.

I suck in a breath when he drags his hand up my back and hooks it around my neck, and he deepens our kiss. He undresses me as I pull down his boxers.

And for the first time, Cristian makes love to me.

His movements are slow.

Gentle.

Like a man worshipping the woman he's in love with.

I jump out of the Suburban when Gigi strolls out of the airport.

People gawk when she passes them—a common occurrence. Beauty runs in the Marchetti family, and Gigi is no exception. Her wild mess of curls blows in the wind as she makes her way toward me. Bruno, her bodyguard, is behind her, carrying their bags.

"There's my best friend," she says, wrapping me in a tight hug. "I've missed you."

"Missed you more," I reply, squeezing her.

She pulls away to hug Benny next and then Luca while Bruno dumps their bags into the back of the SUV.

I've entered a world of having security, as if I were the president. Cristian won't let me leave without always having two men with me. Luca hasn't complained about babysitting again—most likely because he knows it's no longer simple babysitting. He's protecting my life so that another Lombardi situation doesn't happen.

We load into the Suburban—Gigi, Bruno, and me in the back, and Benny and Luca in the front—and Luca drives off.

We go to lunch to catch up, and Gigi teases Bruno about how much he loves Italian macarons. Then, we stop at the bridal store for Gigi to try on her bridesmaid dress.

I've missed my best friend. Now, I just need to figure out how not to make it weird that I'm sleeping with her father.

I'm relaxing in Gigi's bedroom, watching *Bridezillas* and sipping on my vodka and cranberry. When we got back to the mansion, we grabbed snacks, a bottle of alcohol, and mixers. I shift, my feet dangling off the edge of her bed, when my phone chimes with a text. I shove the rest of the Snickers bar into my mouth, wash it down with a drink, and grab my phone to find a text from Cristian.

Cristian: Where are you?

I sneak a glance at Gigi, whose attention is glued to the TV as she dips her hand into a can of Pringles, before replying. It's a slow reply, and I do it with one eye open. *Drunk texting isn't exactly easy.*

Me: Hanging out with Gigi.

Cristian: Find a way to get the fuck out of there and come to me.

Shivers dance up my spine.

Is this a good come to me or a bad one?

Me: Why? I don't like being bossed around.

Cristian: Because I want to fuck you, obviously.

I swallow down the gasp sneaking its way past my lips.

Me: What am I supposed to tell her? BRB, I need to go screw your dad really quick?

Cristian: You're creative. I've seen you in action.

Heat rushes up my face, and I rub my thighs together.

Me: Give me 10 minutes.

Cristian: You have 5.

Me: Or what?

Cristian: Don't test me, sweetheart.

How the hell do I manage this?

Gigi snapping her fingers in my face returns my attention to her. "Earth to Natalia." She exaggeratedly gestures to the TV. "We need to make sure this doesn't become you because I can't do drama queens. Blame it on living with men born with chips on their shoulders and never flicking them away."

"Sorry." I toss my phone down. "Your dad texted, demanding we discuss the wedding." Guilt creeps through me. *I hate lying, but what else can I say?*

She waves her hand through the air. "Let him know we're handling it."

Does Gigi not know her father?

When he wants something, he gets it.

Not even five minutes pass before there's a knock on the door.

"Come in," Gigi yells, grabbing the remote to pause the show.

The door creeps open, and Gretchen strolls in. She blushes as she looks at us.

Gigi smiles at her. "Hey, Gretchen."

Gretchen waves before her gaze quickly darts to me. "Mr. Marchetti asked to speak with you, Natalia."

Chills prick at my skin.

How will I get out of this?

I gulp, searching for excuses. "Tell him I'm busy, and I'll come down when I'm finished."

An expression flashes across Gretchen's face that tells me she'd rather jump out the window than tell Cristian my response. The poor girl already has to deal with one Marchetti man putting her through hell. She doesn't deserve another.

I slide off the bed, proud of myself for not falling on my face. "Where?"

Her body loosens, a sigh releasing from her. "His office."

That's at least better than the bedroom.

"Do you want me to go with you?" Gigi asks.

I shake my head. "No, it's okay. I'm sure it'll be quick."

"I'm totally fine with it." She rises from the bed but stops when her phone rings, and she checks the screen. "Shoot, I need to take this."

"Answer that. I'll be right back."

"Come back with more snacks," she calls to me as I leave her bedroom.

"Thank you," Gretchen says as we walk side by side down the hall.

I playfully bump my shoulder against hers. Gretchen needs a friend, and as someone who didn't have many, growing up—

being the principal's daughter doesn't make you the cool kid—I know how loneliness feels.

We separate at the bottom of the stairs—her walking toward the kitchen and me stopping at Cristian's office. I knock—it's a quick one and nowhere near the nervous ones I once had—and walk in.

Cristian is sitting behind his desk and smiles. "I missed you today."

Since the kidnapping, we've spent most of our days together. I tag along with him to the club, we have lunch together, and he watches movies with me in the evening. And yesterday, we decided I'd work at the club behind the scenes, doing administrative work.

Even though I'd enjoyed working for Bonnie, I don't want to return to the gallery. Bonnie apologized profusely, which I accepted, but walking in there would give me nothing but bad memories.

"You missed me?" I stroll deeper into the office. "Look at my monster, growing a heart."

"I only show that sliver of a heart to you." He rolls out his chair from under the desk and stands. "Otherwise, I'm the heartless bastard others say I am."

"Glad I get to see that side of you."

He circles the desk and leans against the front of it—his usual stance in here. "How is spending time with Gigi?"

"Good." I stretch the word out. "I kind of refrained from talking about us, though."

"What does my daughter think we are?"

"We haven't discussed it."

"She's going to find out about us. It's better to tell her than have her assume we were being deceitful to her."

My shoulders slump.

The problem is, I'm scared to lose my friend.

I'd find it weird if it were the other way around.

Sure, she was okay with us marrying to save my life.

But now that all that's over, will she be?

"Gigi will never hate you," Cristian says, as if reading my mind. "You were there for her during rough times as much as she's been there for you."

He wiggles his finger in a *come here* motion, and I stumble toward him.

"Everything will be fine. I promise." He wraps his arms around my waist as I stare up at him.

I playfully stab at his chest. "Says the guy who will have no repercussions if she's not okay with it."

"Gigi will want to kill me before you." He squeezes my hips. "Now, stop thinking about that."

"You calling me into your office doesn't help matters," I grumble.

"I don't see why it's a problem." His voice thickens. "We will not be hiding this from my daughter. If you think you can't handle that, then I understand. But if you want to do this—*really do this*—Natalia, we need to do it *together*. I will not put my wife in the shadows."

"I know." I sigh. "But she's under the impression that all of this is fake, and we're not spending time together like this. She's even said it'd be weird if we acted like a married couple for real. So … I'm just worried."

"You stabbed a Lombardi in the chest. You are fearless."

"That was different."

"No, that was badass and hot as fuck."

A blush creeps up my cheeks, and I can't stop a smile from stretching across my face.

"We got this, sweetheart." He swipes his hand over my cheek—his touch like my personal relaxant. "Get ready to tell Gigi you're her stepmom."

I smack his stomach. "That's it. I'm calling off the wedding."

He throws his head back and laughs before kissing me. "Mmm … someone has been drinking." He pulls away and licks his lips.

I love this side of Cristian.

The more time we spend together, the more I understand Cristian. He's opening up and sharing his world and childhood with me. Helena said she's never seen him like this in her life.

Cristian is misunderstood by so many. His father taught—no, *beat and bullied*—his son until he formed a thick barrier around his heart so it'd be unusable. If he were alive today, I'd send him the ultimate glare whenever I saw him.

"Just a little bit," I tease. "Now, I gotta go. Gigi demanded I return with more snacks, so I need to raid the pantry."

"I'm sure you'll find plenty of Oreos."

"No, I think you ate most of them, actually."

I smack a quick peck on his cheek.

He stops me when I attempt to pull away from him. "One sec, sweetheart."

"Yeah?"

"A kiss before you leave." Those lips I love to kiss, to feel on me, form a mischievous smile.

"All right." I wiggle my body sarcastically. "I'll take one for the road."

He shifts me back a few steps before dropping to his knees.

What the?

I push at his shoulder as he peers up at me. "Uh, what are you doing?"

"Kissing you," he answers so casually that you'd think this was normal.

I make a circling motion in front of my lips. "My mouth is up here."

"Sweetheart, I never specified *what lips* I'm kissing." He pushes my dress up to my waist and shoves it into the back of my panties so that I'm on full display for him.

My core right in front of his face.

A tremor runs through my body.

This is such a bad idea.

But as Cristian eases his fingers along the seam of my panties, my knees weaken.

Gigi upstairs or not, I can never say no to his mouth between my legs.

"But to clarify," he says, sliding my panties to the side, "the ones between your legs."

I dig my fingers into his hair, pulling at the strands, and use the other to cover my mouth as Cristian drives two fingers inside me.

"Just a quick kiss." He raises my leg, draping it over his shoulder, and flicks his tongue over my clit, setting my nerves on fire.

My breathing is labored as I lower my hand from the desk and clutch the back of his head, holding him in place so he can't move. Cristian pleasures me with his fingers, tongue, and lips until I'm falling apart above him.

"Oh my God," I gasp, tightening my hand over my mouth.

He levels me as my knees buckle. "All right. You can go hang out with my daughter now."

I smack his shoulder as he releases my dress from my panties and smooths it out for me. "You are depraved, you know that?"

"Sweetheart, don't act like you don't enjoy when I corrupt you."

38

CRISTIAN

Benny, Gigi, and Natalia are already seated at the table when I enter the dining room.

I couldn't give two fucks about dinner. My appetite was satisfied in my office with Natalia earlier. I could live off her pussy and be perfectly sated. Normally, we don't have regular dinners like this, but it's Gigi's first night home.

"Daddy," Gigi says, perking up in her chair when she sees me.

I kiss the top of her head as I pass her and then brush a hand over Natalia's bare shoulder before taking my seat. My lips arch when I notice the goose bumps forming on her soft skin. I love how much my touch affects her.

Since Gigi isn't flipping the fuck out, my guess is she's not aware of my and Natalia's change in our relationship.

"How was your trip?" I ask as I spread a napkin over my lap.

"Good." She grins and flips her hair over her shoulder. "Busy. *Lots* of shopping."

My regards to the man she marries because my daughter loves to shop. I've never limited her spending, so she had better marry a man in the same position.

I'll never claim to be father of the year, but people know not to fuck with my children. I've allowed them their freedom before marriage—a rarity for most in this lifestyle. And unlike my father, I won't marry my daughter off to a man I don't trust. Let a motherfucker hurt my daughter, and I'll blow his brains out. After torturing him, of course.

That's why I allow and encourage Gigi to take as many trips to Italy as possible. She stays with my aunt and uncle, who never moved to the States, and is safer there.

Gigi holds up her glass of wine and clears her throat. "First things first. *Cheers* to Dad for murdering Vinny."

Natalia chokes on her water.

"You did a great service to the city," my daughter adds. "No one is sad to see him go."

Thanks to Helena in her life, Gigi is a bit softer than Benny and myself. But Marchetti blood still runs deep in her veins. She grew up in this world, witnessed the dark side of it, and doesn't flinch at the mention of murder. Cross her, and she becomes ruthless.

"Are the Lombardis still after you?" Gigi asks Natalia. "Is that why you two are still marrying?"

Benny snorts into his glass.

I rub my forehead, and Natalia's face burns as her eyes meet mine in panic.

"Natalia doesn't need to worry about the Lombardis," I reply.

"Really?" Gigi stares at me, blinking. "You and Vincent worked out your issues?"

I shake my head. "No, but they know not to cross me."

"They'd marry even if every Lombardi in the world were dead," Benny comments with a shit-eating grin.

Natalia covers her face and sinks down in her chair.

I shoot my son a stern look and rub at the sudden tension in my neck. I'm not concerned about the results of a grudge from my daughter over my being with her best friend. I'm more worried about Natalia's feelings regarding it. I don't want her friendship with my daughter to suffer because of our new relationship.

The dining room turns quiet for a moment as we all wait for where this conversation will lead.

It has to happen—it will happen—but is this the right place?

Gigi signals between Natalia and me, and her face turns horrified. "Wait ... is this a *real*, real thing?"

It seems my daughter didn't think this all the way through when she suggested we get married.

Benny chuckles. "I was hoping I'd be here for this shit."

"Natalia and I are still getting married," I tell her.

Natalia blows out a breath. "I think this is the time where I tell you that your father and I aren't"—she pauses, choosing the best words—"*faking* a relationship."

Gigi's eyes widen, and she takes her glass of wine and chugs it. "You're going to be my stepmom ..."

"You've known this since *you* came up with the idea of us marrying," I tell her.

"At least you won't have to say you hate your stepmother," Benny comments.

"Shut up, Benny," I snap.

The table is quiet for a moment before Gigi looks at me, straight-faced, and says, "You'd better not break her heart, Dad."

I thrum my fingers along my cheek. "That's not something you'll have to worry about."

Natalia clears her throat. "Can we go back to the Italy conversation?"

"Shoot." Gigi snaps her fingers. "I was going to tell you to come with me next time because hot guys and all, but apparently, that's off-limits now."

"Going to Italy? That's fine," I answer my daughter, but my eyes are on Natalia. "Finding hot guys? I'd prefer not to commit murder there. I hear their prisons aren't easy to bribe yourself out of."

"Hiya, Dad," Gigi greets when she strolls into my office after barely knocking on the door.

It seems the women in my life are the ones who believe there are no rules when it comes to my office.

I shove my paperwork to the side and relax in my chair. "Hi, honey."

She rolls her shoulders back as she plops down in a chair. "So … you and Natalia?"

It's not surprising she wants to continue this conversation. She thankfully let it go during dinner, but I figured she'd have more questions … or want to talk more shit to me. Men fear getting attitudes with me, but my daughter acts like it's second nature. Many Mafia men would've corrected that long ago.

My father smacked Helena around plenty of times.

So did other men in my family.

Not me with Gigi.

I had one uncle who *attempted* to raise a hand to my daughter. Rocky held him down while I shot a bullet through each one of his hands.

"Are getting married, yes," I reply, running a hand over my jaw. "Don't give her a hard time on that."

She holds up a finger. "A.) She's my best friend. I'd never." Another finger goes up. "B.) It's better than having a stepmother I can't stand … or one who tells me to eat more vegetables."

I cock my head to the side. "No one has ever told you that."

She's never even had a stepmother.

"Nor do I want it to start." She smirks.

"Get out of here." I shake my head and wave toward the door.

"That was me saying, I approve." She crosses her legs and blows out a breath. "I also appreciate that it gives me a free pass."

"Excuse me?"

"A free pass to date whoever I want because all I'll need to say is, *Well, you married my best friend.*"

"Sometimes, I hate that you're such a Marchetti." I grab a pen and twirl it around my fingers. "Anything else I need to hear you talk shit about?"

Her tone turns serious. "Don't go to war with the Lombardis."

"If they try to fuck with me, I will." My words come out slower. "Is there a reason you don't want me to?"

She pretends to examine her fingernails. "Of course not."

"Gigi, secrets don't stay secrets for long."

"Good night, Daddy." She hops up from her chair. "I'll give you your fiancée back when I'm done hanging out with her."

39

NATALIA

My wedding day depicts the chaos that I'm marrying into. Rain pelts the colors of the stained glass windows in the church's bridal suite.

"Is this a bad omen?" I ask, pinching my pink lips together. "Don't they say rain on your wedding day represents the number of tears a woman will shed during their marriage?"

This is what I get for Googling *bad omens at weddings*.

My father always told me that Google was bad for me.

"No, no, Natalia," Helena says, swatting her hand in front of me, as if smacking the damaging thoughts from my brain. "Rain on your wedding day is good luck."

"She's right." Celine steps behind me and slides the sparkly comb of my veil through my curls. "Rain on your wedding day means the knot you're tying becomes wet and harder to break, making your marriage stronger."

"How about we don't believe in omens?" Gigi stands behind me and squeezes my shoulder. "*Now*, if someone gets shot today, *that'll* be a bad sign."

Helena swats Gigi the same as she did me. "Giana Marchetti! Do not jinx us like that!"

Gigi shrugs. "It's not like it'd be the first wedding shoot-out I've attended."

I grimace. "Oh, yes, because I literally need a *shotgun* wedding."

Violence at our wedding is a concern Cristian and I spoke about yesterday. He told me about his aunt dying from a gunshot at her wedding reception. My hands shook as I asked him why he'd tell me that the night before our wedding. He answered that even though Vinny was dead, there will always be threats, and I need to remain on alert, even on our wedding day.

"Most men wouldn't dare shoot a man *or woman* in the house of God. They'll at least wait until the reception."

Everyone falls silent, and everyone whips around at the unfamiliar voice. Panic smacks into me harder than the rain against the window as I watch a woman move toward us. The room is small, so it doesn't take long until she's behind me.

Gigi blows out a long breath. "Hi, Grandmother."

I've heard stories of Maria Marchetti—none of them detailing her kindness. They say she's as cold as her son and helped mold him into the monster he is today. She's strict, cunning, and wary of outsiders joining the family.

I'm an outsider.

An outsider who dated someone from another family.

I take in Maria through the vanity mirror in front of me. She's short, her back somewhat hunched, but you can tell she does all she can to maintain what youthful appearance she has left. Her face holds random wrinkles, as if fighting with the Botox she's had, and she's dripping in diamonds—from her ears to her necklace to her rings.

I've met nearly every person in the Marchetti family, but her.

When I asked Cristian why I hadn't met his mother yet, he told me the fewer conversations I had with her, the better. Cristian loves and respects his mother—because that's the Mafia way —but that doesn't mean she's a good person.

She further proves that when she says, "I don't approve of you marrying my son." Her words are spit out and hostile.

A nervous sweat forms on my forehead. Anxiety courses through me. Not just because I have Maria Marchetti snarling at me but also because I don't want my makeup to run. There's nothing worse than being nervous about your wedding day and your future mother-in-law saying she doesn't approve.

"Oh," I say.

No one says a word while they wait on Maria's next move.

"But better you than that dead bitch Carmela."

I nearly fall out of my chair at her words.

"Oh," I repeat, the word popping out of my mouth again.

She taps my shoulder and walks away, already finished with me.

These Marchettis are a different breed when it comes to communication.

"Don't worry. She hates me too," Celine says, her tone comforting, when Maria leaves the room and slams the door shut behind her. "She had more choice words for me. Consider yourself lucky."

I blink at her. "Why does she hate you?"

Celine runs her hand down her straight black hair. "I'm the result of her husband having an affair. She'd be happy if I choked to death … and I'm pretty sure she put a hit out on me when I was born until my father put a stop to it."

"That was just a rumor," Helena says.

"*No, it wasn't*," Celine mouths to me and rolls her eyes.

"My mother will come around, Natalia." Helena offers me a reassuring smile. "Your history with Vinny makes her a little uncomfortable. Not many men would marry a woman who was involved with a rival family."

My stomach churns.

Please don't vomit in your wedding dress.

Just when I was getting over my *bad omen* fear, she had to

come in and say she'd rather her son marry me than a dead woman.

"It's time, Natalia," Helena tells me.

Gigi and Celine help me slowly stand from the vanity stool. When I turn and stare at myself in the floor-length mirror, there's no stopping my smile.

The dress is perfect.

How will Cristian compare it to how I explained it to him that night at the club?

The hairdresser left my hair down but pulled half back and curled it to perfection.

And even with all my uncertainties for the future, I'm on top of the world.

By the end of the day, I will be married to Cristian Marchetti. Natalia Marchetti is about to be born.

Gigi grips the train of my dress, carrying it for me as I leave the room. I grin when I see my father waiting for me in the hallway. His face is puffy and red.

"Dad," I squeal, nearly tripping as I lunge forward to hug him tight. "Thank you for coming."

This is my first time seeing him since I told him I'm marrying Cristian. We've spoken on the phone, and he RSVP'd to my wedding. *But* Cristian told me he got in touch and had a conversation with my dad, but wouldn't elaborate further. My father isn't fond of the idea of me marrying Cristian, but he's here because he loves me.

My father takes a step back and holds me at arm's length. "You're a beautiful bride." His eyes are watery as he blinks. "I wouldn't have missed this for the world."

He straightens the black bow tie of his tux and holds out his elbow.

As I loop my arm through his, he dips his head and asks, "Do you love him?"

I nod, my cheeks heating. "I do."

He blows out a harsh breath.

"Cristian might be a little—"

"Batshit crazy?" he says for me. "I just want to make sure this is what you want."

I place my palm over my father's free hand. "He protects me. He makes me feel safe. Cristian is different with me than he is with others. There isn't a better man for me."

"As long as you're happy, then I'm happy for you." His voice cracks at the end. "I wish your mother were here."

I stare up at the ceiling and move our hands to his chest. "She's here. I know she's watching."

My father pulls me tighter to him. "I finally finished my book … I put it in your wedding gift. It's how your mother and I met and fell in love. I want you to be the first to read it."

I kiss his cheek. "I can't wait to read it."

As he slowly walks me down the aisle, a sense of calmness overwhelms me.

The church is filled with people who are here to celebrate our love, our marriage.

This is my fairy-tale ending.

It might not be every girl's, but it's mine.

Happiness sweeps through my stomach. I tune out the music, the guests, and stare at Cristian waiting for me. His black tux is snug against his broad shoulders, his hair is freshly trimmed, and he's biting into his lower lip.

This is it.

I'm marrying this man.

The mob boss of the Marchetti family.

If you'd told me months ago that this would happen, I'd have laughed in your face.

Cristian's eyes are glued to mine as we walk toward him. His face is glowing, and he's holding his arms loose in front of him.

I was nervous about his reaction. I don't expect tears of happiness because this is Cristian Marchetti we're talking about.

But as he looks at me, his face calm and warm, I know I've made the right decision.

Gigi is practically bouncing on her heels when I reach Cristian. My father kisses my cheek before releasing me, shakes Cristian's hand, and then sniffles while taking his seat next to Helena.

Cristian steps forward, leaving hardly any space between us, and the priest widens his eyes.

"*You look beautiful*," Cristian mouths to me.

I grin.

He grows closer—so close—until his lips brush my ear. "I can't wait to see *my wife* out of it later."

All eyes are on us, and I swear, my husband is taking the lead in this wedding thing. The priest hasn't even said a word, and I'm ready for him to swoop me into his arms and take me to the bedroom.

I widen my eyes and jerk my head toward the priest.

He chuckles, retreats a few inches, and then gives the priest the go-ahead.

We say our vows.

Our *I do*s.

Kiss.

And just like that, I'm married to New York's cruelest villain, who's stolen my heart.

40

CRISTIAN

After Benita's death, I swore to never marry again. I was a busy man, had too much on my plate, and didn't need any distractions. But Natalia changed everything when she walked into my office that night.

She's my glass of liquor after a long day of work.

Everything I need to come home to.

I ache to spend time with her.

She views me as more than Monster Marchetti. She doesn't care about my name or position in this city. She just wants me—her husband.

And I see her as more than a pawn and my daughter's best friend.

She makes me laugh—a rarity.

She's pushing experiences on me.

Hell, *we* hosted a movie night at our house, and she invited people over. Shockingly, I enjoyed it. Not that I didn't fake the opposite, though.

Natalia proves that even a cold man like me, a man at my age, can break out of his shell.

I will be a good husband to Natalia because she deserves nothing less.

Bora Bora.
She dragged my ass to Bora Bora.

When I'd told Natalia she had full control of our honeymoon, I hoped it'd be somewhere easy. A short flight, plenty of room to handle business, and a way to return to New York fast, if needed. Oh, and somewhere I could bring my goddamn gun.

But I should've known my wife.

We're in an overwater bungalow in the middle of the ocean.

Benita and I never took a honeymoon. I was too occupied, taking over my father's empire and learning the ropes of being in charge.

But I want to do this husband thing right, and after everything Natalia's been through with me, she deserves a damn honeymoon.

Her decision does give us a distraction-free week in paradise to spend with each other. Natalia might be the only person in this world to get me to do something like this.

Natalia moans my name and writhes underneath me as I stare down at her.

There's no better sight than watching my wife orgasm, to know that I satisfy her this way. I thrust into her two more times before coming inside her and collapsing onto her body. I rain kisses along her chest as we catch our breath.

"What if I get pregnant?" she asks, running her fingers through my hair—a new relaxant for me.

"What about it?" I ask against her skin.

"Would you be mad?"

I slowly pull out of her, rear back, and stare down at her. "Hell no." I run my hand up and down her leg. "Do you want a baby, sweet Natalia?"

She bites into her lower lip and slowly nods.

I grin. "We'd better work on that. Shall we?"

Her face lights up. "Really?"

"Really." I smack a kiss to her lips before slipping my tongue between them. "We can have as many babies as you want."

For a moment, all I hear are the ocean waves outside until she lowers her voice and says, "What if there's already one?"

I jerk back, nearly causing whiplash, and she turns her head to look away from me. Her breathing heightens, now growing louder than outside, and I run a hand over her cheek.

"Natalia, sweetheart, are you pregnant with our baby?"

She opens her mouth, then shuts it, then opens it. "Yes."

A rush of excitement speeds through me like I just scored the biggest deal of my motherfucking life. And I grin. I grin like I haven't grinned in fucking decades.

"Does … does the smile mean you're happy?" she whispers.

"The smile means I'm loving my life right now." I dip down the bed until my face is above her stomach and place a single kiss on it. "This is your dad. I promise to be a good one to you, but your mom? She's going to be the best mom in the world."

Natalia laughs, and tears well in her eyes.

I am the boss of the Marchetti family.

A father.

A husband.

And I will kill anyone who attempts to threaten that.

41

NATALIA

THREE MONTHS LATER

"I wonder how many proposals my father has to get before he decides to finally marry me off," Gigi says, scanning the room of those celebrating Benny's engagement at the mansion.

I pat her arm. "Your dad won't marry you off unless you're okay with it."

"I know." Gigi straightens her stance and runs her hand through her curls. "But eventually, either he'll have to find someone or I'll need to choose someone."

"Or you can be single for the rest of your life and live here with me."

Gigi hasn't returned to Italy, and if I had it my way, she'd stay here. Having her here with me is nice. The more time passes, the less awkward it becomes—my marrying Cristian.

She shakes her head. "Unfortunately, living with my father, who is now married to and bumping uglies with my bestie, doesn't sound like a future dream for me."

"Oh my God." I take a sip of my ginger ale. "Don't say it like that."

Nothing like a good ginger ale at a party.

Do you know what else there's nothing like?
Morning sickness.
Cristian had better be happy he keeps his gun far away from me. Sometimes, when I'm puking my guts up or I have heartburn that could cripple a rhino, I want to shoot him for knocking me up.

She gestures to my growing belly. "Don't get knocked up by my father, and I won't."

"Shush. Don't act like you're not excited to be a big sister."

Monster Marchetti has surprised me.

He's been involved in every step of this pregnancy and baby planning. It's sexy, discussing baby names with him, attending appointments, and hearing him talk nursery furniture and paint colors with our interior designer.

She scrunches her red lips together. "That I am excited about, *but* I can do that from my own place."

"Your dad married your best friend. Use that as an excuse to marry anyone you want."

"Look, you love my father, so you see the best in him. But he's big on loyalty. I need to marry someone loyal to the family … or join a nunnery."

I hold up my arm. "I vote nunnery. You can atone for the family's sins."

She throws her head back and laughs before her face softens. "And poor Benny. He wants to marry like I want Vinny to reincarnate."

"Neomi seems nice," I comment.

Tonight is my first time meeting her.

She was nice to us.

Benny? Not so much.

She hugged Gigi, then me, but then looked at Benny as if she'd rather have a kidney ripped out than hold a conversation with him.

"She's not Benny's type," Gigi says.

"What is Benny's type?"

"Benny prefers women he can boss around, and Neomi is not that woman." She cracks a smile. "I was at a club where she was once. A guy grabbed her ass … and she stabbed him in the shoulder."

"Oh, damn." I whistle. "Benny is in for a treat."

Her smile grows. "That he is."

"What the fuck?"

Our attention travels to outside the foyer at the sound of Benny's voice.

A voice fired with anger.

Gigi grabs my hand, and we scramble out of the foyer toward the commotion flowing out of the billiards room.

"Holy shit," I gasp, clasping my hand over my mouth, praying I don't puke when I see the dead body on the floor.

A man is bleeding out, and no one is attempting to help him.

Gretchen is in the corner crying.

Benny is holding his gun and seething as he stares at Neomi —whose white dress is now splattered with blood.

Neomi is glaring right back at him.

Cristian steps into the room, his eyes leveled as hard on Benny as Neomi's are. When I try to scramble forward to make sure my husband isn't the next man to shoot someone dead, Gigi stops me. She glances at me, shaking her head, and then pays her attention back to the scene in front of us.

"What the fuck happened?" Cristian roars, clenching his fists, his face red.

Severino Cavallaro, Neomi's father, steps to Cristian's side and flexes his fingers.

"Want to know what happened?" Benny begins pacing in front of the dead body.

A dead body no one seems to worry about.

The man could still be alive, fighting for his life, but he's being paid no mind. Obviously, he did *something* wrong if Benny killed him.

But who did the guy come with?

He has to have family here who won't be happy this man attended an engagement party and died.

Benny swings his arm toward Neomi. "I was getting my dick sucked, and she—"

I snort. Gigi gags. Gasps surround me. Cristian curses.

Neomi steps in front of Benny in her spiky black heels. "He was getting his dick sucked by someone who wasn't me—*his fiancée*—I'd like to add."

Neomi's father withdraws a gun from his blazer.

Cristian steps in front of him, blocking Benny from harm, and turns to shake his head at Severino in warning.

"I didn't think it was a problem," Benny yells.

I snort again. Gigi gags again. More gasps.

"Why the hell wouldn't you think it was a problem?" Neomi asks, flipping her straight, dark hair over her shoulder.

"You walked into the room and walked out, so I thought everything was fine," Benny replies, his dark eyes tight.

This time, it's Neomi who snorts.

"*But then*," Benny continues, changing his tone as if he were a game show host, and he pins a death glare toward Neomi, "she comes in with this dead motherfucker here." He kicks the guy's dead body. "Drops to her knees and unbuckles his pants to suck his—"

"Don't you dare fucking say it," Severino screams at Benny.

"An eye for an eye, Benny boy," Neomi argues. "You don't want to be faithful in this marriage, then I don't have to be either."

"That's bullshit," Benny hisses.

"What's bullshit is, you think it's okay for me to walk in and see this woman sucking you off." Neomi does a sweeping gesture toward Gretchen. "You're lucky I didn't kill her." Her eyes hit Gretchen's. "Sorry, not sorry."

Gretchen cries harder, and her lower lip trembles.

My stomach twists.

I understand Neomi's anger. Hell, I'd have the same reaction, but considering Gigi said Neomi stabbed a man in a club, we should get Gretchen out of here unless we want her to be the next victim at this engagement party.

I scan the crowd and see Luca watching the show, shaking his head but smirking.

"Luca," I whisper, waving my hand toward him to come.

He pushes himself off the wall. "What?"

I tip my head toward the corner of the room. "Get Gretchen out of here."

"And miss Benny possibly getting killed?" He frowns. "I vote you save that girl."

"I vote you do it unless you want me to tell Cristian that his pregnant wife asked you for a favor and you declined." I shove his shoulder. "Go be a knight in shining armor."

"Yeah, that's never happening." He scrubs a hand through his hair. "The things you always make me do."

I grin. "You're the best."

Luca walks against the wall to get to Gretchen. At first, when Luca speaks to her, she shakes her head, her face red in fear. But then, eventually, she nods and takes his hand, and he leads her out of the room while Neomi, Benny, and Severino are arguing.

"Oh, I can't wait for this marriage." Gigi rubs her hands together. "This might be more entertaining than my dad and you."

"Let the wedding bells ring," I mutter. "And let's pray no one else dies or gets stabbed."

"Are you sure it's a good idea for Benny and Neomi to marry?" I ask Cristian, spreading my moisturizer onto my face while looking into the bathroom vanity mirror.

Cristian dries his hair with a towel. "Why wouldn't it be a good idea?"

My eyes nearly bulge as I stare at him through the mirror. "Um, did you forget that a man died, Benny and Neomi almost killed each other, and Gretchen could've been murdered too?"

"Benny needs to grow up." Cristian shrugs. "Getting married will be good for him."

"Neomi won't allow him to cheat."

He pulls up his boxer briefs and follows me into the bedroom. "Then, his dumbass had better be faithful."

"Remember when you said you wouldn't be faithful to me?"

I *hmph* when he grabs my wrist and pulls me to him. My back lands against his chest.

"Remember when you said you weren't going to fuck me?" He rests his chin against my shoulder and whispers the words into my ear, causing my skin to prickle. "How long did that last, my sweet wife?"

I swallow. "A super-duper long time."

He chuckles and rubs his nose along my neck. "We both know I was done for as soon as I touched you that first time. Hell, I think I was done for when you fought me in the SUV at L'ultima Cena. You'll never have to worry about that with me."

I lean my head back to look at him. "My monster does have a heart."

He whips me around to face him and runs the tip of his finger against my lips. "Nah, he doesn't. I'll always be a monster, sweet Natalia."

"My monster, though." I circle my arms around his neck and press my lips to his. "My gorgeous monster."

"Who's all yours." He drops his hand and massages my belly. "This monster is yours forever."

ALSO BY CHARITY FERRELL

MARCHETTI MAFIA SERIES
(each book can be read as a standalone)

Gorgeous Monster

Gorgeous Prince

ONLY YOU SERIES
(each book can be read as a standalone)

Only Rivals

BLUE BEECH SERIES
(each book can be read as a standalone)

Just A Fling

Just One Night

Just Exes

Just Neighbors

Just Roommates

Just Friends

TWISTED FOX SERIES
(each book can be read as a standalone)

Stirred

Shaken

Straight Up

Chaser

Last Round

STANDALONES

Bad For You

Beneath Our Faults

Beneath Our Loss

Pop Rock

Pretty and Reckless

Wild Thoughts

RISKY DUET

Risky

Worth The Risk

ABOUT THE AUTHOR

Charity Ferrell is a USA Today and Wall Street Journal bestselling author of the Twisted Fox and Blue Beech series. She resides in Indianapolis, Indiana. She loves writing about broken people finding love while adding humor and heartbreak along with it. Angst is her happy place.

When she's not writing, she's making a Starbucks run, shopping online, or spending time with her family.

Printed in Great Britain
by Amazon